Matter's
End

Gregory Benford

BANTAM BOOKS
NEW YORK · TORONTO · LONDON · SYDNEY · AUCKLAND

MATTER'S END

A Bantam Spectra Book/January 1995

ISBN 0-553-56898-1

Published simultaneously in the United States and Canada

Bantam Books are published by Bantam Books, a division of Bantam
Doubleday Dell Publishing Group, Inc. Its trademark, consisting of the
words "Bantam Books" and the portrayal of a rooster, is Registered in
U.S. Patent and Trademark Office and in other countries. Marca Reg-
istrada. Bantam Books, 1540 Broadway, New York, New York 10036.

PRINTED IN THE UNITED STATES OF AMERICA
OPM   0 9 8 7 6 5 4 3 2 1

Contents

Contents

Matter's
End

Freezeframe

Well, Jason, it'll take some explaining. Got a minute? Great.

Here's the invitation. It's for the weekend, and it's not just the kid's birthday party, no. You and me, we've been out of touch the last couple years, so let me run through a little flashback, okay?

Teri and me, we're world-gobblers. You've known that since you and me were roomies, right? Remember the time I took a final, went skiing all afternoon, had a heavy date, was back next day for another final—and aced them both? Yeah, you got it, fella, aced the date, too. Those were the days, huh?

Anyway, my Teri's the same—girl's got real fire in her. No Type A or anything, just *alive*. And like sheet lightning in bed.

We grab life with both hands. Always have. If you work in city government, like me, you got to keep ahead of the oppo. Otherwise you see yourself hung out to dry on the six o'clock news and next day nobody can remember your name.

Goes double for Teri. She's in liability and claims, a real shark reef. Pressureville. So many lawyers around these days, half of them bred in those barracuda farms, those upgraded speed-curricula things. So we've got to watch our ass.

1

Right, watching Teri's is no trouble, I'll take all I can get. That woman really sends me. We're both in challenging careers, but she finds the time to make my day, every day, get it? Our relationship is stage center with us, even though we're putting in ten-hour days.

That's what started us thinking. We need the time to work on our marriage, really firm it up when the old schedule starts to fray us around the edges. We've been through those stress management retreats, the whole thing, and we *use* it.

So we're happy. But still, about a year ago we started to feel something was *missing*.

Yeah, you got it. The old cliché—a kid. Teri's been hearing the old bio clock tick off the years. We got the condo, two sharp cars, timeshare in Maui, portfolio thick as your wrist—but it's not enough.

Teri brought it up carefully, not sure I'd like the idea of sharing all this wonderful bounty with a cranky little brat. I heard her through, real quality listening, and just between you and me, old buddy, I didn't zoom in on the idea right away.

I mean, we're fast lane folks. Teri's happy poring over legal programs, looking for a precedent-busting angle, zipping off to an amped workout at the gym, and then catching one of those black and white foreign films with the hard-to-read subtitles. Not much room in her schedule to pencil in a feeding or the mumps. I had real trouble conceptualizing how she—much less I—could cope.

But she *wanted* this, I could tell from the soft watery look her eyes get. She's a real woman, y'know?

But the flip side was, no way she'd go for months of waddling around looking and feeling like a cow. Getting behind in her briefs because of morning sickness? Taking time off for the whole number? Not Teri's kind of thing.

What? Oh, sure, adoption.

Well, we did the research on that.

Let me put it this way. We both think the other's pretty damn special. Unique. And our feeling was, why raise a kid that's running on somebody else's genetic program? We're talented people, great bodies, not too hard on the eyes—why not give our kid those advantages?

You got to look at it from his point of view. He should have parents who provide the very best in everything—including genes. So he had to be ours—all ours.

So you can see our problem. Balancing the trade-offs and nothing looks like a winner. We'd hit a road-block.

That's where my contacts came in handy. Guy at work told me about this company, GeneInc.

The corporation was looking for a franchise backer and the city was getting involved because of all the legal hassles. Red tape had to be cut with the AMA, the local hospitals, the usual stuff. No big deal, just takes time.

I did a little angling on the variances they needed and in return they were real nice. We got invited to a few great parties up in the hills. Glitzy affairs, some big media people flown in to spice things up. And that's when we got the word.

Their secret is, they speed up the whole thing. It's entirely natural, no funny chemicals or anything. Purely electrical and a little hormone tinkering, straight goods.

What they do is, they take a little genetic material from Teri and me, they put it in a blender or something, they mix it and match it and batch it. There's this thing called inculcated growth pattern. Just jargon to me, but what it means is, they can *tune* the process, see. Nature does it slow and easy, but GeneInc can put the pedal to the metal. Go through the prelim stages, all in the lab.

Yeah, you got it, fella, you can't see Teri pushing

around a basketball belly, can you? That's why it's like GeneInc was tightwrapped for lives like ours—lives on the go.

So she goes in one Friday, right after a big staff meeting, and with me holding her hand she has the implantation. She overnights in the clinic, watching a first-run movie. Next day she's home. We have dinner at that great new restaurant, T. S. Eliot's, you really got to try the blackened redfish there, and all she's got to do is take these pills every four hours.

Three weeks like that, she's growing by the minute. Eats like a horse. I tell you, we had a running tab at every pasta joint within five blocks of the apartment.

She's into the clinic every forty-eight hours for the treatments, smooth as a press release. Teri's clicking right along, the kid's growing ten times the normal rate.

Before I can get around to buying cigars, zip, here's a seven-pound wonder. Great little guy. Perfect—my eyes, her smile, wants to eat everything in sight. Grabs for the milk supply like a real ladies' man.

And no effects from the GeneInc speedup, not a square inch less than A-max quality. You hear all kinds of scare talk about gene-diddling, how you might end up with a kid from Zit City. Well, the Chicken Littles were wrong-o, in spades.

We figure we'd handle things from there. Maybe send out the diapers, hire a live-in if we could find a nice quiet illegal—Teri could handle the Spanish.

We had the right vector, but we were a tad short on follow-through. Teri started getting cluster headaches. Big ones, in technicolor.

So I filled in for her. Read some books on fathering, really got into it. And I'm telling you, it jigsawed my days beyond belief.

Face it, we had high-impact lives. I gave up my daily racquetball match—and you know how much of a sacrifice that was, for a diehard jock like me, high-school football and all. But I did it for the kid.

Next, Teri had to drop out of her extra course in fastlane brokering, too, which was a real trauma. I mean, we'd practically spent the projected income from that training. Factored it into our estimated taxes, even. I'd already sunk extra cash into a honey of a limited partnership. It had some sweetheart under-writing features and we just couldn't resist it.

Man, crisis time. If she didn't get her broker's license on schedule, we'd be stretched so thin you could see through us.

She couldn't link into the course on home computer, either. Software mismatch or something, and by the time she got it downwired she was too far behind in the course.

See what I mean? Bleaksville.

But we were committed parents. We believe in total frankness, upfront living.

So we went back to GeneInc and had a talk with one of their counselors. Wonderful woman. She takes us into a beautiful room—soft lighting, quality leather couch, and some of that classy baroque trumpet music in the background. Just the right touch. Tasteful. Reassuring.

She listens to us and nods a lot and knows just what we're talking about. We trust her, almost like it was therapy. Which I guess it was.

And we let it all spill. The irritations. Man, I never knew a little package could scream so much. Feeding. No grandparents closer than three thousand miles, and they're keeping their distance. Got their retirement condo, walls all around it, a rule that you can't bring a kid in for longer than twenty-four hours. Not exactly Norman Rockwell, huh? So no quick fix there.

And the kid, he's always awake and wanting to play just when we're stumbling home, zombies. So you cram things in. We had trouble synching our schedules. Lost touch with friends *and* business contacts.

See, I spend a lot of time on the horn, keeping up with people I know I'll need sometime. Or just feeling out the gossip shops for what's hot. Can't do that with a squall-bomb on my knee.

Teri had it even worse. She'd bought all the traditional mother package and was trying to pack that into her own flat-out style. Doesn't work.

Now, the usual way to handle this would be for somebody to lose big, right?

Teri drops back and punts, maybe. Stops humping so hard, let's up. So maybe a year downstream, some younger beady-eyed type shoulders her aside. She ends up targeted on perpetual middle management. The desert. Oblivion. Perpetual Poughkeepsie.

Or else I lower *my* revs. Shy off the background briefings, drop off the party committee, don't sniff around for possible corners to get tight with. You know how it is.

What? No, ol' buddy, you're dead on—not my scene.

But listen, my real concern wasn't my job, it was our relationship. We really work at it. Total communication takes time. We really get into each other. That's just us.

So the lady at GeneInc listens, nods, and introduces us to their top drawer product line. Exclusive. *Very* high tech. It blew us away.

Freezeframe, they call it.

Look, the kid's going to be sleeping ten, twelve hours a day anyway, right? GeneInc just packs all that time into our workweek. Rearranges the kid's schedule, is basically what it is.

Simple electronic stimulus to the lower centers. Basic stuff, they told me, can't damage anything. And totally under our control.

When we want him, the kid's on call. Boost his voltage, allow some warmup—

Sure, Jason. See, he's running at low temperature during the workday. Helps the process. So we come dragging home, have some Chardonnay to unwind, catch the news. When we're ready for him we hit a few buttons, warm him up and there he is, bright and agreeable 'cause he's had a ton of extra sack time. Can't get tired and pesky.

I mean, the kid's at his best and we're at peak, too. Relaxed, ready for some A-plus parenting.

Well, we took the Zen pause on the idea, sure. Thought it over. Teri talked it out with her analyst. Worked on the problem, got her doubts under control.

And we went for it. Little shakedown trouble, but nothing big. GeneInc, they've got a fix for everything.

We boost him up for weekends, when we've got space. Quality time, that's what the kid gets. We've set up a regular schedule. Weekdays for us, weeknights and weekends for him.

Now GeneInc's got an add-on you wouldn't believe—Downtime Education, they call it. While he's sleeping through our days, Downtime Ed brings him up to speed on verbals, math, sensory holism, the works. Better than a real teacher, in many ways.

So we feel that—oh yeah, the invitation.

It's for his big blast. Combo first birthday party and graduation from third grade. We put him on the inside track, and he's burning it up. We couldn't be happier. Our kind of kid, for sure.

Pretty soon we'll integrate him into the GeneInc school for accelerated cases, others like him. There's a whole community of these great kids springing up, y'know. They're either in Downtime, learning up a storm, or getting on-line, first-class attention in Freezeframe weekends.

I tell you, Jason, these kids are going to be the

best. They'll slice and dice any Normkid competition they run into.

And us—it's like a new beginning. We get to have it all *and* we know the kid's not suffering. He'll have a high-school diploma by the time he's ten. He'll be a savvy little guy. And we'll load on all the extras, too. Emotional support, travel, the works.

We'll have him on tap when we want him. That'll stretch out his physical childhood, of course, but speed up his mental growth. Better all 'round, really, 'cause Teri and I totally like him.

See, we want to spread him over more of our lives, keep him for maybe thirty years. Why not have one really top-of-the-line kid, enjoy him most of your life? Efficient.

So look, I got to trot. Map's on the back of the invitation, come and enjoy. No need for a present unless you want to. Teri'll love seeing you again.

And while you're there, I can show you the GeneInc equipment. Beautiful gear, sharp lines. Brochures, too. I've got a kind of little franchise agreement with them, getting in on the ground floor of this thing.

What? Well, that's not the way I'd put it, Jason. This is a class product line.

Calling it a Tupperware Party—hey, that's way out of line. We're talking quality here.

You'll see. Just drop on by. No obligation. Oh yeah, and I got some great Cabernet you should try, something I picked up on the wine futures market.

My God, look at the time. See you, ol' buddy.

Have a nice day.

Mozart on Morphine

As a working hypothesis to explain the riddle of our existence, I propose that our universe is the most interesting of all possible universes, and our fate as human beings is to make it so.

—FREEMAN DYSON, 1988

All theory, dear friend, is grey,
But the golden tree of life springs ever green.

—GOETHE, *Faust*

I read a fragment of God's mind during that summer when He seemed to be trying to stop me.

I realize this is not the usual way such proceedings go, with their pomp and gravity. But please bear with me. I shall try to talk of matters which scientists usually avoid, even though these are crucial to the unspoken rhythms of our trade.

I live in a small community spread before the Pacific like a welcoming grin, thin but glistening in the golden shafts of sunlight. That unrelenting brilliance mocked my dark internal chaos as I struggled with mathematical physics. I worked through the day on my patio, the broad blue of ocean lying with Euclidean grace beyond, perspective taking it away into measureless infinity. Endless descending glare mocked my gnarled equations, their confusion the only stain on Nature.

My habit was to conclude a frustrating day of particle theory by running on the beach. The salt air cleared my mind. The sun hung low and red and I pounded along crisply warm sand, vacantly watching the crumbling, thumping waves. I paid no attention to the small crowd forming up ahead and so when the first shot came it took me completely by surprise.

I saw the teenagers scattering and the scrawny man in his twenties poking the small silvery gun at them, yelling something I couldn't make out. I assumed as an automatic axiom that the gun was loaded with blanks; certainly it wasn't very loud.

The man started swearing at a kid near me, who was moving to my right. I was still doggedly running so when the second shot came I was just behind the kid and the round went *tssiiip!* by my head.

Not blanks, no. I did the next hundred meters in ten seconds, digging hard into the suddenly cloying sand and turning to look back only once. A third thin splat followed me up the beach but no screams—just more swearing from the skinny man, who was backing up the gray concrete stairs and trying to keep the pack of kids from following him.

From a hundred meters away I watched him fire one last time, not trying to hit anybody now, just holding the gang at bay. Then he turned and ran up onto the street beyond.

I thumped back down the beach amid buzzing spectators. It was evidently a drug deal gone bust. The kids had started jazzing the thin man around and he got mad.

The police caught him on the streets above. I

watched them read him his Miranda rights . . . and un-
bidden, my mind gave me a tiny clue about the equations which I had labored over all day. Just like that.

Churchill once said that there was nothing as ex-
hilarating as being shot at and missed.

Perhaps that explained the spurt in my research
through the following week. I found some fresh mathematical tricks, a new conformal transformation. Problems rearranged themselves.

I had been pursuing a model for the universe
which did not begin with any assumption about its di-
mensionality. We are used to our cozy three spatial directions plus ever-flowing time—four dimensions in
all. When God made everything, was this choice forced?
Could the deep laws governing matter work well in, say,
six dimensions? Twenty-six?

The question reeks of arrogance, of course. Just
what or *who* could force God?

Still, my imagination swept on freely. My pencil
scribbled long chains of symbols as I sat on my deck
and contemplated the beach below, where that *tssiiip!*
had flown past.

I interrupted my muse to fly east and visit my parents on their fiftieth wedding anniversary. Alabama
was sultry, the weight of its air somehow reassuring.

If you work in arcane labyrinths, conversations
with parents circle around matters in which all are
equally ignorant—politics, children, economics. I felt
myself falling away from the glide of cool mathematics
that, I knew, underlay everything.

I went with my father to the anniversary reception
after that morning's church service. It was a moist,
sunny day. I lazily breathed in the pine scent as my father pulled up at a stop sign. He started off and something darted in the corner of my vision. It was a car
that a nearby telephone junction box had hidden from
view, coming fast on the right. I yelled, "Dad stop!" as

if it was one word. He hit the brake and the other car smashed into our side.

The windshield cracked into diamondlike shards. Steel jabbed into my head. The pain did not register but blood gushed down my face.

There was yelling and a spreading ache in my temple. My father pulled me across the seat, brushing glass to the floor. Shakily I stood on the tarry road and helped my father tear my shirt off. We used it to stop the bleeding. I kept saying ". . . like a stuck pig . . ." in wonder at the cascade of blood that had soaked me.

The tight knot at my brow was a fist holding my life in. I leaned against the car and felt light, airy. I studied the geometry of the accident and saw that if my father had not stomped down on the brake they would have come smack in on my side of the car and probably right through the door. "It was *that* close," my father murmured to himself.

The people in the other car were badly shaken up. In the hushed moments following the big banging surprise, facts assembled like congealing particles. The other driver wasn't wearing shoes. Her car was borrowed. She had broken her hand. She sat in a red clay ditch, rocking and moaning.

My father took it all quite mildly but my ears rang with alarm. I could smell the pine trees even stronger now. The broad-bladed grass, the azaleas, bright yellow flowers—ingenious implements of a propagating, abundant nature. This impossibly sharp world, and my persistence in it, demanded equally hard-edged explanation.

The vexing riddle of that waning summer stemmed from my reductionist impulse. I share it with all physicists.

The spirit of Einstein moves us still: we try to find the unifying principles behind the universe by looking for symmetries hidden in the laws that govern matter.

The greatest scientists are unifiers—Newton, Einstein—and, indeed, nature often begins its grand works with a simple, unified start. In the beginning, a homogeneous ocean somehow differentiated into cells and microlife, predators and prey. A common ancestry of apes managed to break their smooth symmetry into such as we, with our complicated symbol-scribbling languages and cultures. It is a recurring theme: diversity from unity.

Our bias is to seek that primordial unity. We hope that all of nature once started with just such serene symmetry. A commanding single law fractured as the universe expanded, splitting the unity, spilling forth the four fragmentary forces we now know.

And what odd forces they are. Gravity pins us to our solitary planet. Electromagnetism brings us light which whispers of far galaxies, of strange cosmologies. Stars glow in the boundless black, fueled by fusing atoms which obey the weak force. And underneath the seeming solidity of matter lurks the strong force, a glue binding nuclei.

I labored to find that single, unified parent force. No laboratory experiment can lead us to it, for the energies demanded must rival those of time's first thin instant. So it is up to argonauts on mathematical seas to chart the shadow curve of that Ur-Law.

Consider in turn the breadth of our universe; then the Earth; then a nucleus; finally, a thin wedge called a superstring. Each step downward in scale is by twenty orders of magnitude. That is how remote our theories have become.

Such smallness preoccupied me then. The image of a tiny wriggling string informed my nights, my dreams.

I sometimes awoke, my head still aching from the accident. I was uncomfortably aware that my mind was cradled in a shell of bone, my precarious reason hostage to blunt forces. Intelligence was besieged.

A friend of mine once referred to our brains as "meat computers." She was involved in the study of artificial intelligence, and as the aches slowly ebbed I often thought of her coarse, but perhaps true, remark. Yet my own head still bowed over the intricacies of theory.

In late September I was making my final plans to go to a conference in India when I developed stomach pains. My children had the same symptoms, a standard flu that was going around. I stayed in bed a few days and expected it to go away. I was doing pretty well, running a little fever, though the pain had moved down somewhat.

I went into the university for half a day to see my thesis students. Around noon I was sitting in my office when the pain got much worse. I couldn't stand up. The world contracted to a sphere with me pinned at its center. I called a doctor near the university and made an appointment and waited out the pain. It subsided and I began to think life would resume its linear logic. But in the doctor's office I showed an elevated white blood count and a fever and some dehydration. When she poked my right side a lance drove through me.

She thought it might be appendicitis and that I should go to an emergency room nearby. I thought she was making too much of it and wanted something for my mild pain. I wanted to go to the hospital near my home, where I knew the doctors. She called an ambulance but I was pumped up by then and went out and got into my car and drove very fast, skating down the canyon road. The bleached hills lay beneath a hammering sun.

It was the real thing, of course. Soon enough I watched the fluorescent lights glide by as the anesthetist pushed me into the operating room. He said I must have a high tolerance for pain because the appendix was obviously swollen and sensitive. I asked him how quickly the drugs took effect. He said "Well . . ." and then I was staring at the ceiling of my hospital room and it was half a day later.

I had a good night, slept well. In the morning my doctor told me his suspicions had been right—that when the pain got bad in my office it had been the appendix bursting. By the time they opened me up the stuff had spread. I asked to see the appendix and they brought it up to me later, a red lumpy thing with white speckles all over the top of it. I asked what the speckles were and the aide said casually, "Oh, that's gangrene. It's riddled with the stuff."

The doctor said there was a sixty percent chance the antibiotics would not take out the gangrene that had spread throughout my lower abdomen. Mathematical probability carries little weight in the psyche. Of course I figured I would be in the lucky forty percent.

By the early hours of the next morning I knew I was wrong. A fever swarmed over me. I had stood up and walked around in the afternoon but when the night nurse tried it with me again I couldn't get to my feet. I was throwing up vile sour stuff and the orderly was talking to me about inserting some tubes and then the tube was going in my nose and down my throat and a bottle nearby was filling with brown bile, lots of it, a steady flow.

I couldn't sleep, even with the drugs. There was talk about not giving me too many drugs for fear of suppressing my central nervous system too much. This didn't make much sense to me—but then, little did.

Events ran together. The doctor appeared and said the antibiotics weren't working, my white count was soaring. A man came by and reminded me to use the plastic tube with a ball in it that the nurse had given me the day before. You blew into it and kept a ball in the air to exercise your general respiration. It seemed dumb to me, I could breathe fine, but I did it anyway and asked for some breakfast. I wasn't getting any.

They fed me from an array of bottles going into my IV, and wouldn't give me more than ice chips to suck on.

Quick, watery, white-smocked beings surrounded me. My fever climbed a degree every two hours and my wife patted my brow with a cool cloth and I wanted some food. I didn't see how they could expect a man to get better if they didn't feed him. All they did was talk too fast and add more bottles to the antibiotic array. They started oxygen but it didn't clear my head any. My IV closed off from vascular shock. A man kept punching my arms with needles, trying to find a better way in. Carefully and reasonably I told him to knock it off. And get me something to eat.

They tilted me back so the doctor could put a subclavial tube in close to my heart. It would monitor the flow there and provide easy access for the IV. Then I was wheeling beneath soft cool fluorescents, into a big quiet room. The Intensive Care Unit, a large voice said. I lay for a time absolutely calm and restful and realized that I was in trouble. The guy with the breathing tube and ball was gone, but the nurses made me do it anyway, which still struck me as dumb because I wasn't going to stop breathing, was I? If they would just give me some food I would get better.

After the gusts of irritation passed I saw in a clear moment that I was enormously tired. I hadn't slept in the night. The tubes in my nose tugged at me when I moved. They had slipped a catheter into me, surprisingly painless, and I felt wired to the machines around me, no longer an independent entity but rather a collaboration. If I lay still with my hands curled on my chest I could rest, maybe, and if I could rest I could get through this. So I concentrated on that one irreducible quantum of fact, and on how blissful it felt after the nurse gave me another injection of morphine, on how I could just forget about the world and let the world worry about me instead.

I woke in the evening. I had been dreaming of giant cylinders and pyramids of rolling and thumping on a cool blue plain, enormous geometric buildings jostling merrily on the ocean below my patio.

The next morning my doctor startled me awake. It was as though I came in at midsentence in someone else's life. I was better. They had called in more exotic antibiotics which had stopped the fever's rise, leveling it off at 105 degrees. But I was still in danger and the next day would be crucial.

The room still swarmed with prickly light. My wife came, wearing a peasant dress and ponytail, echoing her artsy college days. I made a joke about this which neither she nor the nurses could understand. At death's gateway there was nothing to do but wrap scraps of tattered wit about us.

She had brought my Sony and a case of tapes. They would shut out the hospital, which was grittily real again, with its bustling all-hours brightness like an airport, its constant rhythm of comings and goings. I wanted to skate on that blue plain of my dreams; something waited there.

I had the nurse put the headphones on me and start a tape. She looked at me oddly and I wondered if I was making any sense. The swirl of a rondo swept me away.

They had me on demand morphine. Every hour or so I called for an injection and lifted off the sheets and spun through airy reaches, Mozart on morphine, skimming along the ceilings of rooms where well-dressed people looked up at me with pleased expressions, interrupted as they dined on opulent plates of veal and cauliflower and rich pungent sauces, rooms where I would be again sometime, among people whom I knew but had no time for now, since I kept flying along softly lit yellow ceilings, above crimson couches and sparkling white tablecloths and smiles and mirth. Toward the blue geometries. Mozart had understood all this and had seen in this endless gavotte a way to loft and sweep and glide, going, to have ample ripe substance without weight.

Physicists don't live in the real world. We have become so decoupled (another physicists' jargon word) that we regard reality's rub as hopelessly crude, an amusing approximation.

From tangible matter we slide easily down to tales of fields and particles. Rubbery, compliant, these fields follow clean differential equations.

Below those lie more profound truths: the symmetry groups which relate fields and particles through deft mathematical twists. Most particle physicists labor in this realm.

But now, I saw, there yawned a deeper level of abstraction: symmetry groups themselves were blunt beings, best seen as states realized in a ten-dimensional space-time. In this larger universe our dull doings in three dimensions, plus time, were as the crawlings of insects.

And still more: superstrings. Their dynamics defined the states possible in that ten-space. The ripple of their motions in that immensely larger universe sent tides lapping into lesser dimensions, wakes spreading like the whorls of passing ocean liners.

That was what I saw in the days that followed. It was all there. Abstractions, yes—but I also felt strumming kinesthetic senses, taking me where the mathematics led. I could tie the superstrings into knots, make of them what I wanted. Unimaginably small, they still had to follow the serene logic of mathematics. I *knew*.

When the doctor took the stitches out a week later he said casually, "Y'know, you were the closest call I've had in a year. Another twelve hours and you would've been gone."

In November I went to India anyway. I hadn't fully recovered, but it seemed important not to let a strange new sense in me, the calm acceptance of mortality, deflect me from life itself.

Without noticing it, I had lost my fear of death. The grave was no longer a fabled place, but rather a dull zone beyond a gossamer-thin partition. Crossing that filmy divider would come in time but for me it no longer carried a gaudy, supercharged meaning. And for reasons I could not express, many matters seemed less important now, little busynesses. People I knew were more vital to me and everything else was lesser, peripheral.

Except the work. I spent time on the patio, watching the classical space defined by the blue sea.

My calculations took only a few weeks. They have proved successful in the limited ways theory can affect the world. Yes, they do predict the particles found in recent Supercollider experiments. True, they are fully consistent with the four forces we already know. Gravity emerges as a manifestation of events in a ten-dimensional space-time.

One of the deeper implications is that there is another kind of time. In that system, our truncated space-time forms a surface in the more general, superstring space-time. To that world, everything we perceive would seem like the surface of a soap bubble, wobbling in air. The bubble has no edge, no boundary—and so we will never, in that higher coordinate system, plunge through an abrupt juncture.

This implies that time, in the larger sense, is never-ending. Of course it is not *our* time, but rather, the duration defined in higher spaces. The existence of this generalized time is perhaps the most startling deduction of the mathematics.

But what does this mean? We search for a completely unified theory, curling the fragmented forces of our hobbled universe into the Ur-Force. Still, even that is just a set of rules and equations.

What is it that breathes fire into the bare mathematics and makes a raw universe for them to describe? Now that we have achieved a unified model, we have in a sense answered the question first posed by the Greeks: *what* is the universe?

My answer is that we experience events in a higher dimension. Our perceived universe is the shadow of a higher realm.

Now we should turn to a grander issue: *why* is the universe? To attack this question is to ask to know the mind of God.

Can we? In comparison with the worldview which emerges from our recent discoveries, our earlier catalog of four forces seems comfy, domesticated. Gravity looms large in the model I have constructed because, though it is the weakest of the four forces, its steady pull can cause matter to collapse in on itself to infinitesimal size.

This may mean that we will never know whether our theories work. How can they be checked? We cannot see down to the skimpy size of a superstring, after all.

Only the chilly beauty of mathematics can lead us. But where does this winding path go?

After all, we cannot even solve exactly for the motion of three bodies acting under Newton's theory of gravity. In my theory, *no* exact solutions are available for *any*thing.

So there is no certainty. Even the most lovely of all models gives us, in the end, a set of equations. But now these squiggles describe events in higher realms, in vast vector spaces where imponderable entities move to their own differential waltzes.

This is profoundly far from the realm of humanity. Yet we who do this are, as I learned, comically human.

We theorists have our homes with a view, our sufficient incomes, our digital stereos and foreign cars, our harassed, ironic wives or husbands—and blithely

seem to have solved the paradox of being thinking animals. But what compass do we have, we who swim in
the backwash of passing, imperceptible ocean liners?

In Agra I rose at dawn to see the Taj Mahal. By
that rosy first glow it was as distant as a ghost.

It shimmered above the lush gardens, deceptively
toylike until I realized how huge the pure curved white
marble thing was. The ruler who built it to hold his
dead wife's body had intended to build a black Taj
also, across the river which lies behind. He would lie
buried there, he planned, a long arcing bridge linking
the two of them.

But his son, seeing how much the first Taj cost,
confined his father to a red sandstone fort a mile away
for the last seven years of his life. When he was too
feeble to sit up, the old man lay in bed and watched
the Taj in a mirror until the end.

I realize this has not been the usual sort of annual
address given to this body. Please do not mistake my
odd approach as a sign of disrespect, however. I deeply
thank the Nobel Committee.

I have tried to speak of the human experience of
science, because we are all finally encased in our individual, truncated selves. If the work for which you
have honored me seems to raise more issues than it
solves, that is our condition. We contend endlessly
against pale immensities.

We seem so small. Yet we have a common, perhaps arrogant impression that we matter, somehow.

There is an old philosopher's joke:

> What is mind? It doesn't matter.
> What is matter? Oh, never mind.

But consider the tiny processes governed by quantum mechanics. There, matter is not inert. It is active,

continually making choices between possibilities, following laws of probability. Mind is present, at least in the sense that nature makes choices.

Let us go one level higher, to our own rains. These fragile vessels amplify the quantum choices made in our heads by molecules. We apply the lever of size to underlying probabilistic events. We are magnifiers.

Now go to vaster scales. The universe itself shows some signs of design, at least in the choice of basic physical constants. If those numbers had come out differently, no life or even stable stars would be possible in the universe.

Or, in the light of my own calculations, consider the reality of other dimensions. Perhaps these dimensions are rolled up like tiny scrolls. Perhaps they simply lie beyond our knowing, except through the effects I have calculated. We do not know—yet.

Still, there emerges now evidence of mental processes at work on many levels of physical reality. We may be part of some larger act. For example, perhaps we contribute remotely to the universe's thinking about itself.

We probably cannot know this with anything approaching scientific certainty—ever. The recent work of myself and others suggests, though, that higher entities affect our times in distant but profound fashion.

The equations can only hint, imply, describe. They cannot tell us why.

I myself suggest that these besieged brains of ours matter. Somehow. Somewhere.

It is all very well, of course, to say that in some far dimension time has no end. But it surely does for us individually, through shootouts and car crashes and disease. ·

Yet we are given a glimmer of perception, through the godly language of mathematics. Maybe, for creatures such as us, that is enough.

* * *

On the broad marble deck behind the Taj Mahal the river ran shallow. To the right lay a bathing spot for Hindu devotees. Some splashed themselves with river water, others meditated. To the left was a mortuary. The better-off inhabitants of Agra had their bodies burned on pyres, then tossed into the river. If one could not afford the pyre, then after a simple ceremony the body was thrown off the sandstone quay and onto the mud flats, or into the water if the river was high. This was usually done in early morning.

By the glimmering dawn radiance I watched buzzards pick apart something on the flats. They made quick work of it, deftly tearing away the cloth, and in five minutes had picked matters clean. They lost interest and flapped away. The Taj coasted in serene eternity behind me, its color subtly changing as the sun rose above the trees, its cool perfect dome glowing, banishing the shadows below. Somehow in this worn alien place everything seemed to fit. Death just happened. From this simple fact came India's inertia. I thought of Mozart and heard a faint light rhythm, felt myself skimming effortlessly over a rumpled brown dusty world of endless sharp detail and unending fevered ferment, and watched the buzzards and the bathers and felt the slow sad sway of worlds apart.

Centigrade 233

It was raining, of course. Incessantly, gray and gentle, smoothing the rectangular certainties of the city into moist matters of opinion. It seemed to Alex that every time he had to leave his snug midtown apartment, the heavens sent down their cold, emulsifying caresses.

He hurried across the broad avenue, though there was scant traffic to intersect his trajectory. Cars were as rare as credible governments these days, for similar reasons. Oil wells were sucking dry, and the industrial conglomerates were sucking up to the latest technofix.

That was as much as Alex knew of matters worldly and scientific. He took the weather as a personal affront, especially when abetted by the 3-D 'casters who said things like "As we all know, in the Greater Metropolitan Area latitudinal overpressures have precipitated (ha ha) a cyclonic bunching of moist offshore cumulus—" and on and on into the byzantine reaches of garish, graphically assisted meteorology.

What they *meant*, Alex told himself as cold drops trickled under his collar, was the usual damp-sock dismality: weather permanently out of whack thanks to emissions from the fabled taxis that were never there when you needed them. Imagine what these streets were like only thirty years ago! Less than that. Imagine these wide avenues inundated to the point of gridlock, that lovely antique word. Cars *parked* along every curb, right out in the open, without guards to prevent joyriding.

"Brella?" a beggar mumbled, menacing Alex with a small black club.

"Get away!" Alex overreacted, patting the nonexistent shoulder holster beneath his trench coat. The beggar shrugged and limped away. Small triumph, but Alex felt a surge of pride.

He found the decaying stucco apartment building on a back street, cowering beside a blocky factory. The mail slot to 2F was stuffed with junk mail. Alex went up creaky stairs, nose wrinkling at the damp reek of old rugs and incontinent pets.

He looked automatically for signs that the plywood frame door to 2F had been jimmied. The grain was as clear as the skin of a virgin spinster. Well, maybe his luck was improving. He fished the bulky key from his pocket. The lock stuck, rasped, and then turned with a reluctant thump; no electro-security here.

He held his breath as the door swung open. Did he see looming forms in the murk beyond? This was the last and oldest of Uncle Herb's apartments. Their addresses were all noted in that precise, narrow handwriting of the estate's List of Assets. The List had not mentioned that Uncle Herb had not visited his precious vaults for some years.

The others had all been stripped, plundered, wasted, old beer cans and debris attesting to a history of casual abuse by neighborhood gangs. At the Montague Street apartment, Alex had lingered too long mourning the lost trove described in the List. Three slit-eyed Hispanics had kicked in the door as he was inspecting the few battered boxes remaining of his uncle's bequest. They had treated him as an invader, cuffed him about and extorted "rent," maintaining with evil grins that *they* were the rightful owners, and had been storing the boxes for a fee. "The People owns this 'parmen' so you pays the People," the shortest of the three had said.

There had been scant wealth in any of the three, and now—

The door creaked. His fingers fumbled and found the wall switch. Vague forms leaped into solid, unending ranks—books!

Great gray steel shelves crammed the room, anchored at floor and ceiling against the earth's shrugs. He wondered how the sagging frame of this apartment building could support such woody weight. Alex squeezed between the rows and discovered wanly lit rooms beyond, jammed alike. A four-bedroom apartment stripped of furniture, blinds drawn, the kitchen recognizable only by the stumps of disconnected gas fittings.

But no—in the back room cowered a stuffed chair and storklike reading lamp. Here was Uncle Herb's sanctuary, where his will said he had "idled away many a pleasant afternoon in the company of eras lost." Uncle Herb had always tarted up his writing with antique archness, like the frilly ivory-white shade on the lamp.

The books were squeezed on their shelves so tightly that pulling one forth made Alex's forearm muscles ache. He opened the seal of the fogged polymer jacket and nitrogen hissed out. A signed and dated *Martian Chronicles*! Alex fondled the yellowed pages carefully. The odor of aging pulp, so poignant and undefinable, filled him. A first edition, too. Pity about the signature; unsigned were more scarce, he remembered.

Still, probably worth a good deal. He slipped the book back into its case, already regretting his indulgence at setting it free of its inert gas protection. He hummed to himself as he inched down the rows of shelves, titles flowing past his eyes at a range of inches.

The Forever War with its crisp colors. A meter-long stretch of E.E. "Doc" Smith novels, all very fine in jackets. *Last and First Men* in the 1930 first edition. Alex had heard it described as the first ontological epic prose poem, the phrase sticking in his mind. He had not read it, of course.

And the pulps! Ranks of them, gaudy spines shouting at customers now gone to dust. Alex sighed. Everything in the twencen had apparently been astounding, thrilling, startling, astonishing, even spicy. Heroines in distress, their skirts invariably hiked up high enough to reveal a fetching black garter belt and the rich expanse of sheer hose. Aliens of grotesque malignancy. Gleaming silver rockets, their prows no less pointed than their metaphor.

The pulps took the largest bedroom. In the hallway began the slicks. Alex could not resist cracking open a *Collier's* with Bonestell full-colors depicting (the text told him breathlessly) Wernher von Braun's visionary space program. Glossy pages grinned at their first reader in a century. To the moon!

Well, Alex had been there, and it wasn't worth the steep prices. He had sprained an arm tumbling into a wall while swooping around in the big wind caverns. The light gravity had been great, the perfect answer for one afflicted with a perpetual diet, but upon return to Earth he had felt like a bowling ball for a month.

Books scraped him fore and aft as he slid along the rows. His accountant's grasp of number told him there were tens of thousands here, the biggest residue of Uncle Herb's collection.

"Lord knows what was in the others," he muttered as he extracted himself from the looming aisles. The will had been right about this apartment—it was all science fiction. Not a scrap of fantasy or horror polluted the collection. Uncle Herb had been a bug about distinctions that to Alex made no difference at all. No novels combining rockets and sword-wielding barbarians, no voluptuous vampires, to judge from the covers.

Alex paused at the doorway and looked back, sighing. Bright remnants of a lost past. He recalled what awe that Brit archaeologist had reported feeling, upon cracking into Tut's tomb. Only this time the explorer *owned* the contents.

He made his way into the chilly drizzle, clucking contentedly to himself. He shared with Uncle Herb the defective gene of bibliophilia, but a less rampant case. He loved the crisp feel of books, the supple shine of aged leather, the *snick snick snick* of flipped pages. But to *read*? No one did that anymore. And surely the value of a collectible did not depend on its mere use, not in this Tits 'n' Glitz age.

In less than an hour Alex reclined on a glossy Korean lounger, safely home, speaking to Louise Keppler on his wall screen. Her face showed signs of a refurb job still smoothing out, but Alex did not allow even a raised eyebrow to acknowledge the fact; one never knew how people took such things. Louise was a crafty, careful dealer, but in his experience such people had hidden irrationalities, best avoided.

"I'd need to see the whole collection," Louise said, peering off camera.

"Certainly. You might be advised to bring your bodyguard, however." He disliked business associates who always seemed to be doing something else when you called, their eyes tracking unseen distractions.

"For that neighborhood I should go in a tank." Louise smiled, eyes at last pinning him with their assessing blue. He thumbed a closeup and found that they were true color, without even a film to conceal bloodshot veins, the residue of the city's delights.

"You got the index?" He wanted to close this deal quickly. Debts awaited, and Uncle Herb had been a long time dying.

"Sure. I ran it through my assessing program just now."

Alex nodded eagerly. So that had been the distraction; she was swift. He shivered and wished he had paid his heating bill this month. His digital thermometer read Centigrade 08. A glance at the window showed the corners filmed by ice. "I hope we can agree on a fair market—"

"Alex, we've dealt before. You know me for no fool."

He blinked. "What's wrong?"

"Books, Alex? Early videos, yes. First generation CDs, sure—nobody realized they had only a seven-year lifetime, unless preserved. *Those* are rare." Her mouth twisted wryly.

"These are even earlier, much—"

"Sure, but who cares? Linear reading, Alex?"

"You should try it," he said swiftly.

"Have you?" she asked sardonically.

"Well . . . a little . . ."

"Kids still do, sure. But not long enough to get attached to the physical form."

"But this was, well, the literature of the future."

"Their future, our past—what of it?" Her high cheekbones lent her lofty authority. She tugged her furs about her.

His knowledge of science fiction came mostly from the myriad movids available. Now that the genre was dead, there was interest in resurrecting the early, naive, strangely grand works—but only in palatable form, of course—to repay the expense of translation into movids.

"They do have a primitive charm," he said uncertainly.

"So torpid! So unaware of what can be done with dramatic line." She shook her head.

Alex said testily, "Look, I didn't call for an exchange of critical views."

"Quite so. I believe you wanted a bid."

"Yes, but immediately payable. There are, ah, estate expenses."

"I can go as high as twelve hundred yen."

"Twelve—" For the first time in his life Alex did not have to act out dismay at an opening price. He choked, sputtered, gasped.

Louise added, "*If* you provide hauling out of that neighborhood and to a designated warehouse."

"Haul—" He coughed a last time to clear his head. Twelve hundred was only two months rent, or three months of heating oil, with the new tax.

"My offer is good for one day."

"Louise! You're being ridiculous."

She shook her head. "You haven't been keeping up. Items like this, they were big maybe a decade back. No more."

"My uncle spent a *fortune* on those magazines alone. A complete set of *Amazing*s. I can remember when he got the last of it, the rare slab-sheeted numbers."

She smiled with something resembling fondness. "Oh yes, a passing technical fancy, weren't they?"

"Expanded right in your hand. Great bioengineering."

"But boring, I'm told. Well past the great age of linear writing."

"That doesn't *matter*," Alex said, recovering slowly and trying to find a wedge in her composure. He drew his coverlet tightly around his numb legs. Should he jump up and shout, to gain some psychological edge, and also to bring blood back into his frozen feet? No, too obvious. He summoned up a stentorian bark instead. "You're trying to cheat me!"

She shook her head slowly, wisely, red curls tumbling. He had to admire her craft; she appeared completely at ease while she tried to rob him. "You don't understand post-literate times, Alex. We've dealt before in posters, antique cars, oldie-goldies, grav-mets. Those are real collectibles. Books aren't."

"There's a wealth of *history* in that apartment. A complete set of everybody, the masters of the high period. Anderson to Zelazny. Pournelle and Aldiss, Heinlein and Lem, everybody."

"And worth damn little. Look, I know the situation you're in. Let me—"

"I don't want charity, Louise." He did, actually, but the best guise was to pretend differently.

"Those other apartments of Herb's, they had really valuable goods." Her eyes drifted off camera, lost in memories. "Unfortunate that he did not secure them better."

"Those were good neighborhoods when he started buying up apartments for storage. With rent control that was a smarter way to use them, after all." If he kept her talking he might think of a way to jack up her price.

"Still is," she said reflectively. "I knew Herb well, and he was a savvy collector. A fine man. I told him to junk the books long ago."

This kind of scuffing around the topic was standard for dealers, but Alex found it only irritating now. He remembered rumors that Uncle Herb had kept several mistresses in the business, and suddenly he suspected that Louise, with her distant gaze and pursed lips, was recalling some fevered trysts.

Her eyes clicked back from the infinite and became analytical. "Okay, fifteen hundred yen. Top offer."

"Absurd!"

"Call me when you calm down, Alex."

And she was gone, trickling away on the wall screen.

He calmed down with a movid. His favorite reader had a buffed leather jacket and a large tubular

spine. He inserted a cylinder of *The Lust of the Mohicans* and contentedly watched the opening segments of
the period piece drama on his enveloping walls, sitting
amid the revelry and swank. Entertainment was essential these forlorn days, when all who could had already
fled to warmer climes. Even they had met with rising
ocean levels, giving the staybehinds delicious, sardonic
amusement.

Alex tired of the main plotthread, distracted by his
troubles. He opened the booklike reader and began
scanning the moving pictures inside. The reader had
only one page. The cylinder in its spine projected a 3-D
animated drama, detailing background and substories
of some of the main movid's characters. He popped up
sidebar text on several historical details, reading for
long moments while the action froze on the walls.
When he turned the book's single sheet, it automatically cycled to the next page.

Alex had been following the intricate braided
story-streams of *Mohicans* for months now. Immersion
in a time and place blended the fascinations of fiction,
spectacle, history, and philosophy. Facets of the tangled
tale could be called up in many forms, while subplots
altered at will. Alex seldom intruded on the action, dis-
liking the intensely interactive features. He preferred
the supple flows of time, the feeling of inexorable con-
vergence of events. The real world demanded more interaction than he liked; he certainly did not seek it in
his recreation.

The old-fashioned segments were only a few para-
graphs of linear text, nothing to saturate the eye. He
even read a few, interested at one point in the menu
which an Indian was sharing with a shapely white
woman. Corn mush, singularly unappealing. The
woman smacked her lips with relish though, as she
slipped her bodice down before the brave's widening
eyes. Alex watched the cooking fire play across her
ample breasts, pertly perched like rich yellow-white

pears in the flickering, smoky glow—and so the idea came to him.

"Alex," the Contessa said, "they're *mar*velous."

"My best," he said, already catching on that the way to handle these people was to act humble and mysterious. "Absolute rarities."

"Hard to be*lieve*, isn't it?" The Contessa gave her blond tresses a saucy little flip. "That people *were* that way?"

Alex had no idea what way she meant, but he answered, "Oh yes, nothing exceeds like excess," with what he hoped was light wit. Too often his humor seemed even to himself to become, once spoken, a kind of pig irony—but the Contessa missed even this much, turning away to greet more guests.

He regarded them with that mixture of awe and contempt which all those who feel their lights are permanently obscured under bushels know all too well—for here was the Mayor and his latest rub, a saffron-skinned woman of teenage smoothness and eyes eons old. They gyred into the ample uptown apartment as if following an unheard gavotte, pirouetting between tight knots of gushing supplicants. The Mayor, a money-eyed rogue, was a constant worldwide talk show maven. His grinning image played upon the artificial cloud formations that loomed over his city at sunset, accompanied by the usual soft drink advertisements.

Impossibly, this glossy couple spun into Alex's orbit. "Oh, we've heard!" the Mayor's rub squeezed out with breathless ardor. "You are *so* inventive!"

The Mayor murmured something which instantly eluded Alex, who was still entranced by the airy, buoyant woman. Alex coughed, blinked, and said, "It's nothing, really."

"I can hardly *wait*," the perfectly sculpted woman said with utterly believable enthusiasm.

Alex opened his mouth to reply, ransacking his mind for some witticism. And then she was gone, whisked away on the Mayor's arm as if she had been an illusion conjured up by a street magician. Alex sighed, watching the nape of her swanlike neck disappear into the next knot of admiring drones.

"Well, *I'*ll talk to you longer than that," Louise said at his elbow.

She was radiant. Her burnt-rust hair softly flexed, caressing her shoulders, cooing and whispering as the luxuriant strands slid and seethed—the newest in biotech cosmetics.

Alex hid his surprise. "It was much longer than I expected," he said cautiously.

"Oh no, you've become the *rage.*" She tossed her radiant hair.

"When I accepted the invitation to, well, come and do my little thing, I never expected to see such, such—"

"Such self-luminosities?" Louise smiled demurely in sympathy. "I knew—that's why I strong-armed the Contessa for an invitation."

"Ah," Alex said reservedly. He was struggling to retain the sense that his head had not in fact left his body and gone whirling about the room, aloft on the sheer gauzy *power* of this place. Through the nearest transparent wall he saw brutal cliffs of glass, perspectives dwindling down into the gray wintry streets of reality. Hail drummed at him only a foot away. Skyscraper, he thought, was the ugliest word in the language.

Yet part of a city's charm was its jagged contrasts: the homeless coughing outside restaurant windows where account executives licked their dessert spoons, hot chestnut vendors serving laughing couples in tuxes and gowns, winos slouched beside smoked-glass limos.

Even in this clogged, seemingly intimate party there were contrasts, though filmed by politeness. In a corner stood a woman who, by hipshot stance and slinky dress, told everyone that she was struggling to make it on the Upper West Side while living on the Lower East. Didn't she know that dressing skimpily to show that you were oblivious to the chilly rooms was *last* year's showy gesture? Alex snuggled into his thick tweed jacket, rented for the occasion.

"—and I never would have thought of actually just making the obvious *show* of it you did," Louise concluded.

Incredibly, Louise gazed at him with admiration. Until this instant he had been ice skating over the moments, Alex realized. Now her pursed-mouth respect struck him solidly, with heady effect, and he knew that her lofty professionalism was not all he had longed for. Around him buzzed the endless churn of people whose bread and butter were their cleverness, their nerves their ineffable sense of fleeting style. He cared nothing for them. Louise—her satiny movements, her ascerbic good sense—that, he wanted. And not least, her compact, silky curves, so deftly implying voluptuous secrets.

The Contessa materialized like one of the new fog-entertainments, her whispery voice in his ear. "Don't you think it's . . . time?"

"Oh. Oh yes."

The crowd flowed, parting for them like the Red Sea. The Contessa made the usual announcements, set rules for the silent auction, then gave a florid introduction. Sweating slightly despite the room's fashionable level of chill, Alex opened his briefcase and brought out the first.

"I give you *Thrilling Wonder Stories*, June 1940, featuring 'The Voyage to Nowhere.' Well, I suppose by now we've arrived."

Their laughter was edgy with anticipation. Their pencils scribbled on auction cards.

"Next, *Startling Stories*, with its promise, 'A

Novel of the Future Complete in This Issue.' And if you weren't startled, come back next issue."

As more lurid titles piled up he warmed to his topic. "And now, novels. *Odd John*, about a super-genius, showing that even in those days it was odd to be intelligent. Both British and American first editions here, all quite authentic."

Louise watched him approvingly. He ran through his little jokes about the next dozen novels. Utopian schemes, techno-dreams.

Butlers circulated, collecting bids on the demure pastel cards. The Contessa gave him a pleased smile, making an O with her thumb and forefinger to signal success. Good. The trick lay in extracting bids without slowing the entertainment.

"I'm so happy to see such grand generosity," Alex said, moving smoothly on. "Remember, your contribu-tions will establish the first fully paperless library for the regrettable poor. And now—"

They rustled with anticipation.

A touch more of tantalizing to sharpen matters, Alex judged: more gaudy magazines. A fine copy of *Air Wonder Stories*, April 1930, showing a flying saucer like a buzz saw cutting through an airplane. Finally, an *Amazing Stories* depicting New York's massive skyline toppling beneath an onslaught of glaciers.

"We won't have that, will we?" Alex asked.

"Nooooo!" the crowd answered, grinning.

"Then let the past protect us!" he cried, and with a pocket lighter bent down to the stack he had made in the apartment's fireplace. The magazines went off first—*whoosh!*—erupting into billowing orange-yellow flame.

Burning firewood had of course been outlawed a de-cade ago. Even disposing of old furniture was a crime. They'd tax the carbon dioxide you exhaled if they could. But no one had thought of this naughtiness . . .

The crisp old pulps, century-dried, kindled the

thick novels. Their hardcover dust wrappers blackened and then the boards crackled. Volumes popped open as the glue in their spines ignited. Lines of type stood starkly on the open pages as the fierce radiance illuminated them, engulfed them, banished them forever from a future they had not foretold.

The chilly room rustled as rosy heat struck their intent faces. Alex stepped away from the growing pyre. This moment always came. He had been doing this little stunt only a few weeks, but already its odd power had hummed up and down the taut stretched cables of the city's stresses. What first began as a minor amusement had quickened into fevered fashion. Instant fame, all doors opening to him—all for the price of a pile of worthless paper.

Their narrowed faces met the dancing flames with rapt eyes, gazes turned curiously inward. He had seen this transformation at dozens of parties, yet only now began to get a glimmer of what it meant to them. The immediate warmth quickened in them a sense of forbidden indulgence, a reminder of lush eras known to their forefathers. Yet it also banished that time, rejecting its easy optimism and unconscious swank.

Yes, there it emerged—the cold-eyed gaze that came over them, just after the first rush of blazing heat. The *Amazing* caught and burst open with sharp snags and pops. On its lurid cover New York's glaciers curled into black smoke.

Revenge. That was what they felt.

Revenge on an era that had unthinkingly betrayed them. Retribution upon a time which these same people unconsciously sought to emulate, yet could not, and so despised. The Age of Indulgence Past.

"Let's slip away," Louise whispered.

Alex saw that the Mayor and his newest rub were entranced. None of these people needed him any longer. His treason was consummated, Uncle Herb betrayed yet again.

They edged aside, the fire's gathering roar covering their exit. Louise snuggled against him, a promise of rewards to come. Her frosty professionalism had melted as the room warmed, the radiance somehow acting even on her, a collector.

As Alex crossed the thick carpet toward the door, he saw that this was no freakish party trick. The crowd basked in the glow, their shoulders squaring, postures straightening. He had given these people permission to cast off the past's dead hand.

The sin of adding carbon dioxide to the burdened air only provided the spice of excitement. Unwittingly, Alex had given them release. Perhaps even hope.

With Louise he hurried into the cold, strangely welcoming night.

Sleepstory

It was at Waterloo that General Cambronne,
when called on to surrender, was supposed to
have said, "The Old Guard dies but never
surrenders!" What Cambronne actually said
was, "Merde!" which the French, when they
do not wish to pronounce it, still refer to as,
"the word of Cambronne." It corresponds to
our four letter word for manure. All the difference between the noble and the earthy accounts of war is contained in the variance
between these two quotations.

> —ERNEST HEMINGWAY,
> *Men at War*

1.

 Airboys had it easy, Russ thought. He did
not have much time to think this, because he
and their ship, the *Asskicker II*, were falling
pretty nearly straight down onto the Ganymede ice fields. Philosophy would have to come later.
If ever.

But atmospheric pilots did have it easier. Air gave
your airfoil some lift. Absence of air—that is, pure

space—at least let you turn easily, let you swivel and fire attitude rockets without trouble.

In between was *this*—the thin, howling scarf of gas boiled out of Ganymede by men. Just enough gas to make trouble, but too skimpy to use for much aerodynamic lift.

It wrenched and slapped at *Asskicker II*. Russ fought them down through the skimpy skin of atmosphere, using the air's rub to brake.

"Secured?" he called.

"Aye!" came shouts. From Zoti and Nye and Kitsov and Columbard, all strapped in, watching their subsystems.

They sounded scared. Usually in this raw war, death came fast and nobody had time to really get their guts snarled up.

But when the snake had hit *Asskicker II* they'd patched the punctures, stopped the engine runaway, saved the electricals. Salvaged a few minutes, maybe.

Certainly they hadn't salvaged the mission. The ship had been venting methane from the aft tanks, a giant fart. They could not possibly complete the dive around Ganymede and lay their egg on Hiruko Station.

The Feds had probably seen the blowout and figured they were dead. So Russ and Columbard had let their ship tumble into Ganymede's upper air, arcing around the rim of the moon so that the main Fed cruiser couldn't see them.

"We gotta get down!" Columbard called.

"Yeah, yeah," Russ answered. His copilot knew the zigs and zags of space nav, but knifing down through this shrieking air rattled her.

"Got one nine zero sec till we come out from behind Ganymede," Columbard said rapidly. "The Feds—"

"Nosing in," Russ said.

He fired their remaining engines. The methane

flared and sputtered and then growled, angry as a damaged hornet.

The sudden hard thrust threw his stomach into his throat. He gulped, eyes watering.

They dipped and banked and the speckled ground was coming up like a big hand, swatting them.

"Slam it!" he called.

Columbard gave them max power. Russ saw a blue-white peak slice by them like a snowy hook. He tried to find a level spot. *Asskicker II* had to come down vertically and had never been designed for more than scooping through the upper layers of atmospheres, to feed its ramscoops.

Damn this soup! he had time to think—and then they hit.

Hard.

And bounced.

And split.

Their reserve air blew out, *whoosh!*, taking debris with it. Russ felt a painful jab in his side and then they flipped over.

Shouts, shrieks.

A bone-jarring, splintering crash.

His board went solid red.

Power gone, armory down, life support—

Columbard's tracer showed red. Then blue.

Outside, Ganymede was a broad dirty-gray plain.

Russ found that a shattered strut was poking him in the ribs. One more centimeter and it would have punched through his skinsuit.

He would be sucking on the whole solar system, trying to inhale it—like Columbard.

He found her in the tangle, legs crushed and her eyes wide open, as though looking into some fresh truth he could not see.

2.

Russ flexed his four-fingered clamp hands and surveyed the landscape. They were on the nightside of Ganymede. Pale crescents of the other moons sliced the darkness, and Jupiter hung like a fat, luminous melon above the distant horizon. He counted three distinct shadows pointing off at angles, each differently colored.

"Maybe these'll help us sneak by optical pattern-recog detectors," he said to Zoti, pointing.

"Shadows?" she asked, puffing up a slope even in the light gravity. She carried a big supply pack. "Think so?"

"Could be." He didn't really think so but at this point you had to believe in something.

"Better get away from here," Zoti said.

"Think the Feds got a trace on us?"

She shook her head, a tight movement visible through her skinsuit helmet. "Our guys were giving them plenty deceptors, throwing EM jams on them—the works."

Russ respected her tech talents, but he never relied on tricks alone. Best thing was to get away before some bat came to check the wreck.

"We'll hoof in three minutes," Russ said.

He looked back at the crushed metal can that a big blue-black ice outcropping had made of *Asskicker II*. It didn't look like a fabulously expensive, lethal bomber now, just a pile of scrap. Nye and Kitsov came up the hill, lugging more supplies.

"Got the CCD cubes?" Russ asked Nye.

"Yeah, I yanked them." Nye scowled. He never said much, just let his face do his complaining for him.

"Think they've got good stuff?" Russ asked.

"Some fighter shots," Nye said. "Then a big juicy closeup of the snake that got us."

Russ nodded. Snakes were the thin, silvery missiles

that their Northern Hemisphere tech jockeys couldn't knock out. "Well," he said, "maybe that'll be worth something."

Kitsov said, "Worth to Command, could be. To Natwork, no."

Zoti said, "Natwork? Oh—look, *Net*work can't use anything that's classified. A snake shot will have TS all over it."

Russ asked, "TS?"

Zoti grinned. "They say it means Top Secret, but as far as we're concerned, might as well be Tough Shit. Means we make no loot from it."

Russ nodded. He hated this mercenary shit. If everything had gone right, *Asskicker II* would have lobbed a fusion head smack onto Hiruko Station. Earthside network royalties for the shot would've gone to them all, with Russ getting twice the share of the others, since he was captain and pilot.

Had that made any difference? You could never really be sure that some subconscious greed hadn't made you rush the orbit a little, shade the numbers, slip just a hair off the mark. Could that be what had let the snake through?

He shook his head. He'd never know, and he wasn't sure he wanted to.

"Still think we'll see a single yen out of it?" Zoti asked him. He realized she had interpreted his shaking head as disagreement. They would be reading him closely now. The crew wanted reassurance that they weren't doomed and he was the only authority figure around. Never mind that he'd never led a ground operation in his life.

"I think we'll get rich," Russ said, voice full of confidence he had dredged up from somewhere. He wondered if it rang hollowly but the others seemed to brighten.

"Is good!" Kitsov said, grinning.

"It'll be better if we get out of here," Russ said. "Come on."

"Which way?" Nye asked.

"Through that notch in the hills there." Russ pointed.

Nye frowned, black eyebrows meeting above his blunt nose. "What's that way?"

"More important, what *isn't* that way," Russ said. "We'll be putting distance between us and Hiruko Station."

Nye's forehead wrinkled. "You sure?"

"We don't have any nav gear running. I had to sight on the moons." Russ said this confidently but in fact he hadn't done a square, naked-eye sighting since tech school.

Zoti said tentatively, "How about a compass?"

"On ice moon?" Kitsov chuckled. "Which way is magnetic pointing?"

"That's the problem," Russ said. "No magnetic field. Let's go."

They moved well in the low gravity. None were athletes but they had kept in shape in the gym on the voyage out. There wasn't much else to do on the big carriers. Columbard had said that Zoti got all her workout in the sack, but then Columbard had always been catty. And not a great enthusiast in the sack herself, either. Not that her opinion mattered much, Russ thought, since she wasn't around anymore to express it.

A storm came sweeping in on them as they climbed away from the wreck. It was more like a sigh of snowflakes, barely buoyant in the thin, deadly methane air. It chilled them further and he wondered if they would all get colds despite the extra insulation they all wore over their combat skinsuits.

Probably. Already his feet tingled. He turned so that his bulky pack sheltered him from the wind.

They'd all get frostbite within a couple of days, he guessed.

If they could survive at all. A man in a normal pressure suit could live about an hour on Ganymede. The unending sleet of high energy protons would fry him, ripping through delicate cells and spreading red destruction. This was a natural side effect of Jupiter's hugeness—its compressed core of metallic hydrogen spun rapidly, generating powerful magnetic fields that whipped around every ten hours. These fields are like a rubbery cage, snagging and trapping protons spat out by the sun. Io, the innermost large moon, belched ions of sulfur and sodium into the magnetic traps, adding to the sleet. All this rained down on the inner moons, sputtering the ice.

Damn it, he was a sky jock, not a grunt. He'd never led a crew of barracks rats on a mud mission.

He kept his mind off his bulky pack and chilled feet by guessing what the Feds were doing. The war was moving fast, maybe fast enough to let a downed bomber crew slip through the Fed patrols.

When Northern Hemisphere crews had held Hiruko Station, they'd needed to work outside, supervising robot icediggers. The first inhabitants of Ganymede instead used the newest technology to fend off the proton hail: superconducting suits. Discovery of a way to make cheap superconducting threads made it possible to weave them into pressure suits. The currents running in the threads made a magnetic field outside the suit, where it brushed away incoming protons. Inside, by the laws of magnetostatics, there was no field at all to disturb instrumentation. Once started, the currents flowed forever, without electrical resistance.

He hoped their suits were working right. *Asskicker II*'s strong magnetics had kept them from frying before, but a suit could malf and you'd never know it.

He fretted about a dozen other elements in a rapidly growing list of potentially deadly effects.

Already he had new respect for the first Hiruko crews. They'd been damn good at working in this bitter cold, pioneering against the sting and bite of the giant planet. They had carved ice and even started an atmosphere. What they hadn't been so good at was defending themselves.

No reason they should've been, of course. The Southern Hemisphere had seen their chance and had come in hard, total surprise. In a single day they had taken all Ganymede. And killed nearly every Northerner.

The bedraggled surviving crew of *Asskicker II* marched in an eerie dim glow from Jupiter. Over half of Ganymede's mass was water-ice, with liberal dollops of carbon dioxide ice, frozen ammonia and methane, and minor traces of other frozen-out gases. Its small rocky core was buried under a thousand-kilometer-deep ocean of water and slush. The crust was liberally sprinkled by billions of years of infalling meteors. These meteorites had peppered the landscape but the atmosphere building project had already smoothed the edges of even recent craters. Ancient impact debris had left hills of metal and rock, the only relief from a flat, barren plain.

This frigid moon had been tugged by Jupiter's tides for so long that it was locked, like Luna, with one face always peering at the banded ruddy planet. One complete day-night cycle was slightly more than an Earth week long. Adjusting to this rhythm would have been difficult if the sun had provided clear punctuation to the three-and-a-half-day nights. But even without an atmosphere, the sun seen from Ganymede was a dim twenty-seventh as bright as at Earth's orbit.

They saw sunup as they crested a line of rumpled hills. The sun was bright but curiously small. Sometimes Russ hardly noticed it, compared to Europa's white, cracked crescent. Jupiter's shrouded mass flickered with orange lightning strokes between the roiling somber clouds.

Ganymede's slow rotation had been enough to churn its inner ocean, exerting a torque on the ice sheets above. Slow-motion tectonics had operated for billions of years, rubbing slabs against each other, grooving and terracing terrain. They leaped over long, strangely straight canyons rather than try to find ways around. Kitsov proved the best distance man, remorselessly devouring kilometers. Russ watched the sky anxiously. Nothing cut the blackness above except occasional scruffy gray clouds.

They didn't stop for half a day. While they ate he ran an inventory on air, water, food. If their processors worked, recycling from the skinsuits, they could last nearly a week.

"How much food you got?" Nye wanted to know while Russ was figuring.

"I'm not carrying any," Russ answered levelly.

"Huh?" Like most cynics, Nye was also a little slow.

"I'm carrying the warhead."

"What!" Nye actually got to his feet, as though outraged.

"Regs, Sergeant," Russ said slowly. "Never leave a fusion head for the enemy."

"We got to survive out here! We can't be—"

"We are," Russ said. "That's an order."

Nye's mouth worked silently. After a while he sat back down, looking irritated and sheepish at the same time.

Russ could almost sympathize with him, perhaps because he had more imagination. He knew what lay ahead.

Even if no patrol craft spotted them, they couldn't count on their carrier to send a pickup ship. The battle throughout the inner Jovian system was still going on—he had seen the flashes overhead, far out among the moons. The Northern Hemisphere forces had their hands full.

He looked down at his own hands—four clamp-fingers with delicate tools embedded in the tip of each. Combat pilot hands, technological marvels. Back on the cruiser they could detach these ceramo-wonders and his normal hands would work just fine.

But out here, in bitter cold and sucking vacuum, he couldn't get them off. And the chill seeping into them sent a dull ache up his arms.

The pain he could take. The clumsiness might be fatal.

"Get up!" he called. "Got klicks to go before we sleep, guys."

3.

They spotted the autotruck the next day at noon.

It came grinding along beside a gouged trench. The trench looked man-made but it was a stretch mark. Ganymede's natural radioactive elements in its core had heated the dark inner ocean, cracking the ice shell.

But the strip beside the natural groove was a route the automated truck used to haul mined ores.

Or so Russ figured. He did know that already, after just over a day of hard marching, his crew was wearing out fast. Zoti was limping. Maybe she *had* spent her gym time on her back. He didn't give a damn one way or the other, but if she slowed them down they might have to leave her behind.

But the truck could change all that. He stopped, dead still, and watched it lumber along. Its treads bit into the pale blue ice and its forward sensors monotonously swept back and forth, watching for obstructions.

Russ was no infantry officer. He knew virtually nothing about flanking and fire-and-maneuver and all the other terms that raced through his head and straight out again, leaving no residue of useful memory.

Had the Feds put fighting machines in the trucks? The idea suddenly occurred to him and seemed utterly logical. He could remember nothing in the flight briefing about that. Mostly because the briefing officer expected them to either come back intact or be blown to frags. Nobody much thought fighter-bombers would crash. Or have surviving crew.

Could the truck hear his suit comm? He didn't know.

Better use hand signals, then. He held up a claw-hand. Nye kept walking until Kitsov grabbed his arm. They all stood for a long moment, looking at the orange-colored truck and then at Russ and then back at the truck again.

One thing was sure, Russ thought. If the truck was carrying a fighting machine, the fighter wasn't so hot. His crew made beautiful targets out here, standing out nice and clean against the dirty ice.

He waved with both arms. *Drop your packs.*

Somewhat to his surprise, they did. He was glad to get the bulk off his shoulders.

The truck kept lumbering along, oblivious. He made broad gestures. *Pincer attack.*

They closed the distance at a dead run. The truck didn't slow or turn.

They all leaped the deep groove in the ice with no trouble. They cleared the next forty meters quickly and Nye had reached the truck when a small popping sound came from the truck rear and Kitsov fell.

Russ was headed for the hatch in the front so he couldn't see the rear of the truck at all. The popping came again and Nye fired his M18 at something, the whole clip at once, *rrrrrrrtttt!*

The popping stopped. Russ ran alongside the truck, puffing, Zoti beside him. Nye had the back of the truck open. Something came out, something all pipes and servos and ripped aluminum. Damaged but still active. Zoti brought up her M18. Nye hit the thing with the butt of his M18 and caved in an optical sensor. The fighter didn't stop. It reached for Nye with a knife that suddenly flipped up, standing straight out at the end of a telescoping arm. Zoti smashed the arm. The fighting machine tumbled out and went facedown on the ice. Russ shot it in the back of its power panel. It didn't move anymore.

"Damn!" Nye said. "Had a switchblade! You ever—"

"Get in front!" Russ yelled, turning away.

"What? I—"

"It's still armed," Russ called, already running. If Nye didn't want to follow orders that was fine with him.

They had all nearly reached the front of the truck when the fighter went off, a small *crump*. Scrapnel rattled against the truck.

"Think it's dead now?" Zoti asked, wide-eyed.

"Leave it," Russ said. He walked to where Kitsov lay facedown.

The man had a big hole in his chest and a bigger one in back. It was turning reddish-brown already. The thin atmosphere was sucking blood out of the body, the stain spreading down the back and onto the mottled ice. It made a pool there which fumed into a brown vapor. He looked at it, his mind motionless for a long moment as he recalled Kitsov once saying some dumb reg made his blood boil. Well, now it was. Clichés had a way of coming true out here.

Russ knew that even the skimpy gear on *Asskicker II* could have kept Kitsov running long enough to get back to the cruiser. Out here there was utterly no hope.

Two days, two crew. Three remaining.

And they had maybe six days of air left. Plenty of time to get their dying done.

4.

They got the truck started again. Its autosystems had stopped at the command of the fighting machine. Apparently the machine didn't send out an alarm, though, so they probably had some time to warm up inside.

He checked the general direction the truck was heading and then let himself relax. They were all exhausted.

"Nye, you're first watch," he said.

"Damn, Cap'n, I can hardly—"

"We're all that way. Just watch the board and look out the front port. I'll relieve you in two hours."

Zoti had already dozed off, sprawled on the deck.

He lay down beside her. Two hours would do more for him if he used the syntha-narrative. He plugged it in and selected a story line. No porno, no. Something as far from this war as he could get, though. Something to give him the combined benefits of subconscious combing and action-displacement.

He settled back and felt the soft buzz of electro-input. First, music. Then a slow, gentle edging into another life, another world . . .

The phone barked her awake. Tina liked the Labrador's warm woofing but her mate did not. She slapped the kill switch and cupped the receiver to her ear, then stumbled in darkness into the bathroom.

It was Alvarez from Orange County Emergency Management. The news was worse than anything she had expected: a break in the Huntington Beach dike.

"I'll send a chopper," Alvarez said in her ear, his tinny voice tight with tension.

"Don't bother—use your choppers to evacuate people. How far is the Metro running from Laguna?"

"To the stop by the river. Traffic's pilin' up there."

She leaned forward in the predawn gloom, letting her forehead press against the cool tile of the bathroom, allowing herself ten seconds of rest.

In four minutes she was walking swiftly toward the bus stop near her apartment in Aliso Viejo. Her hand comm said the next bus was due in two minutes and here it came, early, headlights spiking through the predawn murk.

On the short run into Laguna Beach Tina called the County Overview officer and got the details. The dike had broken badly and the sea was rushing inland, driving thousands before it. Three dead already and calls coming in so fast Operations couldn't even log them.

Tina yanked open a window and looked at the sky. Cloudless. A lucky break—the storm with its high winds had blown through. Had the tail end of it broken the dike?

She sensed flowing by outside the last long strip of natural greenery in the county—the hushed, moist presence of Laguna Canyon. Then Laguna's neon consumer gumbo engulfed the bus and she got off at the station. Walking to Pacific Coast Highway calmed her jittery nerves. As chief structural engineer she had to find out what broke the dike, whether the trouble was a fluke. A thousand lawsuits would ride on the details.

The Metro came exactly on time, humming on its silvery rails. Tina watched the thin crescent of Main Beach vanish behind in the gathering glow of dawn as she called up more details from OC Operations on her comm. The Metro shot north on PCH in its segregated lane, purring up to high speed. They passed the elite warrens bristling with guard stations. The Metro overtook a twencen car, a big job from the seventies with the aerodynamics of a brick. It sluggishly got out of the way. A bumper sticker underlined its splendid chrome extravagance, proclaiming THINK OF THIS AS A KIND OF PROTEST. It trailed greasy smoke.

Heavy traffic buzzed over the helipad at Newport. Cars came fleeing south, horns honking. The Metro slowed as it neared the overpass of the Santa Ana River. Helicopters swooped over a jam up ahead. They blared down orders to the milling crowd that seemed to want to stay, to watch the show.

Tina got off the Metro and walked down the light rail line. People were moving aimlessly, frightened, some stunned and wet.

The dike began here, ramparts rising toward the north as the land fell. Surf burst against the outer wall as she climbed up onto the top walk. She could see all the way to Palos Verdes as daybreak set high clouds afire with orange. A kilometer north the smooth curve of the dike abruptly stopped. She watched ocean currents feeding the break, eagerly exploiting this latest tactical victory in a vast war.

A hovercraft sped toward her along the segmented concrete top of the dike. Alvarez, Tina realized; the man had simply traced the Metro. Alvarez's dark face, split by a grin, called, "Ready for some detective work?" as Tina got aboard.

"I need a good look before the block-droppers get here," Tina said. Alvarez nodded. The hovercraft spun neatly about and accelerated.

The ocean had already chewed away a lot of prestressed concrete. Currents frothed over gray chunks and twisted steel that jutted up like broken teeth.

"A whole segment gave way," Tina said tightly.

"Yeah, not just a crack. Somethin' big happened."

Something deep and serious, she thought. This was the first major break in a chain that ran all the way to Santa Barbara. If there was a fundamental flaw they'd overlooked . . .

Tina clambered down the landward slope of the dike, studying the stubby wreckage, measuring with a practiced eye the vectors and forces that should have held. The sea murmured and ran greedily, the tide rising like an appetite. There were no obvious clues; currents had already erased most evidence. A thin scum clung to the broken slabs and Tina slipped on it.

"Hey!" Alvarez called uselessly. Tina slid down the steep slope. She caught herself at the edge of the rushing, briny flow.

The scum was pale gray goo oozing from fresh cracks in the concrete. It smelled like floor cleaner and stung her fingers. She inched her way back up, hands rubbed raw.

"Been any maintenance here lately?"

"No, I checked," Alvarez said. "Just the biolfilm treatment half a year back."

"Any modifications here?"

"Nope." Alvarez answered his comm, listened, then said, "Big choppers on the way. We better zero outta here."

She disliked losing what frail leads she had. She took a 3-D camera from Alvarez and began snapping holographic shots of the gap. She was still clambering over ruptured concrete when six enormous helicopters came lumbering in from the east, a great rectangular block swaying on cables below each.

Alvarez took the hovercraft down the inward curve of the dike and onto the frothy floodwaters. They sped way, heading inland toward half-submerged buildings. The choppers hovered one at a time and dropped their concrete plugs.

Tina listened to the pilots' running cross talk on the hovercraft comm. They gingerly released their plugs, neatly jamming up the break.

"Think it'll hold?" Alvarez asked, swinging the craft in close for an inspection.

Tina squinted. "Better." No plug was perfect, but this had stopped most of the gushing white plumes of the sea.

They turned inland. Pacific Coast Highway was meters below the water. Signs poking above the swirling water proclaimed that this was Main Street—a district, she remembered, devoted to boutiques and memorabilia from the lost days when this had been a sandy daydream land, blissful surfer country.

They sped along Main, ignoring the shouts of people marooned on roofs. "Safe enough where they are," Tina said. A man in a dirty T-shirt with HOT TO TROTSKY printed on it gave them an obscene gesture. She turned away, trying to think.

The hovercraft growled, cutting toward the north, but the water did not get more shallow. Bedraggled people perched atop cars and houses, looking like drowned rats.

"Hey!" Alvarez pointed. A body floated facedown in a narrow alley. They edged down between garages, water lapping against peeling paint.

Tina hauled in the body, an elderly woman. The arms were already stiffening. Until now Tina had been abstractly precise, gathering data. The woman's sad, wrinkled face sobered her. The brown eyes were open, staring out across the Pacific floodwaters at a distant shore only the dead can see.

They kept on.

Somehow the salty tang of the air lulled her momentarily, as if a part of her wished to withdraw from a world made abruptly raw and solid. She stared into the murky, muddy-brown waters as they skimmed over lawns. She thought of all the sopping rugs and stained furniture inside these elegant homes, the smelly sea's casual embrace. Hunger and an odd lethargy came upon her. The purring hovercraft seemed to drag her down into a soft, gauzy daydream. She often used this dazed state, allowing her subconscious to fumble with a problem when her more alert self could not make progress. The blurred sounds and smells dropped away around her and she let go. Blissful. Falling. Only for a moment.

5.

Russ wondered what shape and size of man had designed the forward seat. He peered forward through a smeared viewport, which barked his knees against the rough iron. The autotruck had been fashioned from Ganymede ore and nobody had bothered to polish rough edges. The seat bit into him through his skinsuit and somehow the iron smelled bitter, as if some acid had gotten in at the foundry.

But, far more important, the cabin was *warm*. The Ganymede cold had seeped into them on the march and they had kept the interior heaters on high, basking in it.

Three watch changes had refreshed them all, and had carried him partway through Tina's vexing puzzle. The detail in the story was riveting—all sights and sounds seemed real, crisp, vivid. It took longer to dream than that "real" time of the story.

The experience was always strange, like drifting through a moist, silky world. The symphony of intricately realized dreaming did something real dreams could not—tap deep wellsprings of the unconscious, while imposing the closure of a concrete story line. He had felt himself caught up in the problems of Tina— real ones, yes, but comfortably distant all the same.

Adventure, he thought wryly, was somebody else doing something dangerous a long way off. Earthside's continuing struggle against the greenhouse effect was quite pleasant, compared with Ganymede.

He sighed and watched the rutted terrain ahead closely. There had been no sign of activity during the day they had ridden in the autotruck. The truck was sluggish, careful, dumb. It had stopped twice to pick up ore canisters from robot mines. The ore came out of a hole in the ground on a conveyor belt. There were no higher order machines around to notice three stow-away humans.

Russ got out of the seat, having to twist over a cowling, and jerked a thumb at Nye to take over. They switched every half hour because after that you couldn't stay alert. Zoti was asleep in the back. He envied her. He had caught some downtime but his nerves got to him after a few hours.

"Helmet," he called. Russ pulled his on and watched Nye zip up. Zoti slept with hers on, following orders. The pleasure of being under full air pressure was hard to give up.

He climbed out the broken back hatch. Nye had riddled it but the pressure seal inside self-healed. Russ used handholds to scramble onto the corrugated top of the truck. He could see much farther from here. Watching the rumpled hills reassured him somehow. Scrunched down below, staring out a slit, it was too easy to imagine Feds creeping up on them.

Overhead, Jupiter eclipsed the sun. The squat pink watermelon planet seemed to clasp the hard point of white light in a rosy glow, then swallowed it completely. Now Europa's white cracked crescent would be the major light in the sky for three and a half hours, he calculated. A rosy halo washed around the rim of Jupiter's atmosphere as sunlight refracted through the transparent outer layers.

He wished he could get the crazy, whirling geometry of this place straight in his head. The Feds had knocked down all nav sats, and he couldn't stay on the air long enough to call for a position check with the carrier. This truck was carrying them away from

Hiruko Station, he thought. It would be reassuring to get some sort of verification, though. No pickup mission would risk coming in close to Hiruko.

He took out his Fujitsu transponder and tapped into the external power jack. He had no idea where the carrier was now, so he just aimed the pistol-grip antenna at the sky and got off a quick microwave Mayday burst. That was all the carrier needed to know they were alive, but getting a fix on them would be tough.

Job done, he sat and watched the slow swirling dance of the sky. No flashes, so maybe the battle was over. Only for a while, though. Neither side was going to give up the inner moons.

Russ grinned, remembering how just a few years back some of his Earthside buddies had said a real war out here was pointless. Impossible, too.

Too far away, they said. Too hard.

Even after the human race had moved into the near-Earth orbits, scattering their spindly factories and cylinder-cities and rock-hopping entrepreneurs, the human race was dominated by nay-saying groundhogs.

Sure, they had said, space worked. Slinging airtight homes into orbit at about one astronomical unit's distance from the sun was—in retrospect—an obvious step. After all, there was a convenient moon nearby to provide mass and resources.

But Earth, they said, was a benign neighborhood. You could resupply most outposts within a few days. Except for the occasional solar storm, when winds of high-energy particles lashed out, the radiation levels were low. There was plenty of sunshine to focus with mirrors, capture in great sheets of conversion wafers, and turn into bountiful, high-quality energy.

But Jupiter? Why go *there*?

Scientific teams had already touched down on the big moons in the mid-twenty-first century, even dipped into the thick atmosphere. By counting craters and tak-

ing core samples, they deduced what they could about
how the solar system evolved. After that brief era of
quick-payoff visits, nobody had gone back. One big
reason, everyone was quick to point out, was the death
rate in those expeditions: half never saw Earth again,
except as a distant blue-white dot.

Scientists don't tame new worlds; pioneers do.
And except for the bands of religious or political
refugee/fanatics, pioneers don't do it for nothing.

By 2050 humans had already begun to spread out
of the near-Earth zone. The bait was the asteroids—big
tumbling lodes of metal and rock, rich in heavy elements. These flying mountains could be steered slowly
from their looping orbits and brought into near-Earth
rendezvous. The delta-V wasn't all that large.

There, smelters melted them down and fed the factories steady streams of precious raw materials:
maganese, platinum, cadmium, chromium, molybde-
num, tellurium, vanadium, tungsten, and all the rare
metals. Earth was running out of these, or else was un-
willing to pollute its biosphere to scratch the last fraction out of the crust. Processing metals was messy and
dangerous. The space factories could throw their waste
into the solar wind, letting the gentle push of protons
blow it out to the stars.

For raw materials, corporations like Mosambi and
Kundusu grubstaked loners who went out in pressur-
ized tin cans, sniffing with their spectrometers at the
myriad chunks. Most of them were duds, but a rich
lode of vanadium, say, could make a haggard, antiso-
cial rockrat into a wealthy man. Living in zero-gravity
craft wasn't particularly healthy, of course. You had to
scramble if a solar storm blew in, and crouch behind
an asteroid for shelter. Most rockhoppers disdained the
heavy shielding that would ward off cosmic rays, figuring that their stay would be short and lucky, so the radiation damage wouldn't be fatal. Many lost that bet.

One thing they could not do without, though, was

food and air. That proved to be the pivot point that drove mankind still farther out.

Life runs on the simplest chemicals. A closed artificial biosphere is basically a series of smoldering fires: hydrogen burns with oxygen to give water; carbon burns into carbon dioxide, which plants eat; nitrogen combines in the soil so the plants can make proteins, enabling humans to be smart enough to arrange all this artificially.

The colonies that swam in near-Earth orbits had run into this problem early. They needed a steady flow of organic matter and liquids to keep their biospheres balanced. Supply from Earth was expensive. A better solution was to search out the few asteroids which had significant carbonaceous chondrites—rock rich in light elements: hydrogen, oxygen, carbon, nitrogen.

There were surprisingly few. Most were pushed painfully back to Earth orbit and gobbled up by the colonies. By the time the rockhoppers needed light elements, the asteroid belt had been picked clean.

Besides, bare rock is unforgiving stuff. Getting blood from a stone was possible in the energy-rich cylinder cities. The loose, thinly spread coalition of prospectors couldn't pay the stiff bills needed for a big-style conversion plant.

From Ceres, the largest asteroid, Jupiter loomed like a candy-striped beacon, far larger than Earth. The rockrats lived in the broad band between two and three astronomical units out from the sun—they were used to a wan, diminished sunshine, and had already been tutored in the awful cold. For them it was no great leap to Jove, hanging there 5.2 times farther from the sun than Earth.

They went for the liquids. Three of the big moons—Europa, Ganymede, and Callisto—were immense iceballs. True, they circled endlessly the most massive planet of all, 318 times the mass of Earth. That put them deep down in a gravitational well. Still, it was far cheaper to send a robot ship coasting out to Jupiter, and looping into orbit around Ganymede, than it was to haul water up from the oceans of Earth. The first stations set up on Ganymede were semiautomatic— meaning a few unlucky souls had to tend the machinery.

And here came some of that machinery now.

Russ slid back and lay down on the truck's flat roof. Ahead a team of robos was digging away. They had a hodgepodge of tracks and arms and didn't look dangerous. The biggest one threw out a rust-red stream of ore which the others were sampling.

One of the old exploration teams, then. He hoped they'd just ignore the truck.

"What'll we do?" Nye whispered over the comm.

"Shut up," Russ answered.

The truck seemed to hesitate, deciding whether to grind over to the robos. A small robo noticed this and came rolling over on balloon tires.

Russ froze. This robo looked intelligent. It was probably the team leader and could relay an alarm.

Still lying flat, Russ wormed his way over to the edge of the truck roof. He brought his heavy pilot's hands forward and waited, hoping he blended into the truck's profile.

The robo seemed to eye the truck with swiveling opticals. The truck stopped. The robo approached, extended a telescoping tube. Gingerly it began to insert this into the truck's external socket.

Russ watched the robo's opticals focus down on its task. Then he hit it carefully in the electrical cowling. His hand clanged on the copper cowling and dented it. The robo jerked, snatching back its telescope arm.

The robo was quick. It backed away on its wobbly wheels, but just a little too fast. They spun. It slewed around on the ice.

Russ jumped down while the robo was looking

the other way. It might already be transmitting an image. He hit the cowling again and then pried up the copper sheet metal. With two fingers he sheared off three bundles of wire.

The robo stopped. Its external monitor rippled with alarm lights. Russ cut some more and the alarms went off. MECHANICAL DAMAGE, the robo's status digitals said.

The other robos just kept on studying the soil.

Zoti was coming out of the rear hatch when he climbed back on the truck. "Back inside," he said. "Let's go."

They got away fast. Those robos had been easy only because no Feds had gotten around to reprogramming them.

Soon enough, somebody would. They were in for a long war out here. He could feel it in his bones.

Trouble was, Earthly interests swung plenty of weight—and mass—even out here. The old north-south division of wealth and ability was mirrored in the solar system, though warped. The Southern Confederation Feds wanted a greater share of the Jovian wealth. So they had seized a few Northern Hemisphere ice-eating bases, like Hiruko Station. Those robos now labored for the Fed factories waiting in near-Earth orbit for the ore.

The shock of actual war, of death in high vacuum and biting, unearthly cold—that had reverberated through Earthside politics, exciting public horror and private thrills.

Earth had long been a leafy preserve, overpoliced and underarmed. Battle and zesty victory gave the great publics of the now-docile planet a twinge of exquisite, forbidden sin.

Here was a gaudy arena where civilized cultures could slug it out, all the while bitterly decrying the beastly actions, the unforgivable atrocities, the inevitable horrific mischances.

And watch it all on 3-D. In full, glossy color.

The economic motivations sank beneath the waves of eager surrogate participation. Unfortunately, the two were not so easily separated in the Jovian system. The first troops guarded the automatic plants on the moons. Thus they and the plants became first targets for the fleets that came accelerating into the system.

Bucks blended with blood. Hiruko Station was the first to fall to the Feds. Now the only way to root them out was to blast the surface, hoping the ice mines would escape most of the damage. That had been *Asskicker II*'s job.

Russ wished he could get news of the fighting. Radio gave only meaningless coded buzzes, flittering through the hiss of the giant Van Allen belts. News would have distracted him from his other preoccupation: food. He kept remembering sizzling steaks and crisp fries and hot coffee so black you had to sip it slow.

Already he had to be careful in dividing up their rations. Last meal, Nye and Zoti had gotten into a petty argument about half a cereal bar. They knew there wasn't much left, even with the packs of Kitsov and Columbard.

He rode along, not minding the cold yet, thinking about fried eggs and bacon. Zoti came topside. She had been copilot and she shared his dislike of the cramped, blind cabin, even if it was warm. They were used to fighting from a cockpit, enveloped in 3-D graphics, living in an all-seeing electronic world.

"I could do without this mud-hugger stuff," Zoti said on short-range suit comm.

"Mud, now that I'd like," Russ said.

"Yeah, this ice gets to me. Brrrr! Pretty, though."

Russ studied the gray-blue valley they were entering. Gullies cut the slopes. Fans of rusty gravel spread from them across the rutted, rolling canyon floor. It did have a certain stern beauty. "Hadn't noticed."

"Wouldn't mind living here."

He blinked. "Really?"

"Look, I grew up in a ten-meter can. Rockrats for parents."

"How you like this grav?"

"A seventh of a gee? Great. More than I ever got on a tether."

"Your parents ever hit it big?"

"Last time I was home, we still measured out our water in cc's."

He waved at an ice tower they were passing. He hadn't been able to figure whether they were eroded remnants or some kind of extrusion, driven by the oddities of ice tectonics. "So to you this is real wealth."

"Sure." She gave him a quizzical glance. "What else is better'n ice? You can make air with it, burn the deuterium for power, grow crops—even swim."

"You ever done that?"

"In grav? Naw—but I sneaked into the water reserve tanks at Ceres once. Strangest thing I ever did."

"Like it better than zero gee?"

She nodded enthusiastically. "*Every*thing's better in gravs."

"Everything?"

"Well"—she gave him a veiled glance—"I haven't tried everything yet."

He smiled. "Try Earth normal sometimes."

"Yeah, I heard it's pretty bad. But grav keeps everything steady. It *feels* better."

He had wrenched his back carrying the fusion warhead and felt a twinge from it as the truck lumbered through a depression. "Not so's I'd notice," he said moodily.

"Hey, cheer up. This's a holiday, compared to fighting."

"This *is* fighting. Just slow motion, is all."

"I love it, ice and gravs."

"Could do with some better rations." It was probably not a good idea to bring up food, but Russ was trying to find a way to keep the talk going. For the first time he was feeling differently about Zoti.

"Hell, at least we got plenty water."

The truck lurched again and Russ grunted despite himself. "Maybe we should carve out some more?"

"Sure," she said lightheartedly. "I'm getting so I can spot the pure water. Tastes better'n cruiser supply."

"Wait'll we get onto the flat. Don't want this truck to speed up and leave you behind."

"Take it off auto." They had already nearly left Zoti once when she laser-cut some water-ice.

"Don't want the risk. We override, probably'll show up in a control system back at Hiruko."

"I don't think the Feds have had time to interface all these systems. Those Dagos don't know zip."

"They took Hiruko pretty easy."

"Snuck up on it! Listen, those oily bastards—" and she was off on a tirade. Russ was a Norther, too, born and bred, but he didn't have much feeling about political roots that ran back to lines drawn on Earth's old carcass. He listened to her go on about the filthy Feds and watched the lurching view and that was when he saw the bat.

It came over the far ice hills. Hard black against the slight haze of a yellow ammonia cloud, gliding when it could, jetting an ivory methane plume when it couldn't.

"Inside!" he whispered.

They scrambled off the truck roof. Zoti went in the rear hatch. He looked over the lip of the roof and saw the bat veer. It had seen them. It dove quickly, head on toward them.

The M18s were lashed to the roof. There wasn't time to get Zoti back out so he yanked an M18 free—making sure he got the one loaded with HE—and dropped off the back of the truck, slipping and landing on his ass. He stooped far over and ran by kicking back on the ice, so that he didn't bounce in the low gravity. He used the truck for cover while he got to the shelter of some jagged gray boulders.

It made one pass to confirm, sweeping in like an enormous thin bird, sensors swiveling. He wedged down among the rocks as it went over. It banked and turned quickly, coming back. Russ popped his helmet telescope out to full extension and saw that it carried rockets under the wings.

The bat lined up on the truck's tail and swooped down. It looked more like a kite from this angle, all airfoil and pencil-thin struts.

The bat was looking at the truck, not at him. He led it a full length and opened up with the HE shells. They bucked pretty bad and he missed with the first two rounds. The third caught it in the narrow fuselage. He saw the impact. Before he could grin a rocket fired from under the right wing and streaked straight for him, leaving an orange trail.

He ducked. The rocket fell short of the truck but close to him. The impact was like a sudden jar. He heard no sound, just found himself flat on his back. Mud and ice showered him.

The bat went on, not seeming to mind the gaping hole in its thin fuselage, but it also didn't rise anymore. Then it started a lazy pitch, yawed—and suddenly was tumbling end over end, like a thrown playing card.

It became a geyser of black fragments against a snowy hill.

6.

Russ had caught all the right signals from her, he thought.

It was dumb, he knew that, and so did she. But somehow the tension in them had wound one turn too many and a mere glance between them set all the rest in motion.

Sure enough, as soon as Nye left by the forward hatch to reconn over the hill, Zoti started shucking her skinsuit. Then her thin green overalls.

He wasn't far behind her. They piled their clothes on the deck and got down on them. He suggested a sitting position but she would have none of it. She was feverish and buoyant in the muted phosphor glow of the cabin, swiveling on him with exuberant soft cries. Danger, sweat, piercing cold—all wedded into a quick, ferocious, hungry battering that they exacted from each other, rolling and licking and slamming among the machine-oil smells and rough iron rub. Fast and then mysteriously, gravely slow, as though their senses stretched time in pursuit of oblivion.

It was over at last and then maybe not and then definitely not and then, very fast this time, over for sure. They smiled at each other through a glaze of sweat and dirt.

"Lord!" she gasped. "The best!"

"Ever?" Frank disbelief.

"Sure . . ." She gave him a sly smile. "The first, too."

"Huh? Oh, you mean—"

"First in real gravity, sure."

"Gravity has a way of simplifying your choices."

"I guess. Maybe everything really is better in gravs."

"Deck of an autotruck isn't the best setting."

"Damn straight. We'll give it a try in someplace better."

"You got a date." He got to his knees and started pulling on his blue long johns.

Automatically he reviewed their situation, shifting back into reality after a blissful time away. He replayed events, trying to see it whole, to look for problems, errors.

They had been forced to override the truck's controls. The bat had undoubtedly reported something, maybe even direct vid images of them. So Zoti and Nye had conferred over the board and got the truck off its designated route.

They left the marked track and ground gears to work their way up among the jagged hills. An hour later two bats came zooming over. By that time Nye had gotten the truck back into a cave. They had left the snow two klicks back, picking their way over rocky ridges, so the bats had no tracks to follow.

They sat there edgily while the bats followed a search pattern, squaring off the valley and then other valleys, gradually moving away.

That had given Russ time to think and get hungry and eat. They didn't have much food left. Or time. Unless the Norther fleet kept Hiruko busy, the Feds would have time to send a thorough, human-led search party.

So they had to change tactics. But keep warm.

Hiruko probably had this truck identified by now. Which meant they needed another truck. Fast.

Once they'd broken the code seal on the truck's guidance, they had access to general tracking inventory. Nye had found the nearest truck, about fifteen kilometers away. They had edged out of the cave when an ivory fog came easing in from the far range of rumpled mountains.

The truck moved pretty fast when its cautious nav programs were bypassed. They had approached the target truck at an angle, finally lying in wait one hill over from its assigned path.

And when Nye went out to reconn the approaching truck, Russ and Zoti had taken one swift look at each other, one half-wild glance, and had seized the time.

Nye came back through the hatch as Zoti tucked her black hair into her neck ring.

"It's coming. No weapons visible." Nye looked from Zoti to Russ, puzzled.

Russ realized he was still flushed and sweaty. "Good," he said energetically. "Let's hit it."

"Better hurry," Nye said, his face narrowing again as he concentrated on tactics. "It just loaded up at a mine."

"Okay. Come out and help me on with my pack," Russ said.

Nye looked surprised. "You still gonna carry that warhead?"

Russ nodded. "Regs."

"Look, we gotta *move*. Nobody's expect—"

"You want to pay for it when we get back?"

Nye shrugged. "Your hassle, man."

"Right," Russ said evenly.

The second truck was moving stolidly down a narrow canyon. It had the quality of a bumbling insect, dutifully doing its job.

"Flank it?" Zoti asked as they watched the truck's approach.

"Okay," Russ said. "You two take it from the sides, just after it passes."

"And you?" Nye asked sarcastically.

"Hit it right where the canyon necks in. See? I'll come in from the top."

It had finally occurred to him that the light gravity opened the choices of maneuver. He leaped from the nearest ledge, arcing out over the canyon and coming down on the top of the truck.

Zoti and Nye fired at the rear hatch, rounds skipping off the thick gray iron. A fighting machine, Class II infantry, popped out the front hatch.

It clanked and swiveled awkwardly. It had heavy guns built into both arms and started spraying the rear of the truck, chipping the metal corners. It hadn't registered Russ yet. When it did a small gun popped out of the machine's top and fired straight at him. He shot the machine three times and it tumbled over and broke in half.

Russ didn't get to see it fall. A heavy round went through his shoulder. It sent a white-hot flower of agony through him and knocked him off the truck. He landed on his neck.

7.

Tina sighed.

Ironies abounded here. Once a sleepy beach town devoted to the elixirs of sun and surf, Huntington Beach's major problem had been the traffic trying to reach the sand on Saturday afternoons. Now the problem was stopping the Pacific from getting to the people.

Tina was thinking furiously, her brow knitted sternly, when the Orange County observation dirigible came humming into view, skimming over a stucco apartment complex. The silvery bullet gleamed in the dawn's crisp radiance.

Nguyen, the head of the Federal Emergency Management Agency, called her on comm and ordered them to come up. Tina had never liked the ride up the spindly cable, but this time she was so interested in the spectacle she scarcely noticed. In the gondola beneath the great silvery belly Nguyen stood stiffly watching the disaster below.

He was short, intense, direct. His first words were, "What happened?"

"Something structural," Tina said. "I want to look at the whole dike from the sea side."

"Okay." He gestured to the pilot. The dirigible purred and moved sluggishly seaward. "Should I declare an emergency all along the line?"

"Wait'll I think this through. And check this out."

She handed him a flake of concrete with a dab of the gray goo on it.

"From here?" Nguyen sniffed at it.

"You're got a portable chem lab in the next deck, right?"

"Yes, but this is plainly an engineering malfunction. What—"

"Just do it."

She put off further questions by moving to the windows. The dark waters reached far inland to Talbert Avenue, sweeping north as far as the wetlands where the Naval Weapons Depot had been. Most buildings had their first floors submerged. Trees ringed most buildings as energy-conserving measures—shade in summer, shelter against cool winds in winter.

She thought wryly about how linked the human predicament was. The worldwide greenhouse effect had forced energy conservation to save burning oil. Global warming had also made the oceans expand and melted ice at the poles, bringing on this flood. And now people were perched in the trees, keeping dry. Maybe the hominids should never have left the trees in the first place.

The dirigible swooped along the dike's northward curve. They could stay up here forever, burning minimal fuel, another saving measure mandated by the Feds. As they swung lower Tina picked out the pale green of the biofilm protectant which was regularly applied to the dike's outer ramparts.

She asked Alvarez, "Anything new about that last painting?"

He consulted his portable data screen. "Nope. Supposed to be better, was all."

"How?"

"Stops barnacles and stuff from eatin' away at the concrete."

"Just a cleaner?"

"Lays down a mat, keeps stuff from growin'."

Now she recalled. Tina knew little about biotechnology, but she understood as an engineer what corrosive seawater did. Biofilm was a living safeguard that stopped sea life from worming its way into porous concrete. It preempted surfaces, colonizing until it met like biofilm, forming a light green shield which lasted years.

"See those splotches?" She pointed at the sea bulwarks near the break in the dike. Gray spots marred the green biofilm.

Nguyen asked, "Seaweed?"

"Wrong color."

Alvarez frowned. "How could li'l microorganisms . . . ?"

"Burrowing back into cracks, growing, forcing them open," Tina said, though her voice was more certain than she felt.

Nguyen countered, "But this product has been tested for over a decade."

"Maybe it's changed?" Alvarez asked.

Nguyen shook his head. "You said this last painting was even better. I don't see how—"

"Look," Tina said, "biotech isn't just little machines. It's *alive*."

"So?" Nguyen asked.

"Life keeps changing. It evolves. Mutates."

Nguyen blinked, disconcerted. "At this one spot?"

"Some microbe goes awry, starts eating concrete," Tina said. "And reproduces itself—there're plenty of nutrients in seawater."

The chemlab report came in then, appearing on the central screen beside the pilot's chair. Even she, an engineer, could see the gray goo wasn't the same as the biofilm.

"We're right," Nguyen said.

She eyed the long curve of the dike toward Long Beach, where offshore wedges protected the beaches. Vast stretches of anchored defenses. Were all these great earthworks being chewed up by the very biotech engineered to protect them? Ironies abounded today.

"Perhaps this is a local mutation," Nguyen said.

"For now, yes," Tina said.

"Means the product's vulnerable, though," Alvarez said, his eyebrows knitted together in worry. "Happened here, could happen anywhere. Those dikes they're puttin' in the Potomac, right by the Lincoln Memorial, f'instance."

Tina looked inland, where the monumental energies of Orange County had filled in the spaces left by 'quake damage. The Big One and the greenhouse effect had hardly slowed down these people.

Their gesture of uncowed exuberance rose in Irvine to the south: the Pyramid. Four-sided and the size of the pharaohs' tombs, but inverted. Its peak plunged into the ground like an impossible arrowhead, gossamer steel and glass, supported at the corners by vertical burnt-chrome columns. Impossible but eerily real, catching the cutting sunrise glow. Its refracting radiance seemed to uplift the toylike buildings that groveled around it.

A brown splotch coated one side of the Pyramid. She saw that it was one of the new biofilm cleaners, working its way around the Pyramid while it absorbed dirt and tarnish. Could that moving carpet go awry, too? Weaken the walls?

"There're going to be plenty of questions to answer," she said distantly.

"Be expensive to replace that biofilm," Nguyen said. "But essential, to avoid such incidents."

"How much you figure this little 'incident' will cost?" Alvarez asked.

"Five, six billion."

"Really?" Tina was surprised. "Six billion yen?"

"Or more," Nguyen said.

Tina hoped there were few dead. This whole incident was dumb, because somebody should have foreseen this biotech weakness. But engineers could not foresee everything, any more than geologists could predict earthquakes. Technology was getting to be as vast and imponderable as natural forces. The world kept handing your dreams back to you as reworked nightmares.

But they had no choice but to use technology—imperfect, human crafts, undaunted gestures before the infinite. The county lived by that belief, and today some died by it. But she knew in her bones that these people blessed by sun and ocean would keep on.

8.

Russ still had to shake his head to jerk himself out of the sunny, airy spaces of Huntington Beach. He had never been there, never even been in North America, but now he longed to be lying on a beach beneath a fireball sun.

Story-sleep wasn't supposed to cling to you like that. Maybe the extremity of his pain had screwed up the effects. Zoti had given him the sleepstory plug in an effort to supplement the autodoc as it worked on him. He could feel the hours of repair work in his left shoulder socket. A patch job, but at least the worst of the pain had ebbed.

Worse, his own memories were warped when he tried to review them. He blinked and could not bring the stale, sweaty cabin into focus. He knew Nye was saying something, but he couldn't make out what it was.

A single picture flitted through his mind. He had crashed in *Asskicker II*, but not on Ganymede. Saturn hung in the black behind the ship. And his helmet was metal, no faceplate. Comically, a road sign pointed to Earthly destinations.

Disturbing. Was the sleepstory intruding into his

long-term memory? Rewriting his life, rubbing out some features, heightening others? He would have to watch himself. If the other two caught on, he wouldn't have much conviction as a commander.

Not that he had a whole lot right now. His head dipped with fatigue and he barely caught himself before his chin struck his chest. He wiped feverish sweat from his eyes with a claw-hand.

Nye, yes, Nye was talking. What . . . ?

"Actually," Nye said with a sly sort of humor, "that shoulder may not be the worst news you got."

Russ let his head clear. He was not in a terrific mood. Nye's wit went unremarked. "What?"

"I got a readout on this truck's itinerary. Didn't have to bust into the command structure to do it, either." Nye grinned proudly.

"Great." His neck hurt worse than his shoulder. The truck's rumbling, shifting progress seemed to provoke jabbing pains all down his spine. The bandage over his shoulder wound pulled and stung. Aside from this he was merely in a foul mood.

"We're going to Hiruko Station," Nye said. "Drop off the ore."

"Well, that doesn't matter," Zoti said. "We'll just jump off somewhere."

Russ nodded blearily. His mouth was dry and he didn't feel like talking. "Right. Steal another. Play musical trucks with the Feds."

"Better hurry. We're less than twenty klicks from Hiruko."

"What?" Russ barked.

Zoti's mouth made a precise, silent O.

"Looks like you had us pointing the wrong way all along," Nye said, his humor dissolving into bitterness.

Russ made himself take a breath. "Okay. Okay." There didn't seem much more to say. He had probably screwed up the coordinates, gotten something backward. Or maybe the first truck took a turn that fouled up his calculations.

It didn't matter. Excuses never did, not unless you got back to the carrier and a board of inquiry decided they wanted to go over you with an electron microscope.

Zoti said carefully, "So close—they will pick us up easily if we leave the truck."

"Yeah," Nye said. "I say we ride this truck in and give up. Better'n freezing our tails, maybe get shot at, then have to give up anyway."

"We bail out now," Russ said.

"You hear what I said?" Nye leaned over Russ, trying to intimidate him. "That's *dumb*! They'll—"

Russ caught him in the face with a right cross that snapped Nye's head around and sent him sprawling. For once his pilot's hands were an advantage, heavy and hard.

Russ was sitting on the floor of the truck cabin and he didn't want to bother to get up. He also wasn't all that sure that he could even throw a punch while standing anyway. So when Nye's eyes clouded and the big man came at him Russ kicked Nye in the face, lifting his boot from the deck and catching Nye on the chin. Nye fell facedown on the deck. Russ breathed deeply and waited for his neck to stop speaking to him. By that time Zoti was standing over Nye with a length of pipe. He waved her away.

"Now, I'm going to pretend you just slipped and banged your head," Russ said evenly. "Because we got to get out of here fast and I don't want to have to shoot you for insubordination or cowardice in the face of the enemy or any of those other lawyer's reasons. That would take time and we don't have time. So we just go on like you never did anything. Got that?"

Nye opened his mouth and then closed it. Then he nodded.

"Do you . . ." Zoti hesitated. "Do you think we *can* get away?"

"We don't have to," Russ said. "We just have to hide."

"Hide and freeze," Nye said sourly. "How's the carrier gonna—"

"We won't hide long. How much time will it take this truck to reach Hiruko?"

"Three, maybe four hours. It's going to a smelting plant on the rim of the first bubble. I—"

"Close enough for government work," Russ said. He felt infinitely tired and irritable and yet he knew damn well he was going to have to stay awake until all this was done.

Zoti said, "Are you sure we can . . . ?"

He breathed in the stale cabin air. The world veered and whirled.

"No, matter of fact, I'm not."

9.

The fusion warhead went off prettily on the far horizon. A brilliant flash, then a bulging yellow-white ball.

Nye had rigged the trigger to go if anybody climbed through the hatch. He further arranged a small vid eye and stuck it into the truck's grille, so they got a good look at the checkpoint which stopped the truck. It was within sight of the rearing, spindly towers of Hiruko Station. The town was really rather striking, Russ thought. Some of the towers used deep blue ice in their outer sheaths, like spouts of water pointing eternally at Jupiter's fat face.

Too bad it all had to go, he thought. The three of them were lying beneath an overhang, facing Hiruko. They ducked their heads when they saw a Fed officer scowl at the truck, walk around it, then pop the for-

ward hatch. He looked like just the officious sort Russ
hated, the kind that always gigged him on some little
uniform violation just as he was leaving base on a
pass.

So he couldn't help grinning mirthlessly when the
flash lit the snow around them. The warhead was a
full 1.2 megs. Of course it was supposed to be a klick-
high air burst, designed to take out the surface structures and Feds and leave the mines. This was a
ground-pounder and it sent a wave they watched coming toward them across the next valley. He didn't have
time to get to his feet so he just rolled out from under
the ledge. The wave slammed into their hill and he felt
a soft thump nearby. Then the sound slapped him hard
and he squeezed his eyes shut against the pain in his
neck.

When he opened them Zoti was looking into his
face anxiously. He grinned. She sat in the snow and
grinned back saucily.

He looked beyond her. The hill had folded in a little and the ledge wasn't there any more. Neither was
Nye.

If it had just been snow that fell on him they
might have had some chance. He had gotten partway
out from under the ledge, nearly clear. But solid ice
and some big rocks had come down on him and there
wasn't any hope. They dug him out anyway. It seemed
sort of pointless because then all they could think to
do was bury him again.

The murky bomb cloud over Hiruko dispersed
quickly, most of the radioactive debris thrown clear off
the moon.

Russ recalled their crash of only a few days before. It seemed to lie far back in a curiously constricted
past. Now anything was possible.

His memory was still stained by the dislocations
he had suffered under sleepstory, though. Sometimes,
when he looked out of the corners of his eye, he would

see that woman, her tanned face creased by a studious frown. Tina, triumphant engineer. People like her were holding the sad, fat Earth together.

While people like himself fought over the baubles of the outer solar system. Was that what his scrambled memory meant? A foreshadowing of himself, standing on a moon of Saturn? Could the war spread that far, leaving him with a steel skull?

He shook his head. Tina would not leave him.

He had always liked historical sleepstories, the immersion in a simpler time. But maybe no era was simple. They only looked that way from a distance. The way cities looked better at night, because you couldn't see the dirt.

They sat in a protected gully, soaking up what sunlight there was, and waited. As a signal beacon the fusion burst couldn't be beat. Carrier ships came zooming over within an hour.

A survey craft slipped in low on the horizon a little later. Only when it was in sight did Zoti produce the rest of their food. They sat on a big flat orange rock and ate the gluelike bars through their helmet input slots. It tasted no better than usual but nobody cared. They were talking about gravity and its myriad delights.

10.

Tina settled into bed, the crisp white sheets caressing her with a velvety touch. The long day was finally over, though crews still worked under floodlights all along the coast. But her job was basically done.

Now the biotech jocks were on the hot plate. The media were making a big deal out of the incident. She had turned down three network interviews already.

She ached for sleep, especially after her long, luxuriant bath. Rachel came in with herbal tea to soothe her further.

But she needed something more. Languidly she reached for the sleepstory module and slipped its pressors to the base of her neck. This would plunge her to the deepest realm of slumber.

Which plot line? Logic said that after the day's events she should choose something soothing. She cocked an eyebrow at the choices. A strong story line, maybe, with a virile male protagonist. She liked someone she could identify with.

She liked war stories and science fiction. Maybe a combination . . .

She thumbed in her choice and lay back with a sensual sigh.

Music, soft at first, then simmering with dissonant strains of tension.

She was on a bleak, rutted plain. A smashed ship lay behind her and cold bit through her thin skinsuit. Jupiter churned on the rumpled gray horizon. She glanced down at her hands, which already ached from the chill, and found that they were four-fingered clamps.

This is going to be quite a delicious adventure, she thought.

Calibrations and Exercises

◆ 1. Alpha awakens 18 minutes earlier than usual. He nudges Beta up from her muzzy slumber. They make love, self-critically. Beta holds that signs of impending interpersonal problems appear first in nuances of caresses, intersections, rhythms. Alpha feels his moves and vectors being calibrated by her. He comes with a curious pressing jerk. Beta makes a deep fluttery sigh; their timed rising signal begins to buzz. Once up, they dispatch their morning tasks with brisk efficiency. Over breakfast Alpha discusses the option clauses in their bonding contract; they are in the second year of a five-year agreement which specifies in gratifying detail the terms of their living together. Alpha asks if she wishes to renegotiate anything. Beta remarks, in a slurred mumble, that he is blocking his transference to her with all this talk. He retorts that he has always regarded psychoanalysis as a disease masquerading as a cure, and then leaves for work, bristling, feeling things have come to a draw.

QUESTION: Is the score truly even?

2. As he reaches the foyer of their apartment building, a man is trying to insert a sheet of plastic into the lock of a side door. Alpha is dressed conservatively in

81

gold and red; the man wears fashionable denims. As he turns toward Alpha, warned by the muffled slide of the elevator doors, Alpha sees that the man is a Mexican-Black mixture (the most common minority associated with crimes of violence in California, Alpha recalls quickly, taking fully 37 percent of the raw totals). The man glowers at Alpha and says curtly, "Delivery man"—clearly a time-buying ruse. Alpha steps out of the elevator, calculating the situation. The plastic slips home. The lock clicks free. The Mexican-Black yanks the door open and darts through it, into the maintenance zone of the building. Alpha feels a sudden surge of adrenaline, a prickling and tingling, as he stares at the vacant doorway; his body's response has come absurdly late. Sheepishly he walks to the house telephone and dials the four-digit code, well memorized, for Security. As he is talking, a hooting alarm begins. Alpha picks up his briefcase and walks out onto Post Street and goes to work.

> PROBLEM: Alpha is 38, in reasonable health, with a
> blood pressure ratio 143/101 in the su-
> pine position. Distance from the elevator
> to the house telephone is 4.3 meters.
> Calculate:
> (a) his adrenaline rush rate;
> (b) time to inform Security.
> (c) Using (a) and (b), estimate the dis-
> tance the Mexican-Black burglar has run
> (in meters) before the alarm sounds.

3. At work Alpha reads the monthly issue of *Predex*, the professional journal for sociometricians. There is a small item about Alpha's recent development of a sophisticated interfacing matrix, for slide-through future projections. The matrix output carries explicit indicators of any value-free assumptions made earlier. *Predex* compares the matrix, in a chatty way, with the legend of Croesus. Alpha smiles.

(Abstract: Croesus frequently consulted the oracle of Delphi on matters of state. The oracle told Croesus that if he went to war against the Persians, he would destroy a great country. He went to war, and soon destroyed his own. *See index for backgrounding references.)*

Alpha reluctantly puts aside *Predex* and sets to work. He is evaluating the load factors of water usage in San Francisco, a chronic problem. The largest fraction of water is flushed away down toilets. Alpha, as a leading sociometrician, has the power to recommend new controls—San Francisco lies within his regional jurisdiction. Alpha spends the morning calculating the optimal flush in a mean-sized private home. Devices in the water closet already keep the maximum mandated flush below 2.3 liters. Alpha soon proves, from parametric analysis, that substantial savings of water (26 percent, minimax) can now come only by not allowing users to flush after every use. The only plausible scenario is to disallow a flush until after three urinations or two defecations, whichever comes first. Alpha is pleased with this result; it promises a considerable saving, when factored through the water grid of the Bay Area.

> PROBLEM: Calculate the mean urine retention rate for an adult male, age 38, blood pressure 143/101. What is the average flush rate he requires? How does he feel about this?

4.   Alpha remembers an aphorism attributed to Murray Gell-Mann: "Everything not disallowed by the laws of nature is compulsory." Gell-Mann intended this sentence to describe nature's richness, the precise implication of physical laws. Alpha feels this statement should apply to social-sexual rules as well. His con-

tract with Beta does not specifically rule out his seeing other women, after all. Thus, quitting work an hour early, he meets Delta at her walkup apartment. She is younger than Beta by 8 years and her waistline is formed of exquisite hyperbolas, viewed from the front, the two curves symmetrically pinching in to a minimum separation of 33 centimeters. Yet when Alpha lies at that place where all parts of her converge, head cradled between thighs, his mind still slips ahead to his planned trajectory. Seeing Delta at this time of day provides a reasonable cover, in case Beta should become jealous of the amount of time he spends with Delta. (Despite her theoretical lack of concern/possessiveness, Alpha senses that Beta can be tipped over the edge on such a point.) With Delta's salty musk aswarm in his nostrils, he regards this issue of sins and sensibility. He can plausibly maintain to Beta that he became trapped in a traffic jam, and spend the extra time with Delta. Private vehicles are now outlawed in San Francisco (Alpha's first major triumph), but the press of buses still slows things to a crawl during peak load times.

PROBLEM: (a) Calculate Alpha's time of arrival at home, given that Alpha and Delta do not pause for the preliminary cocktails they usually share (margaritas). Allow 28 minutes for their copulation.
(b) Calculate the arrival time with margaritas, but with no foreplay.
(c) Redo part (a), adding an air pollution alert from a methyl plant explosion, which halts all commercial buses for 19 minutes.
(d) Estimate the credibility of Alpha's claim, upon reaching home, that his delay was due to part (c) and had nothing whatever to do with Delta.

5. On this particular Saturday, Alpha meets his son (9 years, 4 months), the only testament to his first bonding contract. They participate in the Dad's Day Mercury Hunt. Into the sewers of San Francisco they descend, orange flashlights spiking through the murk. Mercury, now exceedingly rare, commands a price in excess of 1000 New Dollars a kilogram. In earlier, wasteful, uncaring times, commercial-grade mercury was poured down sinks and drains to dispose of it. The heaviest metal (13.5 times the density of water), it immediately sought the lowest spots in the sewer system and pooled there. Alpha and his son wade through the coiled tunnels; other fathers and sons shout gaily in adjacent tubes, and their lights cast sparkling reflections from the wrinkled skin of the flowing waters. His son is clumsy, splashing through puddles and bumping his head on the low curved ceilings. Their conversation sputters along; the acoustics of these concrete tubes seems to make each word have a hollow center. Alpha catches his boot on something and spills into the scum of a standing pond. He curses. His son bends down. In the flashlight's cone they see a seam of tarnished quicksilver. Alpha has stumbled on a crack where two pipes butted unevenly. In the crack mercury gives off its smudged glitter, a thin trapped snake worth at least 400 New Dollars. Alpha slaps his son's back and for the last time that day feels a genuine surge of emotion. Later, outside, they win fourth place in the Dad's Day competition; the profits from collected mercury go to the city's extensive program for abandoned children. As they stand in Golden Gate Park sipping from steaming cups of coffee, feeling the chill bite of the air, Alpha talks and jokes with the other fathers. There is much skeptical discussion of the new Emergency Provisions enacted that week by Congress. Alpha nods earnestly to what the other men say. He waits for a suitable pause in their conversation and then says, "If pro is the

opposite of con, what's the opposite of progress?" His son laughs earnestly at this.

> QUESTION: Does Alpha actually agree with the joke?
> Does his son?

6. He arrives early for his self-defense class. The instructor is not there. She is rarely on time, a fact which Alpha always notices; it is one kernel in his simmering resentment of her. Thoughts of the Mexican-Black man in the foyer swim up to the conscious level once more. In the stale-smelling gym he trundles out the kick target, a padded wafer of canvas which turns about its base as a fulcrum. He adjusts the target. Somewhere he has read that the average weight of muggers in the city is 84.6 kilograms, the average height 1.73 meters. He raises the tan canvas target to where he estimates the throat of a 1.73-meter-high man would be, an idealized spot hanging in the cold air, a disembodied Adam's apple. Alpha backs off and comes at the target from the side, using a high kick, heel turned outward to take the impact. He misses clean. Alpha switches over to his frontal kick, striding innocently toward the target and then whipping his knee up, lashing out and up with his foreleg. The ball of his foot smacks the target with a satisfying thud. Alpha springs back balanced and ready, eyes narrowed, anticipating the canvas bag's recovery. The instructor comes into the chilly room. Alpha feels oddly uncomfortable, anxious, sheepish.

> EXERCISES: Estimate Alpha's height in meters.
> Estimate the instructor's height.

7. Beta's agriresearch project is not going well and fine lines of strain develop in her relations with Alpha. He offers to apply some of his techniques to her problems, on an informal basis, of course. Beta purses her lips and nods. Her eyes flicker once and then become unreadable. Alpha sets to work. Beta is supervising

forced-growth schemes to dramatically raise food production. They have tried high-CO_2 greenhouses for the plants, with indifferent success; similarly, a back-burner project to breed for larger leaves—thus increasing their efficiency of sunlight use—seems to have mixed returns, at best. Alpha tells Beta to drop these programs and deflect the staff from them to better ideas—primarily, fabricated foods. He advocates pushing ahead on the single-cell protein, a football-sized gray dollop grown in synthetic ethyl alcohol. Similarly, glucose can be made from sawdust. Alpha smiles at her, sure of himself on this new ground, and taps his pencil decisively on their organiform dining table. She frowns. After the fabricated goods are grown, Alpha goes on, they can be puffed, salted, sugared, laced with high-fat derivatives for taste, and used to adulterate the corn-based or potato-based mass giveaway foods. This will keep the nutrient density at a respectable level in northern California, he calculates. Problems of zinc deficiency, which worry some of the staff, can be worked out later. Beta blinks, nods, says nothing.

QUESTION: Estimate the probability that Beta wanted any advice at all.

8. By clever management of a trip to the eroding Eastern Seaboard, Alpha arranges to return early and thus spend a night with Delta. They eat at Cambodian restaurant (fluffy vegetables, a sauce like air, dense layered cakes of a white meat) and return to her apartment. It is a high encased space above the city; Alpha fluxes the wall and watches headlights swarm like yellow hornets in the circle below. Delta appears to him as an eddy of warmth. Outside, Xmas is coming; shoppers mill and scatter below; on the gray monolith of an office building a nondenominational angel appears, shimmering. He murmurs to her that she is enough to stiffen a priest, even in these out-moded, discounted holy days. She blows him a snog, he merges into bil-

lowing gold cloud banks of philosophy. Is this Delta?
Or Beta? Later, in the thin light of morning, he lies beside her (Delta it is, indeed) and feels seeping from him
the soft consolations of chemistry that pad the hard
skeleton of facts:

(a) that his hair fell out at age 26, from
    anthracene in the meat preservatives of
    that era;
(b) but still, given (a), a perma-wig suffices;
(c) then, from complications with the anthra-
    cene, he lost his teeth and
(d) now has a removable denture. Molars of
    solemn hardness, eternal, an implied re-
    buke to the easy soft slide of skin around
    them.

Alpha blinks himself into the new day, to confront a
fresh problem. He has not told Delta of his chemical
hair, his ceramic mouth. How to avoid it? His comfortable, familiar life with Beta suddenly beckons: the
known, the anxiety-free. But here he is and, vanity
stretching thin, he does not want Delta to see these
signs of deformity, of aging. He rolls smoothly out of
the gurgling bed and pads to the sink, which lies
within view of her. To remove the denture, yes, scrub
it quietly, getting into the browned crevices (artfully irregular, flawed, human-seeming). In those pockets lurk
the telltale rancid odors; if she smells them upon arising she will know all. Or so he imagines. He runs the
water fast and hunches over, backed turned to that if
she does look she sees mostly ass and bathrobe, a sight
of implied unwelcome. He relies on the politeness that
prevents outright staring at a person performing acts of
maintenance or plumbing, however intimate the two of
them might have been only moments before. He makes
noisy use of the toothbrush, fumbles it into place and

scuttles bedward, all—he notes—without arousing interest, without causing an eyelid to flicker.

QUESTION: Does she know, actually?

9. Alpha has seen the future and found it, by and large, scruffy. Unless, of course, proper methods are employed. Technique is, after all, the whole point. Every major culture has had its way of reading the future. (In ancient Rome, he is fond of pointing out, divination of the future was the function of the College of Augurs, which was still flourishing as late as the fourth century after Christ. Ranging in size from 4 to 16 members, the augurs worked principally in Rome itself—close to the center of power—advising senators, generals, even emperors. Their primary method was to ascend a hill at midnight, to survey a particular quadrant of the night sky and seek omens in shooting stars, clouds and storms, and the flight of birds. Other techniques the augurs employed included the casting of lots and the examination of the entrails of animals, specially disemboweled for the purpose.) Alpha realizes that his earnestness on this point makes him vulnerable to quick stilettoes of wit from Beta. But it helps him in the weekly meeting, such as this one:

The Board reviews his flush-quenching proposal. Ecoaccounting gives it a 93 percent reliability rating; there are few side effects. One of Alpha's rivals, a ferret-faced man, counters that trying a two-defecation minimum between flushes in an office building will cause hostile intergroup relations. Alpha points out that he is only proposing a program for private homes; office environments (where 43 percent of all flushes transpire) are excluded. The usual argument breaks out among the Board: enforcement or education? Alpha adroitly sidesteps the issue, reasoning that one makes only enemies that way.

PROBLEM: Estimate, using standard forecasting methods, the impact of a two-defecation minimum on adolescent dating practices over the next decade.

10.   Alpha accompanies Delta and Beta to the estuaries of the San Francisco Bay, for a holiday of boating. He notes that the influx of seawater into this region has exceeded the allowed parameter space and makes a note to refer this to Enforcement. He and Beta watch a cloud sculpture being carved by a high, darting flittercraft. The pilot chops, prunes, extrudes, and slices the taffy-white cumulus until it takes on the trim features of Lantanya, the current 3-D star. Next to her he sculpts a being: serpentine tail, exaggerated fins, knotted balls of cotton for feet. The act is admirably timed: as the flitter shepherds the remaining puffs into place, to shape the snouted face, the eyes turn ominously dark. They expand, purpling, and suddenly lightning forks from a rolling wall of thunderheads that splits the dragon in two. The sullen clouds churn. Claps of thunder roll over Alpha and Beta.

Somehow, he and Beta end up taking shelter under different boating sheds. Delta comes stumbling in from the spattering avalanche, half soaked. They stand a slight distance away from the rest of the holiday crowd and watch the downpour. Alpha savors the scent of first rain; like popcorn and tobacco, the smell is somehow always better than the reality. As he stands, hands in pockets, Delta tells him. Haltingly at first, she relates how she has just signed a three-year contract with a traveling executive. The executive will stop by when he can, at unpredictable intervals. The man expects her to always be ready, though not necessarily always alone when he appears. So she and Alpha must see each other less frequently, and be more cautious; she does not wish to offend her mate by flaunting her relations with others. Delta wishes things were otherwise, but she really wants to make this contract work. It's time she was beginning a series of more substantial relationships. She says all this with a becoming smile. Her voice is warm and soothing over the drumming of the rain. Alpha's face clenches. She begins to apologize. He says, "Things happen, people do things, and that's it." Meaning: Words are ineffective; only actions matter. She has acted and now he has only words. She murmurs something, but Alpha reels away into the rain, his mind a . . .

QUESTION: Is the story true? or is she trying to get rid of him?

11.   His visits to his father are periodic but not frequent. Before leaving the apartment and the brittle silence that hangs between him and Beta, he wanders restlessly to the kitchen and finds there a raw cabbage, partially cut away. It squats on a sideboard, resolutely natural, as mute rebuke of his advice to Beta about fabricated foods. He slices into its waxy layers and plucks out a bit of the center. He eats it. The sting fills his mouth. He feels in this small fact some new connection to Beta, and kisses her warmly on the way out.

He takes the Bay Area Rapid Transit to the MacArthur station and changes, to go south and then east to Pleasanton. The BART car rattles onto the long bridge which spans a crevasse, mute memory of the Quake. The light and airy filaments flicker by. Alpha reflects that there is a lot of truth in suspension bridges. The impending visit to his father nags at his mind and he turns to reading. He finds it difficult to know, reading popular news magazines, whether one is really thinking about things or simply rearranging one's prejudices. He suspects most news is reported so as deliberately to blur the distinction. He reads of the Exodus of the million from India: freighters jammed with starving human cargo, bound for Australia in a gesture of defiance against the food withholders, the white devil farmer-murderers. One ship has sunk already. Sabotage? Accident? A sly portent from the Australian navy? He suspects the latter; indeed, a scenario cast last month predicted as much. The eternal rule of sociometrics was that all island cultures newly entered on the stage of power are aggressive: Japan, England, dim Crete. Now Australia; it followed as the night the day. Alpha sniffs, turns the page, and reads that what Nietzsche *really* meant when he said God is dead, was that the orgasm had been separated from social usefulness. He closes the magazine abruptly just as the BART car pulls into the station, a mere block from the square white place that encases what is left of his father.

The visit begins with Alpha's ritual offering of forbidden fruits: chocolate almonds, a half bottle of cognac (small enough to hide from the nurses), a snog mistifier. The old man rambles on in a softly intense voice, recounting his clearly seen visions of the 1950s, life histories of people now dead. His eyes are small and cloudy, framed in a crosshatching of wrinkles that shift and crinkle as his lips move. Alpha feels himself slipping away as this man, born in 1935, instructs him in how to live, with stories from ancient eras to illustrate his points. Alpha tries to interject, to make the conversation two-way, but this mottled raisin of a man meanders on, pausing only to crunch an almond, awash in temporocentricity as he shuffles through implausibilities about auto racing, black-and-white movies, new dances, great men glimpsed from a distance, using a firearm to kill an animal for food, cigarettes . . . and Alpha flees, a smoke screen of excuses disguising his abrupt liftoff and exit, something running cold and weak through him as he hurries to the BART station.

He resolves, in the antiseptic BART car, to stop and see Delta on the way home. She seems older now, in the enfolding hand of her executive; his infrequent visits find her brisk and urbane, her conversation a smart rattle of wry observations, insider's jargon, epigrams. He remembers her now, in daydreams, as standing hipshot, the cradle of her abdomen tilted, jaunty. The distance between Beta and Delta is widening. He feels himself suspended between them.

He glances at his watch. Sighs.

PROBLEM: (a) Given random motion and access by Delta's executive, how does the probability of an unpleasant surprise, while Alpha is in her apartment, increase with time? Exclude the executive's lunch hour (he always eats with business associates, for tax purposes), transit time, and occasional illnesses. (Here "occasional" translates as 9/365 of a year.) (b) Estimate the probability that the executive is the Mexican-Black in the foyer.

12. Months later, Alpha takes the bus to work. He glides in a smooth arc around the perimeter of the new public works area, carved from the old Sunset district. The new façades gleam in the lancing sunlight. Alpha recalls vaguely that once there were porches here dotted with people; children playing with sticks and balls in the street; an occasional hearty, blackened tree; small grocery stores; signs in the windows for at-home businesses; knots of dungareed men, hands in hip pockets as they talked and squinted in the sun. Where are they? The streets are clean, safe. Why are the people not here? There are benches provided, far better than uncomfortable stoops and porches. Children could play on the lanes of fresh grass. Alpha frowns. He glances up; a face is bracketed in a window above. The man seems swarthy, familiar; it is the man in the foyer. At that moment the bus surges forward and Alpha stares straight ahead, unsure of what to do.

Shortly thereafter, Beta announces that she wants to terminate their contract prematurely. She agrees to pay whatever unusual expenses this requires of him.

A news item in the fax carries a photo: the

Mexican-Black. He has been charged with assault, convicted, and sentenced to three years in a labor gang.

Predex asks him for a major review article, to be accompanied by Alpha's photograph.

He graduates to a more strenuous self-defense class.

His policy on water use, including the flushing mandates, becomes a Regional Law.

His father dies suddenly of cardiovascular arrest.

Delta is rejected by her executive, her contract bought off. After a week of slammed doors and dropped forks, she makes herself available to Alpha twice a week, no contract demanded.

His problems, which once loomed as a denumerably infinite set, have now shrunk, as though exponentials, to zero. Difficulties disappear, hyperbolically.

And yet, and yet . . . Alpha feels that something is missing.

QUESTION: Can he calculate it?

Leviathan

Something was after them.

This bothered Beth not at all. "Rikki," she said languidly, "what do you smell?"

Rikki curled its prehensile tail around a branch and, with an unconscious display of strength, lifted itself above their luscious jade bower. "Musk. Bitter. Sweaty."

"Air spider?"

"Worse. I know it not."

Rikki cast off in the light gravity, turned an artful flip, and landed with all six legs atop a bristly fern. "Call Mother," it said, ears twitching.

"Oh, all right." With a tug at her ear Beth tuned the microwave antennae tracery in her skull to her mother's wavelengths. She relayed Rikki's misgivings and her mother's silky tones sounded in her head.

"I'm sure the two of you can handle anything aboard the Leviathan," came the smooth, utterly controlled reply. "I've allowed no new species in."

"How 'bout that cat-bat? Took my arm off, Mom."

"But I replaced it." She sounded affronted.

"I know—valuable experience, you said."

"And it was."

Beth raised her orange eyebrows and tuned out her mother. "Rikki-tikki-tavi, what say you?"

"Closer. Smelly. Three of them."

"Let's climb some clouds."

They fled using small jet packs. The tangled yellow-green jungle spread below them and then curved overhead, making a shimmering, distant ceiling. Fog wreathed them as they passed over a glinting lake. They were at the very center of the Leviathan. This bowl of leafy wealth was cut by great air passages, allowing in broad yellow beams of sunlight. Once above the cottony clouds, Beth arrowed toward the air tunnels.

They played swift, darting games as they swooped outward along a radial tube, gaining acceleration from Leviathan's spin. The tube walls were a dense, moist canopy chirping and squealing with life. A sleek skyrat shot up at them from an olive limb. It rode a crosswind, unfurling eggshell-blue mainsails, coming down fast on Rikki.

This proved to be a mistake. Rikki flipped its navigation tail around and extended black claws. The skyrat tried to trim its sails all along the mast which doubled as its spine. Too late. Rikki banked with its nav-tail and slashed a long gash down the sail, leaving a spreading red stain across the gossamer blue tapestry.

"Neat," Beth called as the skyrat screamed and tumbled away.

"Three still coming," Rikki called.

"We'll lose them." They were probably some new adaptation, she thought. Biotechs built up spacelife from Earthly animals. Even this Leviathan had a simple mental template, plus neocortex add-ons.

Beth loved to soar outward, her wings spread to the steady breath of the Leviathan. This hollow spoke in the great rotating cylinder-beast carried gases exhaled by inner layers. Smelly, damp—but alive with migrating minibirds, too, swarming like rainbow splashes in the lofting air.

She loved visiting her mother. The Leviathan was a vast living ship, demanding her mother's intricate eco-control every moment. And because no Leviathan could be made perfectly safe, the very air here murmured with the fevered kiss of danger. This excitement mingled with a warm sense of being in her mother's loving embrace, in a way no mere single body could equal.

They were tired when they reached the Leviathan's skin and found a viewing blister. Rikki snagged boxy, purple fruit and they fell to smacking, licking excess. Through the crystalline blister walls Beth watched the Leviathan's spin bring myriad schools of spacelife coasting by in the outside darkness.

Ugly, yes. Tough, warty, flexible black skins. Huge orange eyes. Panels for collecting the wan sunglow. Tight mouths, stingy with internal gases. Triple spines, adroit geometries more like sailing ships than predators. Yet only a century of biotech yawned between these simple constructions and the Leviathan's vast complexity.

Rikki pointed with a spindly finger. Against the framing blackness Rikki looked more like the mixture of otter and ferret which had been its starting point, but its high forehead and perpetually sardonic mouth implied its true cleverness. "Comet. Catch."

"Ah!" Beth wiped her mouth with the back of her hand. "Mom'll be glad."

To reach the tumbling chunk of ice ahead the Leviathan jetted great yellow-white plumes behind it. Hydrogen peroxide frothed in translucent tubes, meeting catalase in nozzled chambers. Beth felt steady thrust. This far from the sun, with even majestic Saturn only a distant dab of cool blue-white, organic rocketry was the best propulsion.

Chill seeped through even the multiple cystalline

layers of the blister. Beth pushed off, seeking a warm outdraft from Leviathan's belly. The centrifugal gravity here was stronger, deflecting her arc—and this effect saved her.

Something sleek and rust-red flung itself at her. It swiveled tripod legs, bringing around a set of gaping pink jaws and small, glinting teeth.

They snapped shut on air. Beth had windmilled her arms, bringing her legs up, missing the teeth by, literally, a whisker.

She had never seen this horror before. It snapped at Rikki, who had dug claws into its crusty back.

Three of them. And here came the second, out of leafy concealment. Beth threw her knife with an overhand flip. The thing went still, drifting past her with the knife point stuck out the back of its reddening neck.

Rikki had the first in a stranglehold. Beth spotted the third nightmare behind her. Its three legs spun forth a weighted red whip. The whip caught her arm, stinging painfully. Prickly thorns rasped as she tried to jerk free.

If you can't dodge 'em, she thought, join 'em.

Beth yanked on the whip and brought her boots up. She hit with a satisfying crunch and snap; low gravity makes for flimsy construction.

The thing yowled and fled. Rikki's attacker hung limp, its bruised-blue tongue lolling.

"Joy. I joy," Rikki said.

Beth rubbed the yellowing welts on her arm. She called her mother. "Fun's fun, Mom, but that was too close."

"I must have missed that adaptation," the supple voice sounded. "Perhaps they came aboard during the Leviathan breeding as eggs."

"You *mate* Leviathans?"

"They long for it. Easier to breed than to manufacture them."

Beth blinked. "Look—Rikki's hurt."

Rikki flattened its ears in disagreement. "Love duty is."

"No," Beth said, "we should doctor that some."

The three-legged flyer had gashed Rikki's ribs. "You forget," Mother's voice said, "that Rikki is designed for self-repair."

"But Rikki's hurting!"

"Love duty is," Rikki said, brushing away Beth's hands.

"I neglected full craft inventory," Mother said. "I apologize. Here—"

To Beth's surprise, her mother appeared—as well as she could. This manifestation was a flock of ratbirds. They burst in clouds of brown-red from the foliage, coming together in a jostling tapestry. Wings beating the air, calling, they formed a crude human figure. As Mother saw her own shape through Beth's appraising eyes, she sharpened the outline until the hovering bird-cloud approximated the face Beth remembered so well from her childhood. The warm, wry mouth and regal head which had been demolished in the accident. Only her mother's mind and blunt senses remained, managing the Leviathan's intricacies.

Her mother's voice whispered in Beth's mind, "So many details! I'm never done, dear. I fear I was distracted by the comet harvesting. The Leviathan is joyful with its success."

Beth gazed forward as they overtook the cometary head. This far from the sun it was an inert gray-white icesteroid. Beth felt happy for her mother, whose housekeeping duties for the Leviathan occupied every neural circuit of her resurrected brain. Assembling the ratbird replica was a touching gesture. But as the Leviathan began peeling layers from the icesteroid Beth's eyes widened.

"Look at that dark stuff, Mom. That's no ice-head." Beth gestured at the hovering ratbird swarm, though she knew her mother could see better by tapping directly into Beth's own eyes. "See? Scrape off the first few meters, there's nothing but rock underneath."

"Oh . . ." Disappointment laced the silky voice in Beth's head.

Beth's face clouded. Her mother's whole life-support depended on making a profit, on selling ice to the inner planets. The Leviathan had to pay its way.

Beth felt her mother's chagrin—fretting, muddy-brown streams of emotion. That provoked her to kick at the blister wall, calling out to the Leviathan's mind. Beth could sense the Leviathan's sluggish thought patterns lurking behind her mother's.

"Hey, you! You find a nice rich comet head, hear? Right away!"

The Leviathan whimpered and dutifully began firing its rumbling jets.

"It's only an animal, dear," her mother said.

Beth fumed as acceleration took hold. Damn these animals! She needed to appeal to the Leviathan's ancient origins, motivate it. Now what had it been originally? Oh yes—

"Good boy. Now—fetch!"

Shakers of the Earth

1.

1988

Squinting against the slicing sunlight, Dwight Raser shouted, "Lift!"

The excavation crew leaned heavily on crowbars. The heavy-duty winch roared, chains clinked and tightened, dust stirred in the desert breeze—and nothing happened. The crew was already tired from a half day of laborious picking away at the dinosaur vertebrae. They grunted and thrust down harder to free the enormous chunk of pale, sandy fossil.

"Careful!" Mito could not help herself crying out. She reached over and touched Dwight's arm, alarm widening her eyes.

Dwight glanced at her, seeming to be more surprised at this touch from a woman who was normally reserved, compact. "That sucker's heavy, but don't you worry. We'll get it—"

Something broke free at the base of the vertebrae and the winch growled louder. It was mounted on the back of a grimy flatbed truck. Mito watched the big black tires fatten as they took the weight.

Dwight had estimated over three thousand pounds. Why did Americans persist in that antiquated system of units? Mito watched the mass lift with excruciating slowness and translated into kilos. A thousand! How could the winch—

It couldn't. A thick steel-blue bar supporting the chains bent abruptly. The crew scattered—except for one young woman, who held on to her crowbar.

Something snapped. The stony vertebrae lurched, dropped. The woman screamed.

Dust settled as she lay sprawled.

The next few minutes were a fevered blur. Shouts. Attempts to free the woman's leg from under the mass. Recriminations. Angry denials. Sweaty tugs at the crowbars.

Dwight said nothing, just walked around the tilted chunk that had come down to them out of a hundred and fifty million years of pressing silence, and thought. Mito watched him closely, and not merely to distract herself from the contorted face of the woman.

Three young men began digging at the hard-packed soil around her calf but Dwight stopped them. Instead he told the crew to realign the chains. An angle here, oblique tension there, forces vectoring away from the crushed leg—Mito gained fresh respect for the man's quick competence. She was more at home in cool laboratories and had always felt awe for the rough-and-ready elements in science, the rub of the real.

As the crew got ready their faces were drawn, eyes hollow. If the chunk of massive vertebrae slipped again, it could roll.

The woman lay staring blankly up into the piercing winter sun, shock numbing her. She mumbled incoherently. Mito wondered if it was a prayer.

The crew set themselves, digging in. Mito could see wary flickers in their faces as they calculated where they would flee if something went wrong. Following

Dwight's gesture, Mito took hold of one of the woman's shoulders and set her feet to pull. Two men also held the woman. They all looked at each other, nodded, said nothing.

"Lift!" Dwight called again.

This time the massive bulk tilted, escorted by crowbars. The grinding labor of the winch swallowed a chorus of grunts.

The sandy chunk rose a centimeter, two, three—Mito pulled. The woman slid free. They dragged her several meters away and she began yelping with pain.

After a Jeep had taken the woman away for a long, jouncing journey into San Ysidro, she stood with Dwight and watched the crew beef up the hoist assembly. Nobody suggested knocking off for the day.

"Damn stupid, that," Dwight said. "Some kinda introduction for you, eh?"

"You said yourself that it is not easy to estimate the weight of such segments," Mito said.

"Well, I screwed that one up pretty bad." He scuffed at the dust. "This baby's sure bigger than that 'Ultrasaurus' Jim Jensen's been talking about. He found a spine of one a few years ago. They didn't get anybody hurt, though."

The skeleton was mostly uncovered now. The deep trench curved along the brow of a worn sandstone bluff. Dwight's terse report had said it was 140 feet long, bigger than Diplodocus and bigger even than the largest of the plant-eaters, Brachiosaurus.

Mito said, "A set of vertebrae so massive can easily—"

"Two-inch cold rolled steel, too, just gave way."

"Do not blame yourself. That woman was slow." Her voice must have given away the depth of her feeling, for Dwight turned and looked at her with surprise, something fresh coming into his face.

"Thanks for sayin' so," he said quietly. "But it's my fault."

She saw then beneath the gruff manner he was tired and sad and yet undaunted. "My dad, he used to say being fast on your feet was one talent nobody could teach you. Maybe so."

A moment passed between them which she was to remember to the end. A crinkling of his eyes, a wryly sour smile tugging at the corners of his mouth. Brooding, assessing blue eyes. She breathed shallowly, as if to not disturb the currents that brushed between them. She had found Americans confusing, but this man held a kind of limpid mystery.

She had always been drawn to puzzles, and a man like this was doubly odd. A Westerner in both senses of the word, cowboy/scientist, walnut-brown from years of scouring the rocky wastes, yet also known for his precise, meticulous excavations of great fossils.

He had made this remarkable find by dragging an eight-gauge shotgun through these ranges on a wheeled cart. It fired a slug of soft metal into the ground. The slug flattened and sent out a pulse of sound waves. An array of microphones lowered down a drilled hole picked up the waves. A computer unfurled their signals into a three-dimensional picture of the sandstone beneath. Sound sped through bone faster than through stone, and the difference in arrival time cast a sharp sound-shadow. Oak Ridge had developed the shotgun technique to find old sties where drums of radioactive waste had been buried. Dinosaur bones were about the same size, and paleontologists had seized upon this happy accident to extend their grasp.

"This sucker's gotta be ten EEUs, easy," he said.

"Uh . . . EEU?"

"Oh, sorry. Field jargon. Equivalent Elephant Units, a little joke. Elephants weigh about seven and a half tons. This guy's gotta be ten EEUs—that's twice the mass of a Brontosaurus."

"What will you name it?"

"Well . . ." He seemed a bit embarrassed. "I figure

the ground shook when it came by. How 'bout Seismosaurus?"

She allowed herself an amused smile. Her hair was pulled back in a severe black bun held with a blue clasp and she wore a tan field jumper. Dealing with men in such delicate professional matters had never been her strong point, and it was best to not give any unwanted signals.

He led her to the tail dig. They climbed down through nearly three meters of sandstone into the cool trench. The beast had apparently died beside a river and had been quickly buried by drifting sand, she remembered from his report. That kept predators from rending and scattering the bones.

This was a wonderful discovery site, deep inside a federal wilderness area, easy to hide and defend from tourist-vandals. Dirt bikers didn't like the rippling rock formations. This was an upthrust of the Morrison Formation which stretched across the American West. It held the great herbivores, a massive sheet of rock entombing the classic era of giants. They had found possum fossils here within the first few days of scraping, mere minor newcomers on the scale of deep time.

She sneezed from the dust and knelt to follow his description. He had launched into lecture mode, probably to put her at ease, letting her lapse back into her usual air of formality.

"These're Late Jurassic rocks, laid down in a river channel that sliced into older red shale. It's fine-grained sandstone and gray shales with lacings of reddish-brown and tan-yellow. Material was mostly unconsolidated, which accounts for the undisturbed fossil."

It was a beautiful job, stripping away the rock at an inch a day to reveal the smoothly curving, colossal spine.

"These projections, big fat chevrons, see? I figure they helped adjust the weight. Beast like this, carryin' the load's a big problem."

"Thus the hollow bones," she said.

"Huh? How'd you know that?" A sudden scowl.

"Do not patronize me, my colleague." She enjoyed the consternation that flitted across his face.

"Okay, let's cut the socializing. I hoped you Los Alamos types could tell me what I've got here."

"Indeed, I can." Her visiting two-year appointment under the U.S.-Japan exchange program gave her freedom to pursue eccentric ideas. On impulse she had volunteered for Dr. Raser's curiously worded request. He had refused to give away any information about the fossil material he had brought to the laboratory—including the fact that some of it was not fossil at all.

She had prepared her conclusions for a more formal presentation, but somehow, standing here in a shaded trench amid the hammer and clang of the continuing work, sweaty even in the winter sun, skin plated with tangy dust—it all felt sharper, pungent, more earthily real than her antiseptic life amid pyrex precisions.

"I respect your intentions," she said, wishing her tone was not naturally so stiff; a liability of her strict Japanese upbringing, perhaps. "Still, I would have appreciated knowing exactly what I was given to analyze."

He chuckled. "I wanted straight scoop, no preconceptions."

"I knew the scrapings had to be old, of course. Very old."

"How?" His bristly eyebrows knitted together with suspicion. "Somebody leak it?"

"I ran isotope tests. There is a high concentration of uranium."

"Um. Guess it maybe could've concentrated in the bones . . ."

"Not 'maybe'—it did. Scintillation counters do not lie."

"Uh huh." Noncommittal, eyes giving nothing away.

"You gave me some standard fossil material, yes?" He grinned. "Sure. Know which ones?"

"Samples three, seven, and eleven through sixteen."

"Bingo." His grin broadened.

"The signatures were clear. Silica, pyrite, calcite—they had intruded into the bone, replacing the organic matter."

"Standard fossil process, right. I took those samples from the outer segments of the sacrum, pelvis, ribs."

"And the others?"

He smiled slyly. "Not so fast. What'd you find?"

"Very well. Collagen."

She could have laughed at the blank expression on his face. "What's that?" he asked.

"A protein."

"Um." He peered up at the rectangle of blank blue sky, then gave her a guarded look. "What else?"

"No, it is your turn. I suspect you merely gave me fossil samples which had been contaminated—correct?"

"Huh? Contaminated how?"

"By your assistants' handling. Flecks of skin. Human dander."

He shook his head strongly. "Nossir. We took pelvis bones, femur, some spine. Real careful."

"Hollow bones, all?"

"Right. Drilled 'em in vacuum. You got the samples straight from the vac box, believe me."

She felt a strange prickly sensation rush across her skin. A chilly breeze? Here? "How . . . how did you pick the sites for drilling?"

"Most of this fossil was formed by the usual process. Organic molecules were leached out by ground water, then the interstices filled—with quartz, mostly. But the biggest dinosaurs evolved hollow bones to help 'em keep their weight down." He gave her a look of respect. "You looked that up, right?"

"Of course. I became suspicious."

"Look, I'll come clean. It looked to me like the quartz intrusions had sealed up the pores and connections in some of the bones. There was stuff inside—hard but lighter."

"Those were the other samples."

"Right. I figured maybe the solids had trapped some bone in there, preserving it. Real bone, not stuff replaced by minerals. The bones didn't crack, see, so the inside might still be chemically intact. Hell, maybe there's even marrow."

His face had a pensive, almost shy quality. His eyes seemed to plead with her. She had enjoyed playing this game with him, but now there was a tingling in her, a shortness of breath, and she could constrain it no longer.

"I found collagen, yes. Then I performed a thirty-element analysis. Twenty-eight of the elemental abundances matched modern bone to within five percent."

"Ah. Close."

"Very."

His mouth twisted in sudden speculation. "So if bone hasn't evolved a whole lot since the Jurassic . . ."

"There is more. I found twelve other proteins. Clear signatures."

He blinked. His mouth made an O of surprise, then closed.

In the long silence that hung between them she heard, as though coming hollowly down a distant tunnel, the clatter and muted mutterings of the restless human energies around them, delving deeply and with patient persistence, seeking.

"You thinking what I am?" he asked, eyes glinting.

"I believe so. The protein will be broken, of course, by thermal damage."

She was surprised at her voice, still restrained and professional and not giving away a hint of the quickening in her body, of her attraction to this man mingled with the suddenly apparent idea he had begun. He must be thinking along the same lines, or he would not have asked for so specific a series of tests.

The air held a savor of tingling possibility.

"We'll want to be careful."

"Indeed."

"People'll say it's sensationalistic."

"I expect so."

"But we don't want to get scooped, right? Got to be fast on our feet, like my dad said."

She stepped nearer him and caught a heady scent, a sweaty musk that hung in the dry air. Looking up at him, she knew exactly what he was thinking behind his shy smile. His head blotted out the sun. She said quietly, "We can try."

2.

2050

Sixty-two years, she thought. Sixty-two years of trying, of steadily carrying forward their dream. Did they guess then how far it could go? Mists shrouded the decades . . . she couldn't remember.

"Dr. Nakawa?" a young man asked at her elbow. She recognized him: Flores, the microtech specialist. He had made some of the first DNA reconstructions which proved out. That had been a decade ago at least—yet his face was still unlined. Molecular tinkering nowadays corrected many of nature's flaws.

"I was just resting." The pain had passed.

"Your husband is already out in the canyon. He said—"

"I know—hurry up." She made a fierce, comic frown. "He's been pacing around since dawn."

She let the man lead her through the hushed carpeting of the executive offices, past labs and workshops and big work bays. The place had a spruced-up sharpness, part of the half-century observance. She recognized some of the equipment, vastly better than the bulky stuff they had used decades ago to do the first detailed protein chain readings.

The sign over an impressive entrance said Helical Library—a bit of romantic dash, unusual for the bureaucracy-heavy Park Service. She reminded herself that after today she would take some time to browse in there. The flood of new data and ideas made research resemble trying to take a drink from a fire hose, but she was damned if she wouldn't try.

That had been the analogy she and Dwight first used in their grant proposals: the DNA library. For the Seismosaurus they had millions of copies of the same book—DNA segments—but each copy had only a page or two left in it. Worse, the pages weren't numbered. The blind rub of millennia had ripped out all but a few of the Seismosaurus genetic plans.

The trick lay in realizing that each fragment of DNA they found was a book with different pages left. Find enough books, compare the pages, stitch and splice and edit . . . and they could eventually patch together a complete book.

As Dwight often said, after all the talk about molecular groups and amino acids, the library analogy *felt* right. Even a congressman could grasp it.

The young man opened a door—and the fragrance and noise and buzz of the crowd hit her. She blinked at the sudden sun glare. Here were familiar faces, grins, hands to shake, 3-D cams doing zoom-shots. She made perfunctory greetings, smiled a lot. Then they fell away from her as the officials performed their best function, brushing people off. She walked a bit unsteadily through a stand of gum trees, shielding her eyes against the slanting morning light.

"Mito!" Dwight called. He was with a small group of technical people, all carrying field equipment and communicators. She waved and hurried to his side.

"It's almost here," he said. "Ready?"

Then the tech types were talking, checking, reassuring, and she never answered. They all fell silent.

Through the moist air they could hear now the snapping of small trees. A strange, hollow bellowing. And the steps. Long, heavy blows, like a boulder bounding endlessly down a mountainside. Regular, stolid, remorseless.

She had never quite become accustomed to the sight. It was more like a moving jade-green hill, not a living thing at all. Human intuitions of size failed in the face of the great muscle slabs, the smoothly sliding hummocks of fat.

But the hammer blows of its broad, clawed feet belied its grace. The bountiful tail held over eighty vertebrae, tapering to a long, slender whiplash. The beast did not drag such mass, though. The tail arced smoothly upward, pert and buoyant. This weight balanced precisely the pipeline neck that swiveled with lazy grandeur, carrying the head aloft to browse among the tallest eucalyptus.

The improbability of the sight always struck her first. This most massive of land creatures moved with measured, easy elegance. A great deal of its brain dealt with balance and movement because it did not need the sharpened senses and low cunning of the hunters.

They all stepped back involuntarily as it approached. A technician whispered to her, "Don't worry, ma'am, we've done this a thousand times. It'll stop right over there."

Of course, Mito thought, of course. But if everybody's so sure, why are they whispering?

She stepped back anyway, taking Dwight's arm.

The lumbering immensity halted exactly at the right spot. Then a crane lifted the two of them to the prepared chairs perched securely on the broad, leathery back. As all this happened it was as though Mito were two persons, one experiencing the heady swirl of smells and sounds, the other abstractly recalling the many hard struggles and failures they had seen through decades past.

From the proteins in its bone marrow, long before they knew its DNA, she and Dwight had shown that the Seismosaurus was a milk-maker. She turned and watched this mother's brood ambling along nearby, munching small saplings. They were a mere two meters high, tails pointed nearly straight up, perky and alert. One cooed for its mother. Mito knew that today the moving mountain under them would not pause to give suck, however. The control relay rode like a silvery helmet atop the square head, giving carefully programmed orders.

The cheering from below fell away and behind them. Walking was a slow, grave rhythm. The young ones skipped ahead, calling to each other. They were moving appetites, stripping leaves and bark from the copse of gum trees. These babies grew quickly, evolution's best way to offset against predators, but there were none such here.

"You okay?" Dwight asked, concern deepening the furrows in his face.

"I am indulging in memories." She smiled at the passing broad expanse of the canyon as it opened toward the Kansas plain.

"Remember the first ones?"

She laughed. "I thought we would never get one to survive."

"It was you who saw what they needed."

"No, I merely carried it out."

"Nonsense. They had milk but no mothering. And

you were the only one on the whole team who had the guts to mother something like a calf with claws."

She beamed. "All that would have amounted to nothing if you had not suggested feeding them stones."

He shrugged. "*That* didn't take guts."

Even the babies needed stomach stones to crush tough leaves and pine needles, a staple of their diet after the first month. In their antiseptic cages the babies had no way to find any pebbles. Such simple points had eluded the brainy genetic engineers.

Park Service HQ helicopters hissed overhead, but their directives, relayed through the silvery helmet, did not completely offset all natural impulses. Feeding had to be constant, automatic. The beaked jaw was so powerful it could bite into a fat redwood and mash it to pulp in a sawmill of blade-sharp teeth. To work the vast jaws and support the massive skull, thick slabs of muscle worked over an arc of bone back down the thick neck. The cheeks bunched and flowed, chewing perpetually below eyes protected by horned ridges. It fed quickly, not even breaking stride. Its life was a perpetual odyssey, browsing four hundred kilos of leaf and needle a day.

Dwight pointed. "River comin' up."

Her composure slipped along with her smile. "Are you—"

"Just watch. This doll knows her limits."

One of the freshly carved rivers that had remade Kansas rushed and frothed at its banks. The Seismosaurus slowed, apparently working through its slow calculations. Then it waddled into the water. The pipeline neck rose in lofty disregard of the torrent. Currents lapped and swirled higher, higher—and held a meter below their carriage chairs.

"See?"

Dwight always had more confidence in physical matters than she did. "*Her* head is up there. What does she care if her back gets wet?"

"Umm. Rest easy. Feelin' okay?"

Though the pains had returned to her lower abdomen she gave him what she hoped was a sunny smile. "Wonderful."

The beast showed no concern for the churning river. The Sauropods were proving to be astonishingly versatile. They were true land animals, not the pond-loungers envisioned earlier. In the nineteenth century the first discoverers of the huge fossils had thought they were an extinct variety of whalelike reptiles. Bulk was their best defense. Challenged, they could deliver a massive, rib-crushing blow with the strong hind legs or tail.

The young ones crossed the river at a shallows farther down, then raced to join their mother. Swaying, Mito let the summer heat claim her. They worked their way into some undulating hills crowded with the new fast-growth olive trees, which their mount gulped down with gravelly grunts of relish.

They met a Brachiosaurus, russet-red among the shifting silver-greens of the olives. It thudded around a rocky ledge, surprising the humans, but provoking no reaction from the Seismosaurus.

Neither beast displayed hiding behavior, Mito noted abstractly. Only once had any of the Sauropods shown a fighting stance, when surprised by a holo-projection of a model Tyrannosaurus. It had reared onto hind legs like an elephant, claws extended.

The Brachiosaurus was like a smaller edition of their mount, with folds of fat and ribbed colorings of pink and blue. Over the last half century fossil hunters had found organic traces of nearly fifty species, and a dozen now walked the earth. The most startling differences among them were the vibrant splashes of oranges, burnt yellows, milky blues, and rich browns that each species displayed as soon as they were weaned, as their reproductive patterns took hold. Mito watched the Brachiosaurus approach, appreciating the contrast of colors, when suddenly a powerful explosion jarred her.

"What—" Dwight jerked around, alarmed.

The great tail curled high above them. Fierce bellows boomed. The tail descended, a blur that abruptly sent forth a hammer-hard crack.

The Brachiosaurus jerked, daunted. Its massive feet pounded as it turned, a sight which brought laughter from them, and then it beat a hasty retreat.

"Protecting its grazing rights," Mito said.

"And here I always thought it used that tail as a weapon."

"The best weapon is one you do not have to use."

Dwight blinked as their mount gave a loud parting shot. "Damn impressive."

"You see what this means? We humans thought we were the first creatures to break the sound barrier. But a great whip like this—it must, yes?"

He thought a moment. "Suppose so. The dinos beat us to it by one hundred fifty million years."

What she most loved about her life was the way surprises abounded. To bring true a deep human dream, to conjure forth the great lizards again, would have been quite enough, even without the cornucopia of amazements that followed.

Who would have guessed, she thought, that the Sauropods' pursuit of mass as a defense against the meat-eaters would in the fullness of time give them immortality? The quest for sheer weight had led them to the efficiencies of hollow bones. Cradled in those chambers, the dinosaur genetic heritage slumbered for over a million centuries . . . while the solid-boned meat-eaters' legacy trickled away, the helical chains besieged by the salts of ground water. Finally, the meek did inherit the earth.

The stabbing pain returned, catching at her breath.

They rose over the last line of slumped hills and

there before them spread the center of the park. The fresh, glittering river rapids lay like a string of white-water jewels in a verdant setting. Dinosaurs grazed all along the broad, lush plain, their splashes of color like gaudy ornaments. Amid the fields of tan wheat and stretching orchards were discreetly positioned cameras, observers, elite guests. Even the grandest class of all dinosaurs could spook and run, given provocation, as more than one trampled specialist had learned.

As they descended along a slow-sloping hillside, something strong and dark welled up in her. Perhaps it was the ancient sway of the great beast, or her mounting suspicions about the pain that had ebbed and returned in her now for days. Medicine had prolonged life in the best possible way: lengthening the robust days, then ending them with a sudden, sure collapse. There was little to do at the end, which was a final kindness. And if she kept her serene outer glaze, Dwight would not guess and worry until the last possible moment.

So long as it fell after *this* day, she reminded herself. A happy accident, that the Park could open at the half-century mark, and that they had both labored into this era. They could have been caught beneath the blundering incoherence of one of the first rebirths, crushed by the malformed beasts made in the first few years of experiments. Several of the unwary had been.

But no. Now the immense mass beneath them had been harnessed with skill and love.

As they descended a cheer rose all down the ample plain, thousands of voices giving them greeting. The sky itself swarmed and lit with the new electro-display she had heard about but never witnessed.

KANSAS SAUROPOD PARK
OPENING CEREMONIES
DEDICATED TO MITO NAKAWA AND DWIGHT
RASER
THEY OPENED OUR PAST

It was a dazzling iridescent display. The letters loomed across the pewter sky bowl, yellow cascading into orange.

"Y'know, I still wish we'd patented the Seismosaur DNA," Dwight said.

She laughed; he could always make her do that.

With a sudden swelling of emotion, she felt herself let go of all her concerns. This might be the last of days but it would certainly be one of the greatest. Her heart thumped with love of the man next to her, and with love for the rough beast beneath them, slouching into their strange world.

As she made ready to depart, it was arriving, brought forth from the pressing solemn silence of a million centuries, into a territory free of the predators its kind had borne for so long. Humans might tinker all they would, but they could not with any genetic certainty reconstruct the great Tyrannosaurus, or all the rest of that blood-drenched legion which had bedeviled these vast, simple creatures.

She grasped Dwight's hand and drew in a breath containing scents unsensed for longer than humans had walked the world.

They would evolve, of course. But this time they would have a shepherd.

Proselytes

 It was the third time something had knocked on the door that evening. Slow, ponderous thuds. Dad answered it, even though he knew what would be standing there.

The Gack was seven feet tall and burly, as were all Gacks. "Good evening," it said. "I bring you glorious word from the stars!"

It spoke slowly, the broad mouth seeming to shape each word as though the lips were mouthing an invisible marble. Then it blinked twice and said, "The true knowledge of the universe! Salutations of eternal life!"

Dad nodded sourly. "We heard."

"Are you certain? I am an emissary from a far star, sent to bring—"

"Yeah, there's been two others here tonight already."

"And you turned them away?" the Gack asked, startled.

Junior broke in, leaving his homework at the dining-room table. "Hey, there's been *hundreds* of you guys comin' by here. For *months*."

The Gack blinked and abruptly made the sound that had given the aliens their name—a tight, barking sneeze. Something in Earth's air irritated their large red

118

noses. "Apologies, dear ignorant natives, from a humble proselyte of the One Patriarch."

Dad said edgily, "Look, we already heard about your god and how he made the galaxy so you Gacks could spread his holy word and all, so—"

"Oh, let the poor thing finish its spiel, Howard," Mom said, wiping her hands on a towel as she came in from the kitchen.

"Hell, the Dodgers' game'll be on soon—"

"C'mon, Dad," Junior said. "You know that's the only way to get 'em to go away."

The Gack sniffed appreciatively at Junior and started its rehearsed lecture. "Wondrous news, O Benighted Natives! I have voyaged countless of your years to bring . . ."

The family tuned out the recital. As Dad stood in the doorway he could see dozens of Gack ships orbiting in the night sky. They were like small brown moons, asteroid-sized starships that had arrived in a flurry of fiery orange explosions. Each had a big flat plate at one end. They were slow, awkwardly shaped, clunky—like the Gacks themselves.

They had come from a distant yellow star and all they wanted was free rein to "speak to the unknowing," as their emissary had put it. In return they had offered their technology.

Dad had been enthusiastic about that, and so had every government on Earth. Dad's half interest in the Electronic Wonderland store downtown had been paying very little these last few years. An infusion of alien technology, whole new racy product lines, could be a bonanza.

But the Gacks had nothing worth using. Their ships had spanned the stars using the simplest possible method. They dumped small nuclear bombs out the back and set them off. The ship then rode the blast wave, with the flat plate on one end smoothing out the push, like a giant shock absorber.

And inside the Gack asteroid ships were electronics that used vacuum tubes, hand-cranked computers, old-fashioned AM radio . . . nothing that humans hadn't invented already.

So there would be no wonder machines from the stars. The sad fact was that the aliens were dumb. They had labored centuries to make their starships, and then ridden them for millennia to reach other stars.

The Gack ended ponderously with, "Gather now into the outstretched loving grasp of the One True Vision!"

The Gack's polite, expectant gaze fell in turn on each of the family.

Mom said, "Well, that was *very* nice. You're certainly one of the best I've heard, wouldn't you agree, Howard?"

Dad hated it, how she always made *him* get rid of the Gacks. He began, "Look, we've been patient—"

"*They're* the patient ones, Dad," Junior said. "Sittin' in those rocks all those years, just so they could knock on doors and hand out literature." Junior laughed.

The Gack was still looking expectantly at them, waiting for them to convert to his One Galactic Faith. One of its four oddly shaped hands held forth crudely printed pamphlets.

"Now, now," Mom said. "We shouldn't make fun of another creature's beliefs. This poor thing is just doing what our Mormons and Jehovah's Witnesses do. You wouldn't laugh at them, would you?"

Dad could hold it no longer. The night air was cold and he was getting chilled, standing there. "No thanks!" he said loudly, and slammed the door.

"Howard!" Mom cried.

"Hey, right on, Dad!" Junior clapped his hands.

"Just shut the door in its faith," Dad said, making a little smile.

"I still say we should always be polite," Mom persisted. "Who would've believed that when the aliens came, their only outstanding quality would be patience? The patience to travel to other stars. We could learn a thing or two from them," she added sternly.

Dad was already looking in *TV Guide*. "We should've guessed that even before the Gacks came. After all, who comes visiting in this neighborhood? Not that snooty astronomer two blocks over, right? No, we get hot-eyed guys in black suits, looking for converts. So it's no surprise that those are the only kinds of aliens who're damn fool enough to spend all their time flying to the stars, too. Not explorers. Not scientists. Fundamentalists!"

As if to punctuate his words, a hollow thump made the house creak. They all looked to the front door, but the sound wasn't a knock.

Another boom came down from the sky and rattled the windows.

When they went outside, the night sky was alive with darting ships and lurid orange explosions.

Junior cried, "The Gack ships! See, they're all blown up."

"My, I hope they aren't hurt or anything," Mom said. "They're such *nice* creatures, truly."

Among the tumbling brown remnants of the Gack fleet darted sleek, shiny vessels. They dived like quicksilver barracuda, sending missiles that ripped open the fat bellies of the last few asteroid ships.

Dad felt a pang. "They were kinda pleasant," he said grudgingly. "Not my type of person, maybe, and their technology was a laugh, but still—"

"Look!" Junior cried.

A sleek ship skimmed across the sky. A bone-rattling boom crashed down from it.

"Now *that's* what an alien starship oughtta look like," Junior said. "Lookit those wings! The blue exhaust—"

Behind the swift craft huge letters of gauzy blue unfurled across the upper atmosphere. The phosphorescent words loomed with hard, clear purpose:

GREET THE CLEANSING BLADE OF THE ONE ETERNAL TRUTH!

"Huh?" Junior frowned.

Dad's face went white.

"We thought the Mormons were bad," he said grimly. "Whoever thought there might be Moslems?"

Touches

Today, at work, he thought of the Game incessantly.

He had been playing it for some years now.

At first he had sought mere mild entertainment. There were, of course, the electronic games that one saw in public places—pitiful things, a few moments of shallow amusement bought with a quarter. That was as far as most people went—or could go, given their skills.

He had tried those numbing, repetitive contests, and quickly abandoned them with disdain. They rewarded quick motor skills and elementary tactical sense, but were painfully limited. Nothing like the Game.

He had a board meeting in the morning. It dragged unmercifully. Then came lunch with some business associates. They were confident, seasoned fellows, their seamed faces at ease. As they discussed recent events he thought mildly that politics was the intelligent man's weather; an inexhaustible subject, forever new and forever purposeless. He studied the brown liver spots on his hands and said nothing.

He found their talk of money matters kept drifting in and out of his attention, dreamlike, as if their numbers and analysis were unreal, airy, and only his memory of the Game was concrete.

That afternoon he lost track entirely during a conference with his own counsel. The man gave him a puzzled look as they chatted.

He left early and went directly home. This would be a particularly fine evening, he hoped. He would have ample time to himself, since his lady had arranged to have supper with friends. Over an early cocktail he made polite, bland conversation with her, introducing no fresh topics on his own. After she left he had a light supper, dismissed the servants, and went to his study.

He settled into his favorite leather armchair, pulling the massive board to within easy reach. The display screen nearly obscured the view out the wide windows. The rich lawn beyond was a vibrant yellow-green swath. Birds trilled their twilight calls among the trees that marched down to the river. Dogs romped near the gate.

He sat with his back to the study door, to discourage any passing servant from disturbing him. He had a fresh drink at his side and his mind was alert.

The Game began. He lounged back, making his first moves, knowing at this stage he had ample time. The tranquillity of his study made immersion in the growing complexities easy, and heightened even the simple victories of the opening contests. He never had difficulty at this stage any longer.

It was very much like learning the characters and setting in a novel. Each time the Game featured different cultures, different assumptions about the importance of wealth, of power, of love, of life itself. Each Game was fresh.

The pitiful electronic games that the public played were monotonous to him. In the decades since their introduction, the public amusements had improved somewhat, but they were inevitably dominated and limited by their audience—adolescents who had the time to play, but not the sophistication to demand anything better.

Tonight the scheme was particularly engrossing. The social matrix was modified Late Marxist, with class divisions reemerging. He liked this motif better than the more common PseudoCap, where acquisitive urges were openly acknowledged, but often undercut by mildly socialist jargon. Late Marxism contained the fruitful seeds of deep, true hypocrisy—always a stimulus, and often a valuable fulcrum for turning an opponent's hand.

He played the role of a young man, restive and ambitious—his customary choice.

In the first challenge he had to maneuver himself into the Party apparatus. Simple enough. There were impediments, of course. At the People's Training Camp the physical challenges translated into quick, deft motions on the board. He learned to excel at single combat, neatly setting up his opponents in the Maze-Delay and then—*touch*—one button, pressed at the right instant, did them in.

Idealology—the study of ideals, as a predictor of others' behavior—came naturally to him. He used it to unmask some clumsy players, consigning them to the oblivion of jobs as clerks, functionaries, laborers.

He particularly enjoyed the turns and ironies introduced into the Game by the advance of current events. Eastern Europe was undergoing its convulsions of thought, a low-motion train wreck of principle upon the tracks of necessity. Regimes proclaimed themselves the new vanguard of this or that notion, and then sank with agonizing struggles in the swamps of economics, weighed down by their leaden ideals.

Tonight's Game, for example. Its underpinning was positively antique. Socialist Man—that marvelous, hoary phrase—was the ideal paid lip service in tonight's Game. So in principle these losers were embarking on virtuous careers. This pleasurable blend of irony and hypocrisy he relished.

Atmospherics appeared on side screens. Dingy streets, gray concrete buildings like inflated bunkers, buses hissing by in the light rain. Crowd murmurs, sharp scents of sausage and sauerkraut from a corner restaurant.

Moving through this twentieth-century miasma proved exciting and oddly moving. The past was inherently touching, with its air of solidity and purpose, unknowing of its fate.

Or was this the past? In idealology, yes—Socialist Man was at one with the dinosaurs—but occasional unsettling nuances poked through the atmospherics.

A pornographic magazine flaring like a rose amid a newsstand of stolid newspapers. A fancy Japanese automobile slithering through the pallid city streets. A blue-haired woman wearing only a halter and shorts, oblivious of the air's thin chill.

Mere glimpses. He brushed them aside in his eagerness.

He secured a good middle-level post. The steps upward were clear, his responses deft. For a young man he was doing quite well.

He relaxed for a moment. Time to relish some of the rewards appropriate to his age. He indulged himself.

He became involved with Lisa, the mistress of a Regional Commissioner. Lust drove him—the Game knew his likes by now, and the gaudy, rippling images of Lisa held his eyes even when he knew he should be absorbing other information from the board. Her face was a composition of serene curves, and her moist skin glowed.

He had to keep the affair secret. The Commissioner was known to be jealous and vindictive; the man had learned of Lisa's earlier affairs, and had adroitly framed each of her past lovers for offenses against the state. Most of them had vanished in mysterious circumstances.

Dusk darkened into night outside as he felt his way through this society. There were advantages he knew from experience—some black marketing here, a neat dodge there: a controversial report filed with the Party at the right moment, which forced his immediate superior to resign.

The Game was expensive, and that, too, enhanced his enjoyment. The Game was as intelligent as a human—perhaps more so—within its tight, circumscribed universe. Huge computer resources hummed to match his mental agility. He stretched leisurely in the armchair, feeling the warm caresses of worn leather, languidly letting the familiar study slip away, entering the Game more deeply with each move he made.

Touch—he moved up a notch in the system.

Touch—and he made contact with some members in the Opposition. Dangerous, but exciting. Worth many additional points, if he could make use of it in events somewhere downstream.

Timing, that was it. A moment too soon, and the flow of events across the board would unmask his moves, make his intentions obvious. Too late, and a missed opportunity would be picked up by an underling, gnawing away his position.

Much of this was displayed in moving patterns of crystalline colors, in currents of probability. His decisions—*touch*—came quickly.

Tactics. Maneuver. He felt himself skimming over white-water rapids, a zesty sting in his nostrils. His attention flicked from point to point on the board, sizing up each maneuver—moving, always moving.

Tonight the Game was better than ever. It presented him with problems at work, intrigues of Party politics, chances for black market gains. Risky, but inventive.

He could lose at any moment. But he didn't. No

matter how many moves the Game thought ahead, he anticipated. There was always an out, a way to gain, or at least to avoid defeat. That was the one rule: there must be a solution.

At some points the Game was slower than usual. He knew this was because his skill was matching the ability of the entire system. The Game had to simulate life in all its complexity, and provide patterns of play not used before.

Any sufficiently complex network comes, in time, to seem like an independent entity. It was helpful to think of it as sentient.

The intricate computer linkages had a personality of their own, and they did not like to lose. Through the years, he liked to think, a relationship had formed between himself and the constantly improving computer net. They had sharpened their wits on each other.

Now he was straining it to the limit. When that limit was passed, he could win. And tonight he knew he would.

He met Lisa at an apartment he rented, under a false name, for that purpose alone. Their nights together inflamed his imagination. The system served him lacquered images from their couplings, stirring old urges. The scenes were lit by tranquil colors, as warm as jewels seen through oil. Her hands moved with assured grace and her touch ignited a roaring in him. At each caress the world became incandescent with promise.

Leaving the apartment at sunrise, however, he noted a sign that he was being followed.

There were several explanations. Someone in the police, perhaps. A leak in the Opposition?

Or an underling, trying to uncover some scrap of scandal? Possibly.

The grim, gray concrete of the city framed itself about the question.

Here was a place to be deft, subtle. Just a touch . . .

He laid traps for these two eventualities.

Nothing happened.

He continued meeting Lisa, as often as she could arrange to slip away from the Commissioner. The man often kept her at his country estate, making her wait until he had time for her.

She got away to the city as often as possible. Their arrangements were elaborate and as secure as his years of experience could make them.

Still, there were more signs. He tended to his growing personal empire, his network of informants, his associations with those whom he could help and who would be willing to return the favor.

All this he had done before in earlier Games. But this time, tonight—he had to glance up at the black study windows to remind himself—there were undercurrents he could barely sense, subtle shifts, pivots, flows of money and power that he did not understand.

He was oblivious now. He did not notice the gathering chill from the great windows of the study, or even feel the rub of warm, familiar leather. He was fully, vibrantly alive, his prickly instincts alert for warning nuances in his work, in his customary social relations, in everyday detail.

A singing vibrancy gripped him and the past years of routine fell away. The Game was excelling itself tonight. He could sense its brooding intelligence behind the board, feeling him out, retreating when he lunged, never giving itself away. Patient. Unforgiving.

The computer had a style, as did he. The Game avoided the obvious, brutal methods. It usually let him run a given tactic for a while, studying it, before adroitly deflecting it. Done skillfully and often, this alone could rob him of momentum and verve.

The Game favored responses that turned the logic of his strategy back upon itself. Inversion. Subversion.

Often it seemed to be playful, ingenious, as if to say, *Have you considered it* this *way?*

It was Lisa who noticed the small error. She recognized one of the Commissioner's limousines parked in the distance, a man sitting at the wheel. The man was not looking at the two of them on the balcony above, of course. Nothing that obvious. And he drove off a moment later, after picking up a dumpy, overweight woman who might quite plausibly be his wife.

Though Lisa had met the man only in passing once before, she had a remarkable memory for faces. The Commissioner had probably thought using him was a negligible risk.

Fear was part of the Game as well. It would have been simple to abandon Lisa, to back away and try another path to success. After all, there were many women.

He rejected the idea. By now he was linked to her in ways he could not describe even to himself. To slink away, losing face when confronted by the electronic intelligence behind the Game—

No. He began playing with great speed, nimbly repeating patterns of the past.

It was important to appear unafraid. To continue using tactics that had his usual style. To give no hint of his preparations.

He had to eliminate the Commissioner. The brittle intelligence within the Game would anticipate that, though probably it would not seem a likely move.

His personal style ran more to the gradual techniques—a slow piling up of advantages, until the moment of resolution came. Let the Party demote the Commissioner, or have him transferred. Nothing too direct, nothing flagrant or gaudy.

The Game would expect something like that.

Therefore, do the opposite.

Instead of carefully marshaling resources, strike swiftly, boldly, in a way uncharacteristic of his usual methods. But use the computer's expectations against it. *Seem* to be following a customary pattern. Carry on a series of slower moves, moves that the Game would expect.

He set about constructing a reasonably devious plot, involving a dozen officials. It aimed at implicating the Commissioner in treasonous securities exchanges with a nearby country. Something that would be unseemly in even a PseudoCap society. He had used a similar device before with great success.

Beneath this, he laid a subplot. It had to involve a minimum of people. Lisa was the only one he could trust. His style was always to use conventional pathways, so the subplot had to be unusual, swift, and daring.

Touch.

Their paths intersected at twilight, at an old inn in the tranquil countryside. He had abandoned his own auto on the other side of the city, taken a bus, then returned speedily on a maglev train. Lisa had just come from the Commissioner's estate.

She left the pyramid-shaped thing on a table in the foyer, keeping her eyes straight ahead, and then went in to dinner. She did not so much as glance at him. The timing was perfect. He palmed the pyramid on his way out, a moment later.

The man with Lisa—the Commissioner's usual guard for her—stayed in the limousine, reading a newspaper. She was meeting friends for dinner and he would be out of place. The man did not even look up as a shadow flitted from a side door and into the trees nearby.

He ran the two kilometers through dense woodland as dusk deepened into night. Branches scratched his face. An owl hooted at him but there was no sign of detection. Panting, he thought of Lisa dining, taking her time, extending the interval until the pyramid key would be needed to readmit her to the estate. He remembered her black hair, the high arch of her cheek-bones, the vivid, hypnotic passion of her.

In the blackness he had only starlight and the remembered locations of the alarm system monitors—information purchased at great risk and cost—to guide him.

Soon the bulky silhouette of the central command unit rose before him. He approached from the correct angle and used the pyramid key to disarm it. Ahead, he recognized the small hill near the river and ran around it, keeping in cover.

There was the line of trees leading to the great house. The downstairs rooms were not supposed to be in use, and indeed, as she had promised, they were dark. Two windows glowed burnt yellow, like living eyes in a skull. There the Commissioner would be, relaxing after his indulgent dinner. Perhaps he would be dulled by wine.

The servants were in their own quarters by now. No dogs barked.

He used the pyramid key at the gate again. It slid open silently, a black ribwork gliding in the night.

He crept up the driveway, avoiding the gravel, and around to the back.

The kitchen door yielded. No one about.

Through a side room, where polished silverware awaited galas to come, its curves seeming to gather the wan light.

Turn left. Yes—the dining room, an echoing cavern. Everything seemed larger in the gloom.

He felt his way. Yes, a hallway lined with scowling portraits. Good.

Warm, cloying air. Lush carpeting that led to a stairway. His footsteps made no sound going up.

He took out the gun. Pressed against flesh, it delivered a nerve poison. Death was swift and untraceable. But not painless. That would be too much to ask. Or perhaps too much to give, tonight.

Turn here to the left. A closed door. From under it seeped yellowish light. No sound from within.

He turned the knob slowly. Well oiled, as she had arranged. The latch slid free.

Now he moved quickly. The images came at him in a rush.

—A brown armchair. Books lining the study. Large windows, filled with blackness.

He stepped forward, raising the gun.

—The head of the older man, white-haired, strangely fragile, not resting back against the leather but instead tilted forward, concentrating on the gaming board before him, the wrinkled neck exposed, the face intent and pensive, focused, as if waiting for—

Touch.

Nobody Lives on
Burton Street

I was standing by one of our temporary command posts, picking my teeth after breakfast and talking to Joe Murphy when the first part of the Domestic Disturbance hit us.

People said the summer of '78 was the worst ever, what with all the pollution haze and everything was kicking up the temperatures, but here it was a year later and getting worse than '78. Spring had lost its bloom a month back and it was hot, sticky—the kind of weather that leaves you with a half-moon of sweat around your armpits before you've had time to finish morning coffee. The summer heat makes for trouble, stirs up people.

I was getting jumpy with the waiting. I walked back toward the duplex apartment set away from the street, trying to round up my men. The apartment was deserted, of course, so I wasn't listening for anything special from the bedroom. I walked right in on them.

Johnson, a kid from the other side of town, was sprawled across the bed with a skinny little black girl. He was really ramming it to her, grunting with each thrust. She had her legs wrapped around him like a snake in heat, sobbing each time he went in, eyes rolled up.

Yeah, I knew that one; rolled with her a few times myself last year. She was a groupie, really, always following our squads around with that hungry look in the eyes. She just liked to hump the boys, I guess, like some girls go for Marines. She had her skirt bunched up around her waist while Johnson was working on her, hands wrapped around her ass so he could lift her up with each lunge. They were really going at it.

"Okay, fun's over," I said, and gave Johnson a light kick in the butt. "Finish it off and form up."

"What th—" he said as he rolled over, still clutching her to him and jerking. Then he saw me and shut up. The girl—Melody, I think her name was—looked at me with big round eyes and squirmed all over Johnson, getting him to hurry up. I made a mental note to get back to her one of these days; she was skinny, but she had a good way of twisting around that really got me off.

I turned and walked back out onto the roof where we had our command post.

We knew the mob was in the area, working toward us. Our communications link had been humming for the last half hour, getting fixes on their direction and asking the computers for advice on how to handle them when they got there.

I looked down. At the end of the street were a lot of semipermanent shops and the mailbox. The mailbox bothers me—it shouldn't be there.

From the other end of Burton Street I could hear the random dull bass of the mob, sounding like animals.

We started getting ready, locking up the equipment. I was already working up a sweat when Joe came over, moaning about the payments on the Snocar he'd been suckered into. I was listening with one ear to him and the other to the crowd noise.

"And it's not just that," Joe said. "It's the neighborhood and the school and everybody around me."

"Everybody's wrong but Murphy, huh?" I said, and grinned.

"Hell no, you know me better than that. It's just that nobody's *going* anyplace. Sure, we've all got jobs, but they're most of them just make-work stuff the unions have gotten away with."

"To get a real job you gotta have training," I said, but I wasn't chuffing him up. I like my job, and it's better than most, but we weren't gonna kid each other that it was some big technical deal. Joe and I are just regular guys.

"What're you griping about this now for, anyway?" I said. "You didn't used to be bothered by anything."

Joe shrugged. "I dunno. Wife's been getting after me to move out of the place we're in and make more money. Gets into fights with the neighbors." He looked a little sheepish about it.

"More money? Hell, y'got everything you need, we all do. Lot of people worse off than you. Look at all those lousy Africans, living on nothing."

I was going to say more, maybe rib him about how he's married and I'm not, but then I stopped. Like I said, all this time I was half listening to the crowd. I can always tell when a bunch has changed its direction like a pack of wolves off on a chase, and when that funny quiet came and lasted about five seconds I knew they were heading our way.

"Scott!" I yelled at our communications man. "Close it down. Get a final printout."

Murphy broke off telling me about his troubles and listened to the crowd for a minute, like he hadn't heard them before, and then took off on a trot to the AnCops we had stashed in the truck below. They were all warmed up and ready to go, but Joe likes to make a final check and maybe have a chance to read in any new instructions Scott gets at the last minute.

I threw away the toothpick and had a last look at my constant-volume joints, to be sure the bulletproof plastiform was matching properly and wouldn't let anything through. Scott came double-timing over with the diagnostics from HQ. The computer compilation was neat and confusing, like it always is. I could make out the rough indices they'd picked up on the crowd heading our way. The best guess—and that's all you ever get, friends, is a guess—was a lot of Psych Disorders and Race Prejudice. There was a fairly high number of Unemployeds, too. We're getting more and more Unemployeds in the city now, and they're hard for the Force to deal with. Usually mad enough to spit. Smash up everything.

I penciled an OK in the margin and tossed it Scott's way. I'd taken too long reading it; I could hear individual shouts now and the tinkling of glass. I flipped the visor down from my helmet and turned on my external audio. It was going to get hot as hell in there, but I'm not chump enough to drag around an air-conditioning unit on top of the rest of my stuff.

I took a look at the street just as a gang of about a hundred people came around the corner two blocks down, spreading out like a dirty gray wave. I ducked over to the edge of the building and waved to Murphy to start off with three AnCops. I had to hold up three fingers for him to see because the noise was already getting high. I looked at my watch. Hell, it wasn't nine A.M. yet.

Scott went down the stairs we'd tracted up the side of the building. I was right behind him. It wasn't a good location for observation now; you made too good a target up there. We picked up Murphy, who was carrying our control boards. All three of us angled down the alley and dropped down behind a short fence to have a look at the street.

Most of them were still screaming at the top of their lungs like they'd never run out of air, waving whatever they had handy and gradually breaking up into smaller units. The faster ones had made it to the first few buildings.

A tall Negro came trotting toward us, moving like he had all the time in the world. He stopped in front of a wooden barbershop, tossed something quickly through the front window, and *whump!* Flames licked out at the upper edges of the window, spreading fast.

An older man picked up some rocks and began methodically pitching them through the smaller windows in the shops next door. A housewife clumped by awkwardly in high heels, looking like she was out on a shopping trip except for the hammer she swung like a pocketbook. She dodged into the barbershop for a second, didn't find anything, and came out. The Negro grinned and pointed at the barber pole on the sidewalk, still revolving, and she caught it in the side with a swipe that threw shattered glass for ten yards.

I turned and looked at Murphy. "All ready?"

He nodded. "Just give the word."

The travel agency next door to the barbershop was concrete-based, so they couldn't burn that. Five men were lunging at the door and on the third try they knocked it in. A moment later a big travel poster sailed out the front window, followed by a chair leg. They were probably doing as much as they could, but without tools they couldn't take much of the furniture apart.

"Okay," I said. "Let's have the first AnCops."

The thick acrid smell from the smoke was drifting down Burton Street to us, but my air filters would take care of most of it. They don't do much about human sweat, though, and I was going to be inside the rest of the day.

Our first prowl car rounded the next corner, going too fast. I looked over at Murphy, who was controlling the car, but he was too busy trying to miss the people who were standing around in the street. Must have gotten a little overanxious on that one. Something was bothering his work.

I thought sure the car was going to take a tumble and mess us up, but the wheels caught and it rightened itself long enough for the driver to stop a skid. The screech turned the heads of almost everybody in the crowd and they'd started to move in on it almost before the car stopped laying down rubber and came to a full stop. Murphy punched in another instruction and the AnCop next to the driver started firing at a guy on the sidewalk who was trying to light a Molotov cocktail. The AnCop was using something that sounded like a repeating shotgun. The guy with the cocktail just turned around and looked at him a second before scurrying off into a hardware store.

By this time the car was getting everything—bricks, broken pieces of furniture, merchandise from the stores. Something heavy shattered the windshield and the driver ducked back too late to avoid getting his left hand smashed with a bottle. A figure appeared on the top of the hardware shop—it looked like the guy from the sidewalk—and took a long windup before throwing something into the street.

There was a tinkling of glass and a red circle of flame slid across the pavement where it hit just in front of the car, sending smoke curling up over the hood and obscuring the inside. Murphy was going to have to play it by feel now; you couldn't see a thing in the car.

A teenager with a stubby rifle stepped out of a doorway, crouched down low like in a western. He fired twice, very accurately and very fast, at the window of the car. A patrolman was halfway out the door when it hit him full in the face, sprawling the body back over the roof and then pitching it forward into the street.

A red blotch formed around his head, grew rapidly, and ran into the gutter. There was ragged cheering and the teenager ran over to the body, tore off its badge, and backed away. "Souvenir!" he called out, and a few of the others laughed.

I looked at Murphy again and he looked at me and I gave him the nod for the firemen, switching control over to my board. Scott was busy talking into his recorder, taking notes for the write-up later. When Murphy nudged him he stopped and punched in the link for radio control to the fire-fighting units.

By this time most of Burton Street was on fire. Everything you saw had a kind of orange look to it. The crowd was moving toward us once they'd lost interest in the cops, but we'd planned it that way. The firemen came running out in that jerky way they have, just a little in front of us. They were carrying just a regular hose this time because it was a medium-sized group and we couldn't use up a fire engine and all the extras. But they were wearing the usual red uniforms. From a distance you can't tell them from the real thing.

Their subroutine tapes were fouled up again. Instead of heading for the barbershop or any of the other stuff that was burning, like I'd programmed, they turned the hose on a stationery store that nobody had touched yet. There were three of them, holding on to that hose and getting it set up. The crowd had backed off a minute to see what was going on.

When the water came through it knocked in the front window of the store, making the firemen look like real chumps. I could hear the water running around inside, pushing over things, and flooding out the building. The crowd laughed, what there was of it—I noticed some of them had moved off in the other direction, over into somebody else's area.

In a minute or so the laughing stopped, though.

One guy who looked like he had been born mad grabbed an ax from somewhere and took a swing at the hose. He didn't get it the first time but people were sticking around to see what would happen and I guess he felt some kind of obligation to go through with it. Even under pressure, a thick hose isn't easy to cut into. He kept at it and on the fourth try a seam split—looked like a bad repair job to me—and a stream of water gushed out and almost hit this guy in the face.

The crowd laughed at that, too, because he backed off real quick then, scared for a little bit. A face full of high-velocity water is no joke, not at that pressure.

The fireman who was holding the hose just a little down from there hadn't paid any attention to this because he wasn't programmed to, so when this guy thought about it he just stepped over and chopped the fireman across the back with the ax.

It was getting hot. I didn't feel like overriding the stock program, so it wasn't long before all the firemen were out of commission, just about the same way. A little old lady—probably with a welfare gripe—borrowed the ax for a minute to separate all of a fireman's arms and legs from the trunk. Looking satisfied, she waddled away after the rest of the mob.

I stood up, lifted my faceplate, and looked at them as they milled back down the street. I took out my grenade launcher and got off a tear gas cartridge on low charge, to hurry them along. The wind was going crosswise so the gas got carried off to the side and down the alleys. Good; wouldn't have complaints from somebody who got caught in it too long.

Scott was busy sending orders for the afternoon shift to get more replacement firemen and cops, but we wouldn't have any trouble getting them in time. There hadn't been much damage, when you think how much they could've done.

"Okay for the reclaim crew?" Murphy said.

"Sure. This bunch won't be back. They look tired out already." They were moving toward Horton's area, three blocks over.

A truck pulled out of the alley and two guys in coveralls jumped out and began picking up the androids, dousing fires as they went. In an hour they'd have everything back in place, even the prefab barbershop.

"Helluva note," Murphy said.

"Huh?"

"All this stuff," he waved a hand down Burton Street. "Seems like a waste to build all this just so these jerks can tear it up again."

"Waste?" I said. "It's the best investment you ever saw. How many people were in the last bunch—two hundred? Every one of them is going to sit around for weeks bragging about how he got him a cop or burned a building."

"Okay, okay. If it does any good, I guess it's cheap at the price."

"If, hell! You know it does. If it didn't they wouldn't be here. You got to be cleared by a psycher before you even get in. The computer works out just what you'll need, just the kind of action that'll work off the aggressions you've got. Then shoots it to us in the profile from HQ before we start. It's foolproof."

"I dunno. You know what the Consies say—the psychers and the probes and drugs are an in—"

"Invasion of privacy?"

"Yeah," Murphy said sullenly.

"Privacy? Man, the psychers are public health! It's part of the welfare! You don't have to go around to some expensive guy who'll have you lie on a couch and talk to him. You can get better stuff right from the government. It's free!"

Murphy looked at me kind of funny. "Sure. Have to go in for a checkup sometime soon. Maybe that's what I need."

I frowned just the right amount. "Well, I dunno, Joe. Man lets his troubles get him down every once in a while, doesn't mean he needs professional help. Don't let it bother you. Forget it."

Joe was okay, but even a guy like me who's never been married could tell he wasn't thinking up this stuff himself. His woman was pushing him. Not satisfied with what she had.

Now, *that* was wrong. Guy like Joe doesn't have anywhere to go. Doesn't know computers, automation. Can't get a career rating in the army. So the pressure was backing up on him.

Supers like me are supposed to check out their people and leave it at that, and I go by the book like everybody else. But Joe wasn't the problem.

I made a mental note to have a psycher look at his wife.

"Okay," he said, taking off his helmet. "I got to go set up the AnCops for the next one."

I watched him walk off down the alley. He was a good man. Hate to lose him.

I started back toward our permanent operations center to check in. After a minute I decided maybe I'd better put Joe's name in, too, just in case. Didn't want anybody blowing up on me.

He'd be happier, work better. I've sure felt a lot better since I had it. It's a good job I got, working in public affairs like this, keeping people straight with themselves.

I went around the corner at the end of the street, thinking about getting something to drink, and noticed the mailbox. I check on it every time because it sure looks like a mistake.

Everything's supposed to be pretty realistic on Burton Street, but putting in a mailbox seems like a goofy idea.

Who's going to try to burn up a box like that,

made out of cast iron and bolted down? A guy couldn't take out any aggressions on it.

And it sure can't be for real use. Not on Burton Street.

Nobody lives around there.

Dark Sanctuary

The laser beam hit me smack in the face.
I twisted away. My helmet buzzed and went
dark as its sunshade overloaded. *Get inside
the ship*. I yanked on a strut and tumbled
into the yawning, flourescent-lit airlock.

In the asteroid belt you either have fast reflexes or
you're a statistic. I slammed into the airlock bulkhead
and stopped dead, waiting to see where the laser beam
would hit next. My suit sensors were all burned out,
my straps were singed. The pressure patches on knees
and elbows had brown bubbles in them. They had blis-
tered and boiled away. Another second or two and I'd
have been sucking vac.

I took all this in while I watched for reflections
from the next laser strike. Only it didn't come. Whoever had shot at me either thought *Sniffer* was disabled, or else they had a balky laser. Either way, I had
to start dodging.

I moved fast, working my way forward through a
connecting tube to the bridge—a fancy name for a
closet-sized cockpit. I revved up *Sniffer*'s fusion drive
and felt the tug as she started spitting hot plasma out
her rear tubes. I made the side jets stutter, too, putting
out little bursts of plasma. That made *Sniffer* dart
around, just enough to make hitting her tough.

I punched in for a damage report. Some aft sensors burned out, a loading arm melted down, other minor stuff. The laser bolt must have caught us for just a few seconds.

A bolt from *who*? Where? I checked radar. Nothing.

I reached up to scratch my nose, thinking, and realized my helmet and skinsuit were still sealed, vacworthy. I decided to keep them on, just in case. I usually wear light coveralls inside *Sniffer*; the skinsuit is for vac work. It occurred to me that if I hadn't been outside, fixing a hydraulic loader, I wouldn't have known anybody shot at us at all, until my next routine check.

Which didn't make sense. Prospectors shoot at you if you're jumping a claim. They don't zap you once and then fade—they finish the job. I was pretty safe now; *Sniffer*'s strutting mode was fast and choppy, jerking me around in my captain's couch. But as my hands hovered over the control console, they started trembling. I couldn't make them stop. My fingers were shaking so badly I didn't dare punch in instructions. *Delayed reaction,* my analytical mind told me.

I was scared. Prospecting by yourself is risky enough without the bad luck of running into somebody else's claim. All at once I wished I wasn't such a loner. I forced myself to think.

By all rights, *Sniffer* should've been a drifting hulk by now—sensors blinded, punched full of holes, engines blown. Belt prospectors play for *all* the marbles.

Philosophically, I'm with the jackrabbits—run, dodge, hop, but don't fight. I have some surprises for anybody who tries to outrun me, too. Better than trading laser bolts with rockrats at thousand-kilometer range, anyday.

But this one worried me. No other ships on radar, nothing but that one bolt. It didn't fit.

I punched in a quick computer program. The

maintenance computer had logged the time when the aft sensors scorched out. Also, I could tell which way I was facing when the bolt hit me. Those two facts could give me a fix on the source. I let *Sniffer*'s ballistic routine chew on that for a minute and, waiting, looked out the side port. The sun was a fierce white dot in an inky sea. A few rocks twinkled in the distance as they tumbled. Until we were hit, we'd been on a zero-gee coast, outbound from Ceres—the biggest rock there is—for some prospecting. The best-paying commodity in the Belt right now was methane ice, and I knew a likely place. *Sniffer*—the ugly, segmented tube with strap-on fuel pods that I call home—was still over eight hundred thousand kilometers from the asteroid I wanted to check.

Five years back I had been out with a rockhound bunch, looking for asteroids with rich cadmium deposits. That was in the days when everybody thought cadmium was going to be the wonder fuel for ion rockets. We found the cadmium, all right, and made a bundle. While I was out on my own, taking samples from rocks, I saw this gray, ice-covered asteroid about a hundred klicks away. My ship auto-eye picked it up from the bright sunglint. Sensors said it was carbon dioxide ice with some water mixed in. Probably a comet hit the rock millions of years ago, and some of it stuck. I filed its orbit parameters away for a time—like now—when the market got thirsty. Right now the big cylinder worlds orbiting Earth needed water, CO_2, methane, and other goodies. That happens every time the cylinder boys build a new tin can and need to form an ecosystem inside. Rock and ore they can get from Earth's moon. For water they have to come to us, the Belters. It's cheaper in energy to boost ice into the slow pipeline orbits in from the Belt to Earth—*much* cheaper than it is to haul water up from Earth's deep gravity well. Cheaper, that is, if the rockrats flying vac out here can find any.

The screen rippled green. It drew a cone for me, *Sniffer* at apex. Inside that cone was whoever had tried to wing me. I popped my helmet and gave in to the sensuality of scratching my nose. If they scorched me again, I'd have to button up while my own ship's air tried to suck me away—but stopping the itch was worth it.

Inside the cone was somebody who wanted me dead. My mouth was dry. My hands were still shaking. They wanted to punch in course corrections that would take me away from that cone, *fast*.

Or was I assuming too much? Oresniffers use radio for communication—it radiates in all directions, it's cheap, and it's not delicate. But suppose some rocker lost his radio, and had to use his cutting laser to signal? I knew he had to be over ten thousand kilometers away—that's radar range. By jittering around, *Sniffer* was making it impossible for him to send us a distress signal. And if there's one code rockrats will honor, it's answering a call for help.

So call me stupid. I took the risk. I put *Sniffer* back on a smooth orbit—and nothing happened.

You've got to be curious to be a skyjock, in both senses of the word. So color me curious. I stared at that green cone and ate some tangy squeeze-tube soup and got even more curious. I used the radar to rummage through the nearby rocks, looking for metal that might be a ship. I checked some orbits. The Belt hasn't got dust in it, to speak of. The dust got sucked into Jupiter long ago. The rocks—"planetesimals" a scientist told me I should call them, but they're just rocks to me—can be pretty fair-sized. I looked around, and I found one that was heading into the mathematical cone my number-cruncher dealt me.

Sniffer took five hours to rendezvous with it—a big black hunk, a klick wide and absolutely worthless.

I moored *Sniffer* to it with automatic moly bolts. They made hollow bangs—*whap, whap*—as they plowed in.

Curious, yes. Stupid, no. The disabled skyjock was just a theory. Laser bolts are real. I wanted some camouflage. My companion asteroid had enough traces of metal in it to keep standard radar from seeing *Sniffer*'s outline. Moored snug to the asteroid's face, I'd be hard to pick out. The asteroid would take me coasting through the middle of that cone. If I kept radio silence, I'd be pretty safe.

So I waited. And slept. And fixed the aft sensors. And waited.

Prospectors are hermits. You watch your instruments, you tinker with your plasma drive, you play 3D flexcop—an addictive game; it ought to be illegal—and you worry. You work out in the zero-gee gym, you calculate how to break even when you finally can sell your fresh ore to the Hansen Corporation, you wonder if you'll have to kick ass to get your haul in pipeline orbit for Earthside—and you have to like it when the nearest conversationalist is the Social/Talkback subroutine in the shipboard. Me, I like it. Curious, as I said.

It came up out of the background noise on the radar scope. In fact, I thought it *was* noise. The thing came and went, fluttered, grew and shrank. It gave a funny radar profile—but so did some of the new ships the corporations flew. My rock was passing about two hundred klicks from the thing and the odd profile made me cautious. I went into the observation bubble to have a squint with the opticals.

The asteroid I'd pinned *Sniffer* to had a slow, lazy spin. We rotated out of the shadow just as I got my reflex-opter telescope on-line. Stars spun slowly across a jet-black sky. The sun carved sharp shadows into the rock face. My target drifted up from the horizon, a funny yellow-white dot. The telescope whirred and it leaped into focus.

I sat there, not breathing. A long tube, turning.

Towers jutted out at odd places—twisted columns, with curved faces and sudden jagged struts. A fretwork of blue. Patches of strange, moving yellow. A jumble of complex structures. It was a cylinder, decorated almost beyond recognition. I checked the ranging figures, shook my head, checked again. The inboard computer overlaid a perspective grid on the image, to convince me. I sat very still. The cylinder was pointing nearly away from me, so radar had reported a cross section much smaller than its real size. The thing was seven goddamn kilometers long.

I stared at that strange, monstrous thing, and thought, and suddenly I didn't want to be around there anymore. I took three quick shots with the telescope on inventory mode. That would tell me composition, albedo, the rest of the litany. Then I shut it down and scrambled back into the bridge. My hands were trembling again.

I hesitated about what to do, but they decided for me. On our next revolution, as soon as the automatic opticals got a fix, there were *two* blips. I punched in for a radar Doppler and it came back bad: the smaller dot was closing on us, fast.

The moly bolts came free with a bang. I took *Sniffer* up and out, backing away from the asteroid to keep it between me and the blip that was coming for us. I stepped us up to max gee. My mouth was dry and I had to check every computer input twice.

I ran. There wasn't much else to do. The blip was coming at me at better than a tenth of a gee— incredible acceleration. In the Belt there is plenty of time for moving around, and a chronic lack of fuel—so we use high-efficiency drives and take energy-cheap orbits. The blip wasn't bothering with that. Somehow he had picked *Sniffer* out and decided we were worth a lot of fuel to reach, and reach in a hurry. For some reason they didn't use a laser bolt. It would have been a simple shot at this range. But maybe they didn't want to chance my shooting at the big ship this close, so they put their money on driving me off.

But then, why chase me so fast? It didn't add up.

By the time I was a few hundred klicks away from the asteroid it was too small to be a useful shield. The blip appeared around its edge. I don't carry weapons, but I do have a few tricks. I built a custom-designed pulse mode into *Sniffer*'s fusion drive, back before she was commissioned. When the blip appeared I started staging the engines. The core of the motor is a hot ball of plasma, burning heavy water—deuterium—and spitting it, plus vaporized rock, out the back tubes. Feeding in the right amount of deuterium is crucial. There are a dozen overlapping safeguards on the system, but if you know how—

I punched in the command. My drive pulsed, suddenly rich in deuterium. On top of that came a dose of pulverized rock. The rock damps the runaway reaction. On top of *that,* all in a microsecond, came a shot of cesium. It mixed and heated and *zap*—out the back, moving fast, went a hot cloud of spitting, snarling plasma. The cesium ionizes easily and makes a perfect shield against radar. You can fire a laser through it, sure—but how do you find your target?

The cesium pulse gave me a kick in the butt. I looked back. A blue-white cloud was spreading out behind *Sniffer,* blocking any detection.

I ran like that for one hour, then two. The blip showed up again. It had shifted sideways, to get a look around the cesium cloud—an expensive maneuver. Apparently they had a lot of fuel in reserve.

I threw another cloud. It punched a blue-white fist in the blackness. They were making better gee than I could; it was going to be a matter of who could hold out. So I tried another trick. I moved into the radar shadow of an asteroid that was nearby, and moving at a speed I could manage. Maybe the blip would miss me when it came out from behind the cloud. It was a gamble, but worth it in fuel.

In three hours I had my answer. The blip homed in on me. *How?* I thought. *Who's got a radar that can pinpoint that well?*

I fired a white-hot cesium cloud. We accelerated away, making tracks. I was getting worried. *Sniffer* was groaning with the strain. I hadn't allowed myself to think about what I'd seen, but now it looked like I was in for a long haul. The fusion motor rumbled and murmured to itself and I was alone, more alone than I'd felt for a long time, with nothing to do but watch the screen and think.

Belters aren't scientists. They're gamblers, idealists, thieves, crazies, malcontents. Most of us are from the cylinder worlds orbiting Earth. Once you've grown up in space, moving on means moving *out,* not going back to Earth. Nobody wants to be a ground-pounder. So Belters are the new cutting edge of mankind, pushing out, finding new resources.

The common theory is that life in general must be like that. Over the last century the scientists have looked for radio signals from other civilizations out among the stars, and come up with zero results. But we think life isn't all that unusual in the universe. So the question comes up: if there *are* aliens, and they're like us, why haven't they spread out among the stars? How come they didn't overrun Earth before we even evolved? If they moved at even one percent the speed of light, they'd have spread across the whole damn galaxy in a few million years.

Some people think that argument is right. They take it a little further, too—the aliens haven't visited our solar system, so check your premise again. Maybe there *aren't* any aliens like us. Oh, sure, intelligent fish, maybe, or something we can't imagine. But there are no radio-builders, no star-voyagers. The best proof of this is that they haven't come calling.

I'd never thought about that line of reasoning much, because that's the conventional wisdom now; it's stuff you learn when you're a snot-nosed kid. We stopped listening for radio signals a long time ago, back around 2030 or so. But now that I thought about it—

Already, men were living in space habitats. If mankind ever cast off into the abyss between the stars, which way would they go? In a dinky rocket? No, they'd go in comfort, in stable communities. They'd rig up a cylinder world with a fusion drive, or something like it, and set course for the nearest star, knowing they'd take generations to get there.

A century or two in space would make them into very different people. When they reached a star, where would they go? Down to the planets? Sure—for exploration, maybe. But to live? Nobody who grew up in fractional gee, with the freedom the cylinder world gives you, would want to be a ground-pounder. They wouldn't even know *how*.

The aliens wouldn't be much different. They'd be spacefarers, able to live in vac and tap solar power. They'd need raw materials, sure. But the cheapest way to get mass isn't to go down and drag it up from the planets. No, the easy way is in the asteroids—otherwise, Belters would never make a buck. So if the aliens came to our solar system a long time ago, they'd probably continue to live in space colonies. Sure, they'd study the planets some. But they'd live where they were comfortable.

I thought this through, slowly. In the long waits while I dodged from rock to rock there was plenty of time. I didn't like the conclusion, but it fit the facts. That huge seven-kilometer cylinder back there wasn't man-made. I'd known that, deep in my guts, the moment I saw it. Nobody could build a thing like that out there and keep it quiet. The cylinder gave off no radio, but ships navigating that much mass into place would have to. Somebody would have picked it up.

So now I knew what was after me. It didn't help much.

I decided to hide behind one rock heading sunward at a fair clip. I needed sleep and I didn't want to keep up my fusion burn—they're too easy to detect. Better to lie low for a while.

I stayed there for five hours, dozing. When I woke up I couldn't see the blip. Maybe they'd broken off the chase. I was ragged and there was sand in my eyes. I wasn't going to admit to myself that I was really scared this time. Belters and lasers I could take, sure. But this was too much for me.

I ate breakfast and freed *Sniffer* from the asteroid I'd moored us to. My throat was raw, my nerves jumpy. I edged us out from the rock and looked around. Nothing. I turned up the fusion drive. *Sniffer* creaked and groaned. The deck plates rattled. There was a hot, gun-metal smell. I had been in my skinsuit the whole time and I didn't smell all that good either. I pulled away from our shelter and boosted.

It came out of nowhere.

One minute the scope was clean and the next—a big one, moving fast, straight at us. It *couldn't* have been hiding—there was no rock around to screen it. Which meant they could deflect radar waves, at least for a few minutes. They could be invisible.

The thing came looming out of the darkness. It was yellow and blue, bright and obvious. I turned in my couch to see it. My hands were punching in a last-ditch maneuver on the board. I squinted at the thing and a funny feeling ran through me, a chill. It was *old*. There were big meteor pits all over the yellow-blue skin. The surface itself glowed, like rock with a ghostly fire inside. I could see no ports, no locks, no antennae.

It was swelling in the sky, getting close.

I hit the emergency board, all buttons. I had laid out good money for one special surprise, if some prospector overtook me and decided he needed an extra ship. The side pods held fission-burn rockets, powerful things. They fired one time only and cost like hell. But worth it.

The gee slammed me back into the couch. A roar rattled the ship. We hauled ass out of there. I saw the thing behind fade away in the exhaust flames. The high-boost fuel puts out incredibly hot gas. Some of it caught the yellow-blue thing. The front end of the ship scorched. I smiled grimly and cut in the whole system. The gee thrust went up. I felt the bridge swimming around me, a sour smell of burning—then I was out, the world slipping away, the blackness folding in.

When I came to, I was floating. The boosters yawned empty, spent. *Sniffer* coasted at an incredibly high speed. And the yellow-blue thing was gone.

Maybe they'd been damaged. Maybe they just plain ran out of fuel; everybody has limitations, even things that can span the stars.

I stretched out and let the hard knots of tension begin to unwind. Time enough later to compute a new orbit. For the moment it simply felt great to be alone and alive.

"Ceres Monitor here, on 560 megahertz. Calling on standby mode for orecraft *Sniffer*. Request microburst of confirmation on your hail frequency, *Sniffer*. We have a high-yield reading on optical from your coordinates. Request confirmation of fission burn. Repeat, this is Ceres Monitor—"

I clicked it off. The Belt is huge, but the high-burn torch I'd turned loose back there was orders of magnitude more luminous than an ordinary fusion jet. That was one reason I carried them—they doubled as a signal flare, visible millions of klicks away. By some chance somebody had seen mine and relayed the coordinates to Ceres.

All through the chase I hadn't called Ceres. It would have been of no use—there were no craft within range to be of help. And Belters are loners—my instinct was always to keep troubles to myself. There's nothing worse than listening to a Belter whining over the radio.

But now—I switched the radio back on and reached for the mike to hail Ceres. Then I stopped.

The yellow-blue craft had never fired at me. *Sniffer* would have been easy to cripple at that range. An angry prospector would've done it without thinking twice.

Something prevented them. Some code, some moral sense that ruled out firing on a fleeing craft, no matter how much they wanted to stop it.

A moral code of an ancient society. They had come here and settled, soaking up energy from our sun, mining the asteroids, getting ices from comets. A peaceful existence. They were used to a sleepy Earth, inhabited by life-forms not worth the effort of constant study. Probably they didn't care much about planets anymore. They didn't keep detailed track of what was happening. Suddenly, in the last century or so—a very short interval from the point of view of a galactic-scale society—the animals down on the blue-white world started acting up. Emitting radio, exploding nuclear weapons, flying spacecraft. These ancient beings found an exponentially growing technology on their doorstep.

I tried to imagine what they thought of us. We were young, we were crude. Undoubtedly the cylinder beings could have destroyed us. They could nudge a middle-sized asteroid into a collision orbit with Earth, and watch the storm wrack engulf humanity. Simple. But they hadn't done it. That moral sense again?

Something like that, yes. Give it a name and it becomes a human quality—which is in itself a deception. These things were *alien*. But their behavior had to make some sort of sense, had to have a reason.

I floated, frowning. Putting all this together was like assembling a jigsaw puzzle with only half the pieces, but still—something told me I was right. It fit.

A serene, long-lived, cosmic civilization might be worried by our blind rush outward. They were used to vast time scales; we had come on the stage in the wink of an eye. Maybe this speed left the cylinder beings undecided, hesitant. That would explain why they didn't contact us. Just the reverse, in fact—they were hiding. Otherwise—

It suddenly hit me. They didn't use radio because it broadcasts at a wide angle. Only lasers can keep a tight beam over great distances. That was what zapped me—not a weapon, a communications channel.

Which meant there had to be more than one cylinder world in the Belt. They kept quiet by using only beamed communications.

That implied something further, too. We hadn't heard any radio signals from other civilizations, either—because they were using lasers. They didn't want to be detected by other, younger societies.

Why? Were the aliens in our own Belt debating whether to help us or crush us? Or something in between?

In the meantime, the Belt was a natural hideout. They liked their privacy. They must be worried now, with humans exploring the Belt. I might be the first human to stumble on them, but I wouldn't be the last.

"Ceres Monitor calling to—"

I hesitated. They were old, older than we could imagine. They could have been in this solar system longer than man—stable, peaceful, inheritors of a vast history. They were moral enough not to fire at me, even though they knew it meant they would be discovered.

They needed time. They had a tough decision to face. If they were rushed into it they might make the wrong one.

"Orecraft *Sniffer* requested to—"

I was a Belter; I valued my hermit existence, too. I thumbed on the mike.

"Ceres, this is *Sniffer*. Rosemary Jokopi, sole officer. I verify that I used a fission burn, but only as a part of routine mining exploration. No cause for alarm. Nothing else to report. Transmission ends."

When I hung up the mike, my hands weren't shaking anymore.

Side Effect

 FROM: BIOENGINEER CHIEF CLAY
TO: DR. SANDERS, OASIS CRATERS,
INC.
(ONE-WAY VOICE TRANSMISSION,
MARS-EARTH COMPRESSED SQUIRT)

It worked like a charm, sir. The orbital guys brought the icesteroid right in on sked. How they can deliver ice hunks the size of a football field, clear from the rings of Saturn, and drop them smack on target on Mars, I dunno. But they did.

You shoulda seen it! Like God got mad and finally put His foot down. The icesteroid blasted a hole a kilometer wide. We were hunkered down in a bunker 'way over the horizon and I still couldn't hear right for an hour.

They took three hole punctures at the dome in Hellas Central, and that's five hundred klicks away. That bio-teched dog you sent us was the first out onto the plain to watch the show. He scampered around in the streams and mud, yapping and carrying on. We sure liked him, sir, and we think he's the forerunner of a whole line of products that'll really hit it big here.

I was in the first tractor that reached the lip of the crater. It was just like you'd said in the brochures—all the sub-tundra ice melted, big pretty yellow geysers, mud flowing like chocolate rivers. I got good footage. Lassie—that's the dog—took off, those big lungs sucking in the oxy and nitrogen liberated by the impact. Frisked, barked—one of your best beasts, sir.

We got right to work rigging the plastic projectors along the crater rim. Took a day, but when we sighted them in and blew the bubble, it worked fine, just fine. The crater was still outgassing real well, so we just let it fill the bubble, pull it tight. Lot faster than when we blew the Hellas Central dome, I tell you.

So then we spread the biomat, just like you said. That blue algae stuff flat-out loved the fog bubbling up everywhere. Had to throw down a patch and step back quick, 'cause it grew fast as it could eat. Just sopped up the UV and gorged on the free chemicals. Beautiful foamy geysers spewed up like fountains all over the floor of the crater. That watered the mats even more.

And you were right about the rocks, too. I could feel the heat through my glove. That impact warmth made the biomat grow like crazy. In two days those patches of yours spread out and covered the whole crater. We got clouds forming at the top of the bubble dome, and then rain—the first on Mars in a couple billion years.

Right now we're sowing that new wheat you sent. Looks like a good product, uses the UV real well. Planted a field right next to the central lake. I figure we got a century's worth of water here, all from tundra ice. Dome pressure is half an Earth atmosphere. I can walk around in just long johns and an oxy mask. Yesterday at sunset we got an actual rainbow inside the dome, both ends standing on the crater rim.

So I figure it's an unqualified success, sir. You can see that from the attached data. Time to franchise the operation, I'd say. I hope those Saturn ring guys can deliver a hundred or so icesteroids per year, 'cause we can blow bubbles for that many right now—and you just wait'll the whole crater oasis idea catches on!

Well, almost unqualified. We lost track of Lassie in all the rush. I figured, hell, where can he go, right? He ran off into the crater, happy as any bio-teched beastie I ever saw.

We were having trouble with the biomat then so I got busy. Thing was, it was *too* good. Gobbled up mud and grew, spreading like a carpet everywhere. Could hardly beat it off with a stick. Thick, too. Wearing steel boots, I walked over it like it was a rug, looking for Lassie.

So maybe you're going to have to do some fine-tuning on the mat. Or on Lassie 2, assuming there'll be an update in that product line.

We finally found out what happened to Lassie, sir, and I want you to know all of us here are real sorry. We don't like to lose equipment. After all, that cuts into our profit sharing, too.

But I'm afraid, sir, that the rug ate your dog.

Knowing Her

When we first met it was 1998 and we were both twenty-six. I had stepped outside, into the garden, away from the swirling party.

She stood watching water drip from a thick-lipped urn and spatter on brown stones below.

The back of her long neck seemed ghostly, frosted. We had been introduced inside but now, in the still garden, I became unsure of myself. Her head swiveled intently, studying the lazy fountain as though it possessed subtle secrets. And the objects themselves seemed stilled, as the hare freezes before the snake.

I coughed. She turned toward me.

"I have more life than that crowd in there," she said abruptly. "That's why you followed me out."

Judicious, as a screen for lingering uncertainty, I murmured, "Could be."

"Energy attracts, isn't that what you physicists say?"

"You've got it scrambled." (It was a year for being precise.)

She wrinkled her nose with an artful disdain. In the evening light her face was veiled in a dusty blue. "Still, I probably make more sense than that mumbling over there."

She nodded toward Coleman, who was explaining

162

the sudden dieback in South America, his audience a ragged crescent on the patio.

"He speaks carefully, like he's putting together a fine watch," she said. "But by the time he's through you don't care what time it is."

I smiled. Behind us the crowd inside muttered and shifted. I said something meant to be observant.

She considered my words for a moment. Her face was pooled in shadow and I could not read her expression.

"Perhaps you did not approach me for the right reason. Do you prefer beauty or focus of person?"

I laughed.

"You'd rather love me for my warts, then?"

I knew she moved in circles distant from my own. She was swift, beautiful, popular, totally unlike the people I knew. Yet when I looked at her I was seized by an idiot joy. I told her who I was, what I did, odd lumpy facts of pleasures and dislikes, the ornamental facets of public personality.

She gave me a quotation: "Life can only be understood backward, but it must be lived forward." I blinked. "Sören Kierkegaard, you know him?" she said.

I nodded, lying.

"I slept with my first husband last evening."

I said nothing. In the chill air our breath made small clouds.

"Do you think I seem changed for it?"

"I didn't know you were married."

"I'm not. But I'm young enough to do it."

I said that I thought it odd that she would say young, instead of old. Did not—?

"I shall be Subtracted soon," she said. "Does that make me more beautiful to you now? Or only younger?"

I remarked that she did not need to subtract years yet. She made a hollow laugh.

At that moment some friends approached and saluted us loudly. I lost the thread. A moment later, engaged in conversation, I missed seeing her smoothly slip away.

Later I walked through the garden again, but without finding her. And throughout the warming drone of the party that evening I did not see her face again.

It was some time after that before I realized that, in some cool analytical way, she had been trying me out as a possible candidate for the position of first husband.

We met in Toronto six years later. I was attending a scientific conference and that morning had given my invited paper. Lunch finished, I found the afternoon papers boring, the long narrow rooms stultifying. I left the hotel and went for a walk. Most of the damage from the guerilla war had been repaired by this time, though occasionally I came upon a gutted building, stark and raw and naked in the shimmering July sunlight.

I strolled aimlessly and eventually wandered into a broad, comfortable park. I thought a figure in the distance seemed familiar. She was arrowing to my left, legs scissoring the air with purpose. I moved to intersect and with Euclidean perception we met beneath the statue of a dead politician.

"And have you studied Kierkegaard yet?" she said as we approached.

"Probably not enough."

"I'm past all that now. You either act or read, but not both."

I parted my lips to agree, and stopped. In my home, long shelves of Princeton University Press editions of Kierkegaard rested, some of them well thumbed. I loved the clean stiff pages, thick with words. Some of Kierkegaard's spirit seemed invested in them, splintered into footnotes, epigraphs, italics that shouted from the page, heavy German philosophical jargon with a weight like layered cake. The austere formal march of words—was that what she'd seen in Kierkegaard?

I paused as I thought this, and she said, "I see you haven't changed."

"Some of us don't."

"All of us do." She folded her arms and stood hip-shot, arms white as thighs against the burnished cloth. She smiled teasingly and crinkled her eyes against the sunlight. "You really should have yourself Subtracted, you know."

"We are still young."

"You were quite stupid not to follow me then, that night. It was a crucial moment."

"You married him, I saw."

"Yes, and it was all right for a while."

"I saw that his bill was defeated in the House last week," I said, searching for neutral ground.

"The Conversationists are losing everything these days. It was clear to me they were on the way out a year ago. My divorce came through last spring."

"Oh, I—"

"—didn't know," she finished wryly. She glanced up at the granite politician above us, now the colleague of pigeons. "I couldn't have gone any further with him." She sighed prettily. "You were really very stupid, you know. You might have gotten me out of all this."

I frowned, puzzled. She was youthful, undeniably so. Yet a thin weary air clung to her. Her movements, so light and sure, seemed to echo other thoughts, other times well memorized.

"Surely there are many others," I said casually.

"Quite so. They stand in line. This next one is very important to me," she said briskly. "I must be Subtracted again."

"That requires a great deal of money."

She nodded. "The money is the easiest part."

"You mean getting through to the government. I

thought the moratorium on Subtracting had been
lifted."

"It has, but no clinic will give the treatments without government approval."

"Simply because public opinion is so much against
it?"

"Of course! Look at that fellow Samuelson. The
mob killed him. And he'd only been in for three treatments. They hate it that we can buy years with
money."

"We? You perhaps, not me. I can't afford it. I've
never made that much money grinding out equations."

"Maybe that's the point. We never would have
worked out, then, I suppose. To get any treatments at
all I need connections, and you don't have connections.
That's what I'm working on now." She gestured ele-
gantly and my eyes followed, looking down a pathway
bristling with hedges, flanked by knotted chain bor-
ders. A small group of people stood chatting there, occasionally glancing in our direction. The air was like
soft, cloying wax, rippling the light; I could not see
them clearly.

"No, I couldn't do that for you," I admitted.

"They can. They *move* things."

"I see."

"There are no other people like them."

"I see."

She shuffled nervously. "And I must get over
there. I am probably late already. They don't like people who are late."

"I know. I can see the strings."

Her face hardened. She began to walk away. My
breath caught.

"But wait. Can't we, ah, correspond?"

She made a thin smile and shook her head. Gods
don't answer letters.

I watched her quick, spiked pace as she left. I felt
a sudden warm rush of emotion and studied her in-

tently, framing her there in my memory—a beautiful woman, moving away with clean strides. An image of—what? A worldly beauty on her way to an assignation? Perhaps. So much purpose in her motion, such muscled drive. Her world seemed enclosed in brackets and heightened by invisible coefficients.

Some nine years later I attended the late evening party of an acquaintance, scarcely thinking I would stay long. I had dribbled away my day in analyzing experimental data. Physics is like a rough, uncharted landscape choked with brambles, cut through by yawning canyons, most of it impassible even on foot. Across this terrain slice smooth freeways of theory, where everything is under control and the traveler scarcely notices the chaos to either side. An experiment lands one in the wilderness; someone must then hack a tortured path to the nearest highway. If he succeeds, we sigh in relief and say that the data more or less agree with known theory. I had been through a day of this, a less successful one than most, and I was tired.

I stood on a narrow balcony watching the sprinkle of city lights below, sipping a drink. When I glanced up she was there.

She was turning away, as though to go back inside before I had seen her. "No, wait," I said.

She forced a smile and the electricity of it caught at my heart. "Ah, I didn't recognize you." Her lips had the same exquisite red brightness I remembered, but her words had an automatic, machinelike edge to them.

I began conversationally, "I suppose you have—" and broke off, because she tugged with her left hand and brought into view her reluctant companion. He was a short, sturdy man, swarthy, black hair, probably Arab. He nodded and smiled formally at me with carefully measured grace.

"Mr. Samyan," she said, drawing him forward a

little more. I put on my public face and made my own introduction, guessing that she would stumble over my name, or not remember it at all.

Mr. Samyan had none of the intent businessman's myopia I had expected. He made a few artful remarks, mostly the preliminary sniffing one does at parties to find out what the other person does, to place everyone in a context. Then, glancing sideways at her fidgeting, he excused himself with a mumbled word about going for drinks.

"He's very smooth, just right for you," I said.

"I am pretty sure he had never read any Kierkegaard. That's what I like."

"You have grown thinner."

"I'm busy," she said lightly. "I do things. I work."

She shrugged and the motion caused her helical sleeve to shift upward for an instant. There was a hint of pink on her elbow. She caught my glance and abruptly said, "Oh, listen. Remember that one?" She cocked an ear to the thumping music.

It was some number by the Rolling Stones from the middle 1960s. I vaguely recognized it. It was from before my time and certainly before hers as well. We both knew that.

She adjusted her clinging dress and the sleeve drooped, exposing for one long moment the red-rimmed crater in her elbow. I knew that sort of thing was now almost acceptable, that I should not be shocked to see it in public—but I could not take my eyes away. She saw me looking and hastily covered the elbow.

"It's not a crime," she said. It was the first defensive remark I had ever heard her utter.

"No, of course not. But—why you? I know they pay well, still—"

"Money isn't it," she said harshly. "There are some places they can't even pay people to plug into.

Filthy jobs, high security jobs, plugged into insidious machines. The operators have to be trustworthy."

"The tactile nerve endings near the socket, don't you lose those?" My glance rippled down her almost involuntarily, and knowing what to look for, I saw the telltale bulges at wrists, knees, ankles. The open wounds of sockets at every jointed nerve nexus. Coupling points for machines.

"Oh, yes," she said wryly, watching my eyes. "I have them everywhere. They require that. And yes, I lose the feeling here and there. Nothing substantial, compared to what I get."

I frowned. "Not money, then, just—"

"Obligations. I accumulate obligations. Which they discharge by letting me have more Subtraction." She smiled cynically. And I noticed that, yes, of course, she was precisely the same. A beautiful girl suspended in the amber of time.

"I am still beautiful, I still have that energy, don't I?" She leaned forward, wetting her lips. The answer was important. "You don't think the socketing makes me ugly?"

I had to say, "No, by no means." And inside I meant it, for the lovely delicate blending of her features was the same. The blue intensity of her eyes shone through me.

"I suppose you know you should not repeat this." She paused. "It is illegal to have as many treatments as I have . . ."

"Of course." There was a pause between us and I heard the slow sway of music from within. "I would have imagined Mr. Samyan could get the treatments for you, without . . ."

"Without my having to get myself punched?" she said sharply. "I tell you, it's not money. You have to give them what they want, and bureaucrats don't need money. They need people who are willing to sweep up

their messes. Who'll run cyborgs that some people—
the newspapers, certainly—think are immoral."

"And are they?"

She looked suddenly to the side, out at the jeweled
city lights, blinking rapidly. The gesture opened a
chasm in her. For an instant I saw through, into the
brambles and uncharted chaos. Into vast disorder. And
felt beneath my feet a sure, hard blacktop of the highway. In her beautiful face I had seen something very
old.

Before I could say anything the noise from inside
suddenly grew louder. We turned and Mr. Samyan was
coming through the door carrying drinks. She closed
her eyes for a moment, collecting herself, and I mumbled thanks to her companion. Mr. Samyan continued
with his impersonal partygoer's conversation and I re-
sponded in kind, both of us politely not noticing that
she had moved an impenetrable few meters away,
watching the city. My mind was still churning from
what she had told me and I could scarcely keep my
eyes from her. Samyan's glance flickered across at the
woman intermittently and I knew we were both
equally uninterested in talking to the other. I began to
contrive a polite exit. Once I had, the rest of the party
seemed to move by in a glazed fog, leaving me to my
own thoughts. Indeed, a year later I could scarcely remember where the party had been, but every word she
had said repeated itself in my mind.

Several times over the next few years I had the recurring feeling that she was out there waiting for me to
make a move, a gesture. But I did nothing. I attended
to my research and the mainstream of my private life.
It came as a shock when I received the invitation to her
Freezing.

It was fashionable then to have a party that ran
on, even as one was entombed in liquid nitrogen. I felt
it echoed unpleasantly of the pharaohs, even though

realizing my views were already considered provincial. I hesitated over whether to go, and hence arrived late, after immersion. Most of the guests were already arrayed in the conversation pit, drinking and talking of other matters. The long wall of plastic and steel bubbled to itself.

A butler intercepted me quietly, probably alarmed at my stony face. I was led over; I peered through the frosted glass at her. She hung some distance away, hair clipped, arms and legs bound, encased in a white cloak. She swam in the clear brilliant nitrogen. She was still young, beautiful, her features molded with perfection. Through the fog I could not tell if she smiled or not.

A waiter offered me a goblet; I refused. The soft warm carpet, molded chairs, cunningly placed lighting—we stood in the path-space of the living. A centimeter away was the cold place, where she floated, to me still a place of death. I felt as if in a dream.

I turned to go. Someone called my name.

Mr. Samyan caught up with me at the door and tugged at my sleeve. "Stay, stay," he said. "She wondered if you would come."

"I came," I said dumbly. I hung suspended between the doorway and the awful warmth of the room. His hand did not move. I struggled with my shyness, and not wishing to insult him, I moved into a corner of the reception room at his request. I remained standing, clutching a goblet I had somehow acquired, and ignored the crowd behind me.

"She said she hoped that you would understand, sir. You are a scientist."

"I was only a sort of vague friend," I said stiffly.

"You must understand. She sought life. To remain young. It is what every American wants."

"Some." I felt a sudden fullness in my throat. My voice broke. "She was so beautiful."

"She wished to stay that way."

"I suppose I can understand that. When you have something, you want to keep it." I thought of my own career. What would happen when I could no longer form the delicate web of inference, see the way through a maze of facts and calculations? "But why does she have to run away from all of us? To be Frozen?"

He brightened at my response, his round face creased by a smile. "The youth, the beauty, that was the raison d'être. But you are a scientist, you will understand what that means."

"I am not a doctor."

"Ah, the Subtracting is fine, you know, it can go on and on. As she did. On her waltz through the world. She has been doing that all her life, the dance. To be young was everything. That is what attracted me to her. And you . . . ?"

He let the sentence trickle away, hoping I would pick it up. I shook my head. "Pointless. Our average lifespan is nearly a hundred now, we're all young long enough."

"But that is not *life*, that is only *aging*. To be the person she knew how to be, she had to be *young*. It was very American," he mused. "Very appealing. It took her into the highest circles. She found it was the only card she had."

"Then why Freeze? Why run away?"

"To live. Perhaps in the future they can cure her, fix the cancer."

"What?" I felt a tremor of surprise. "We can cure that now."

"At a price. A cost to the body. You are a scientist, you understand, to cure the disease it is necessary to match the tumor. They select and program the antigens with their scopes and clever chemistry. But they cover only certain—ah"—he struggled for the word in a tongue foreign to him—"species of the cancer. The

Subtracting inhibits the immune response, as you say. Not in all cases, but in hers, yes."

I stood dumbly, unable to speak. Mr. Samyan shifted uneasily and peered down at his rich black leather shoes. Around us the party moved, murmuring to itself, unchanging and eternal.

"Do not think so hard upon it, sir," he said with sudden gusto. "She is not gone, truly. She merely seeks youth. She always has. She will be young again. To stop the growth of the cancer it would have been necessary to stop the Subtracting, and she could not bear that."

He gestured to a passing waiter. "Here, have another drink. She ordered that the reception go on for hours."

"I see."

"She lives, sir," the small man said.

"No," I said with sudden absolute conviction. "She has been dying ever since I knew her."

Stand-In

 By the time I got to the party the unicorn was talking to a girl in ballet tights and the liquor was already gone.

Never throw an open house party in San Francisco. It's a town full of people who like to drink and talk talk talk, and the only ones who give parties are masochists who like trampled rugs and depleted refrigerators.

Not that I'm not one of them. I'm a man who likes people, work, responsibility, the whole bit. That's why I put on parties every once in a while—without a few of us the social life of the city would fall apart. Occasionally I think it's people like me who carry the world on their shoulders.

As I finished mauling the hors d'oeuvres I looked up and saw Marge on the other side of the room. The one in the unicorn costume would probably be a better bet, but I went over to pay my respects to the Old Flame In Residence first.

A cat would have broken an ankle trying to get through the people sprawled on pillows in the middle of the floor, looking like extras from a Cecil B. deMille Roman orgy, but I circumnavigated the bar and made it.

"It has a certain dualistic quality that lends the

mode a touch of the mystical," a thin-shouldered little man was saying to her. Marge gave me a warm, glazed look and a greeting, apparently not noticing that he was rocking back and forth on his toes, trying to look down the front of her dress.

"You're an iconoclastic synthetic-ist, then," I said, to divert his attention. Not that I blamed him for trying. When Marge walks a room it looks like chipmunks fighting inside a burlap sack.

"Well, yes," the artist grumbled.

"Excuse me, what's that?" a husky, deep voice said. It was the girl in the unicorn costume, breaking in.

"It's a new school," he said. "We believe the only fitting medium for this crass, materialistic society is the artificial, the cheap, anything that shows the decadence of the age. True art must be done now with purely synthetic materials."

He fished a green bathroom tile out of his coat pocket. Lines webbed across it, drawn on with purple ink in random patterns.

"Ugly," the unicorn said.

The word was short, the word was apt.

"It's a whole new mode of expression," Thin Shoulders said. Marge gripped his arm protectively and gave the girl a look that would have made Hannibal think about taking the next elephant back to Carthage.

The unicorn moved off. I could stay with Marge, but I'd been that route before. She had been weighed in the balance and found wanton. I followed the unicorn.

"Pretty nice costume," I said, trying to look down her throat and see who was inside. Are unicorns supposed to have tonsils? This one did.

"Thank you," she said. "I have it brushed twice a day."

"What?"

"My coat, of course, silly." She gave a demure little whinny, undeniably feminine. For the first time I noticed that the coat was a soft, warm gold, only slightly lighter than the funny little horn in the middle of her forehead.

"You mean this isn't a costume? Your coat is real?"

As it developed, not only was she a unicorn, and real, but a good conversationalist, too. I won't make the obvious remark about the people you meet at parties—my motto is just accept everything, don't try to figure out the situation, and see what develops. Still, unicorns don't turn up every day.

"I thought you were extinct," I said.

"Oh no," she batted golden eyelashes at me. "Technically, we never existed, so we couldn't become extinct."

"Then how . . . ?"

"It's one of those proverbial long stories. If you have the time . . ."

A hint, of course, almost classic in its form. I never thought I'd get one from something that looked literally like a horse, though.

I looked around. A lot of old and new faces were mingling with each other, with the standard party types. The Quarreling Couple were trying not to make a scene, there was the Symbolic Negro, the Informed Source, and The Girl Who'll Have Hysterics Later. And as I said, no drinks. Nothing particularly to hold me.

"Yours or mine?"

Hers was an ordinary walk-up with a few tacked-on pretensions. The smell of money hung over the interior, though, and I had to wade through inch-thick rugs to reach the couch.

"It's a matter of necessity," she said, settling into a strange hammocklike affair of cloth and wrought iron.

"Human beings are always thinking up things

they can't have, or think exist somewhere else. It's a habit they have, although I must say I don't quite understand it. Seems like a waste of time."

I looked at a carefully manicured hoof and tried to pay attention.

"We're from all the neighboring stars, and as soon as we achieve space travel the sensitive ones among us are drawn here by the emotional waves your mixed-up psyches give off. Once we're here we can't get out. Your race doesn't understand what it's doing, but there's no way we can stop you."

" 'We'?"

"Oh, I'm not really like this," she gestured at the glistening golden body. "It's the form I'm forced to take. By this."

She pressed a button on a side table and the wall at the other end of the room slid aside. It was one long panel of dully blinking lights, chemical feeder tubes, and spinning magnetic tapes. A worn panel near the top had the name UNIVAC almost scratched out.

"UNIVAC? That was dismantled long ago."

"True. We have to make do with what we can, and some of the old parts are easier to get. It's more than a computer—it synthesizes the chemicals I live on, keeps this body functioning, and gives me my instructions. I'm just in training now, before I get to work."

I felt like somebody had put my head on the wrong way. "What the . . . ?"

"I can see this form bothers you. Perhaps you would feel more at home with my surrogate body—the one left over from Helen of Troy?"

"*Helen* is a myth?"

She nodded and pressed a stud on the wall, spoke into a microphone for a moment. "You humans have remarkable faith that anything written down on a piece of paper constitutes history. A charming belief— but here's Helen."

Another panel opened and she stepped out. The

face seemed to fit the image, but the body looked like
a reflection in one of those mirrors at a fun house that
makes everyone look fat. Except with Helen, it wasn't
fat, just all woman. They'd also forgotten to add any
clothes.

"She's been around ever since I did that part for a
few weeks as a fill-in. Without my personality superim-
posed on her, she's a completely new person, suscepti-
ble to any command or suggestion."

Helen walked over to my chair and curled up on
the arm. She gave me a dazzling smile and didn't say
anything. "I don't get it," I said. "Why all this?"

"Because you and your vivid imaginations—the
worst in the galaxy—have drawn us into your fanta-
sies, right out of our own lives. The emotional pull is
too strong, so we have to go along." Helen slid off the
arm into my lap, brushing my cheek with lush red lips.
I tried to keep my mind on what the unicorn was saying.

"But it's a strain. None of us can last very long in
any one role. There have been four unicorns before me,
and we've had dozens of those Norse gods—they're
terrible on one's health, with all that throwing lightning around. Even a comparatively civilized character,
like Sherlock Holmes and his morphine, can wear us
down."

Helen murmured something into my ear, but I
don't think it had anything to do with Sherlock
Holmes. "But so?" I put out my hand in a questioning
gesture and a warm, white breast popped into it. Not
all of it—from where I was, it looked like it would
take two hands to hold on—but it was enough to
make me lose the thread of the argument.

"So that's why I wanted to talk to you. We've
never been very healthy, and there aren't many of us
who can take this for long." The unicorn nodded at
Helen and she gave me a coy little look, up from under
with heavy eyelashes thrown in.

"Yes," she said, "there are a number of vacancies . . . and rewards. With just a slight modification, your body can fit the part quite well."

"Rewards? For helping you complete this compulsion of yours?" I was still a little dense.

"We can't pay much, of course. But there's always Helen."

Helen gave me a slow smile and reached down and made a gesture that started my body temperature rising. "Batman is open," the unicorn said softly. "King Lear, James Bond, Don Juan . . . and Atlas."

So you can see how I got this job.

Like I said, I'm one of those people who carry the world on their shoulders.

Time Guide

 Herewith gives a few Milieu Menu selections from the immensely popular but extremely disorienting Age of Appetite.

This Catalog is only sampler. More exotic Milieus require permission of Psychological Counselor. Full instructions await those who file full credit voucher.

See cautionary notes at end and be warned.

MILIEU—STATIONARY AMBIENCE H8BSigmaFive-Alpha (Core Index)—
Degree of Significant Cultural Fluctuation: ± .076 *(Prime Rating)* 7/0/58 to 3/12/79 Stable. Region ± 2.36 yrs. varistable, within adjustable parameters. Region downstream 1.62 years of 8/23/81 carries possibility of detection by locals; *not advised*.

* * *

Sociomatrix info necessary for reducing detection possibility to 10^{-6} or less is appended, in varifax form. Tourists following these mandates are under insurance umbrella, unless deviation from pattern exceeds ± .16 Raleigh.

* * *

Now follows mood-fixing input. Is trying to transsub lacing dancing tremor of pasttime, pastrhyme, prior to launching customer thru iris. *Is following:*

. . . Drive a station wagon or a pickup truck. Carry in the back a bag of cement, a Coleman lantern, two wood saws wrapped in an oily rag, and the first issue of *Playboy.*

Be able to screw (trans: *flex; frapange; cop*) in a sleeping bag, using any of 4 different positions.

Always go around with girls who have short, blond hair and look vaguely like Doris Day used to.

Try to pick up a waitress in a coffee shop. Then drink a lot of beer afterward when you don't succeed. *(Sex change not formal option here.)*

Say that George Wallace makes a lot of sense, when you think about it. (Compare with Thos. Jefferson, Ambience B69J.)

Know a lot about yogurt or yak's milk before any of those health food nuts did.

Smoke Camels. Call them "cigs."

Play Johnny Cash records, esp. when parties are crowded. Try to dance to them, using girlfriend of guy you've just met. Always buy Coors when available. (Do not buy a "Coors—Breakfast of Champions" T-shirt, unless your role is modeled at under-15.)

Call everyone else's car a "Chevy." Prefer the chopped '58 model, but know three major design errors in the transmission.

Always crush used beer cans with one hand, laughing and gritting your teeth a little. Say that guy Hemingway is pretty good but doesn't really know a damn thing about shooting.

Call potatoes "spuds." Make a point of referring to all businesswomen as "gals." Call marijuana "hemp" but do not smoke any of it.

Use the line "as the actress said to the bishop" at least three times every day.

Never move to New York.

Say you've heard of the East Coast, but you don't believe it.

* * *

BERKELEY, CALIFORNIA, NORTH AMERICA
MISSED REVOLUTION MILIEU
STATIONARY AMBIENCE 6/4/66 to 3/16/71. Suggest restrict visit to 6 ± 2 days for proper saturation. Adaptive guises necessary.

Is following flexings:
. . . Either wear your hair very long or shave it all off—no compromises. Drive a tiny foreign car (if you must), but be sure no one can identify quite what it is. Hitchhike if possible. Deny reading anything. If someone mentions R. Crumb and the underground comics *(Collectors option here)*, say you look at Huckleberry Hound on morning TV every once in a while to catch the really subtle head stuff they're running these days.

Find an Eisenhower jacket and wear it constantly—even in bed.

Cultivate a dreamy, dislocated expression; occasionally don't finish your sentences. *(Option;* every once in a

while, wander away into traffic and have to be led
back to the sidewalk.)

When Kennedy and the assassination come up in conversation, say, "Yeah, who was that he ran against?"
and then put on a Rolling Stones record.

Be very serious about films. Sample sentence: "I've
been trying to get beyond *Clockwork Orange* for a
year now."

Always have wood chips, wrinkled brown organic rai-
sins, old doorknobs, etc. in your pockets. Occasionally
leave a pile of them at a friend's house for safe keeping.

Sample praise: "McDonald's is really, you know, in the
here and now. The people's food."

When meeting a local radical political figure for the
first time, stare at him/her intently for thirty seconds
and then say slowly, "I see it, yeah, now I see it," and
move away, distracted.

Cultivate an obscure rock band, tout them as "the new
Beatles," and two days later, when they come up in
conversation on Telegraph Avenue, mutter "Plastic.
Lost it all now," and change the subject.

Have a theory of history that compares, very ob-
scurely, Timothy Leary to Oliver Cromwell.

When someone passes illegal dope to you, murmur
"No man, don't want it to bring me down."

Pretend not to know where New York is.

* * *

EAST COAST, NORTH AMERICA
(Care Advised)
STATIONARY AMBIENCE 11/8/84 to 6/7/93
(Themes: Humor of Combat; Joy of the Thrust; Urban
Adrenaline Chemistry)

. . . contemplating the surge of action while remaining
in the lofting joyful moment, knowing we are both
with the past and beyond it. The hunt, after all, is only
pleasurable when one knows clearly who, precisely, is
the hunted and who the hunter . . .

> (from the attached program notes for the
> traveler, establishing the milieu and reflex
> motor-muscle coordination necessary for the
> age)

* * *

Is flexings:
Laugh a lot in the hollow concrete canyons, often hyster-
ically. When meeting others for the first time, refuse to
shake hands but then say "Scored big" enigmatically and
roll your eyes around. Wear either tweeds or a T-shirt.
Refuse to take off either, no matter how often heating
subsystems overload, or the air-conditioning fails. Smile
wanly as the sweat drips from your oily nose.

Say that what the big Eastern cities need is somebody
like, well, that guy Daley who used to run Chi. (Always say "Chi.")

Be able to trace the histories and triumphs, however
minor, of five separate and mutually antagonistic political factions on *The New York Times Review of
Books*. Regard these divisions as far more important
than "city issues" and believe, when pressed, that
Marx probably predicted it all anyway.

Useful positions: "War is the clashing of two parties with the goal of separating the conqueror from the conquered. There is no significant child's game which does not spring from the love of war. Now, to apply this to our problem . . ." (at this point you will be interrupted, so there is no need to complete the phrase)

Be able to recognize the mayor of New York City when he appears at the Central Park Rally of the People to explain the latest cutbacks in Survival Benefits, but avoid the Rally itself until the armored units arrive.

Know the subways very well, but don't go on the subways.

When visitors come in from the Midwest, ask them what they think, what the answers are. Smile tolerantly without actually laughing as they speak.

When you leave, tell people you are moving to California.

* * *

—is ending transmission here. Catalog terminates. Attempts to find stable social ambience in the years following 1999, which could be safely visited and their essence plucked, have failed. Time travelers are reminded that we of the dancing skittering hive do not promise more than a glancing, mind-warming intersection with these past ambiences. Remember, these flights connect the sliding rippling Truth we know today to a world totally unlike ours, in which people and society are frozen by custom to paths and patterns and habits, unmindful of the stochastic nature of Truth.

Taste these juicy moments.

Lick of the stationary realm.

Know the past, sensing that it is once more a present
a mere second wide, with a future nonexisting.

> *Postdate Note:* No inquiries about the once-
> available visits to the Red Sea of New
> Jersey, circa 2013, are now entertained.
>
> Attempts to make contact among the
> Red Sea Barges failed. It was not possible
> to define a stable sociomatrix, to share
> the skipping joy of mirth with the stoop-
> shouldered sailors. The Late TwenCens
> became blinded to our views. They could
> not see their times as the necessary
> quicksand of events we now all know;
> could not skate; were forced to walk.
> Unable to live lightly on the earth, to
> dance with grace, they sank.
>
> *(Group rates to the Apocalypse availa-
> ble. Passengers must wear pajamas.)*

We Could Do Worse

Everybody in the bar noticed us when we came in. You could see their faces tighten up. The bartender reached over and put the cover on the free-lunch jar. I caught that even though I was watching the people in the booths.

They knew who we were. You could see the caution come into their eyes. I'm big enough that nobody just glances at me once. You get used to that after a while and then you start to liking it.

"Beer," I said when we got to the mahogany bar. The bartender drew it, looking at me. He let some suds slop over and wiped the glass and stood holding it until I put down a quarter.

"Two," I said. The bartender put the glass in front of me and I pushed it toward Phillips. He let some of the second beer slop out too because he was busy watching my hands. I took the glass with my right and with my left I lifted the cover off the free-lunch jar.

"No," he said.

I took a sandwich out.

"I'm gonna make like I didn't hear that," I said and bit into the sandwich. It was cheese with some mayonnaise and hadn't been made today.

I tossed the sandwich aside. "Got anything better?"

"Not for you," the bartender said.

"You got your license out where I can read it?"

"You guys is federal. Got no call to want my liquor license."

"Lawyer, huh?" Phillips asked slow and steady. He doesn't say much but people always listen.

The bartender was in pretty good shape, a middle-sized guy with big arm muscles, but he made a mistake then. His hand slid under the bar, watching us both, and I reached over and grabbed his wrist. I yanked his hand up and there was a pistol in it. The hammer was already cocked. Phillips got his fingers between the revolver's hammer and the firing pin. We pulled it out of the bartender's hand easy and I tapped him a light one in the snoot, hardly getting off my stool. He staggered back and Phillips put away the revolver in a coat pocket.

"Guys like you shouldn't have guns," Phillips said. "Get hurt that way."

"You just stand there and look pretty," I said.

"It's Garrett, isn't it?"

"Now don't never you mind," Phillips said.

The rest of the bar was quiet and I turned and gave them a look. "What you expect?" I said loud enough so they could all hear. "Man pulls a gun on you, you take care of him."

A peroxide blonde in a back booth called out, "You bastards!"

"There a back alley here?" I asked the whole room.

Their faces were tight and they didn't know whether to tell me the truth or not.

"Hey, yeah," Phillips said. "Sure there's a back door. You 'member, the briefing said so."

He's not too bright. So I used a different way to open them up. "Blondie, you want we ask you some questions? Maybe out in that alley?"

Peroxide looked steady at me for a moment and

then looked away. She knew what we'd do to her out there if she made any more noise. Women know those things without your saying.

I turned my back to them and said, "My nickel."

The bartender had stopped his nose from bleeding but he wasn't thinking very well. He just blinked at me.

"Change for the beers," I said. "You can turn on that TV, too."

He fumbled getting the nickel. When the last of *The Milton Berle Hour* came on the bar filled with enough sound so anybody coming in from the street wouldn't notice that nobody was talking. They were just watching Phillips and me.

I sipped my beer. Part of our job is to let folks know we're not fooling around anymore. Show the flag, kind of.

The Berle show went off and you could smell the tense sweat in the bar. I acted casual, like I didn't care. The government news bulletins were coming on and the bartender started to change the channel and I waved him off.

"Time for *Lucy*," he said. He had gotten some backbone into his voice again.

I smiled at him. "I guess I know what time it is. Let's inform these citizens a li'l."

There was a Schlitz ad with dancing and singing bottles, the king of beers, and then more news. They mentioned the new directives about the state of emergency, but nothing I didn't already know two days ago. Good. No surprises.

"Let's have *Lucy*!" somebody yelled behind me.

I turned around but nobody said anything more. "You'd maybe like watchin' the convention?" I said.

Nobody spoke. So I grinned and said, "Maybe you patriots could learn somethin' that way."

I laughed a little and gestured to the bartender. He spun the dial and there was the Republican convention, warming up. Cronkite talking over the background noise.

"Somethin', huh?" I said to Phillips. "Not like four years ago."

"Don't matter that much," Phillips said. He watched the door while I kept an eye on the crowd.

"You kiddin'? Why, that goddamn Eisenhower almost took the nomination away from Taft last time. Hadn't been for Nixon deliverin' the California delegation to old man Taft, that pinko general coulda won."

"So?" Phillips sipped his beer. A station break came and I could hear tires hissing by outside in the light rain. My jacket smelled damp. I never wear a raincoat on a job like this. They get in your way. The streetlights threw stretched shapes against the bar windows. Phillips watched the passing shadows, waiting calm as anything for one of them to turn and come in the door.

I said, "You think Eisenhower, with that Kraut name, woulda picked our guy for the second spot?"

"Mighta."

"Hell no. Even if he had, Eisenhower didn't drop dead a year later."

"You're right there," Phillips said to humor me. He's not a man for theory.

"I tell you, Taft winnin' and then dyin', it was a godsend. Gave us the man we shoulda had. Never coulda elected him. The Commies, they'd never have let him get in power."

Phillips stiffened. I thought it was what I'd said, but then a guy came through the doors in a slick black raincoat. He was pale and I saw it was our man. Cheering at the convention came up then and he didn't notice anything funny, not until he got a few steps in and saw the faces.

Garrett's eyes widened as I came to him. He pulled his hands up like he was reaching for something under his coat, or maybe just to protect himself.

I didn't care which. I hit him once in the stomach to take the wind out of him and then gave him two quick overhand punches in the jaw. He went down nice and solid and wasn't going to get back up in a hurry.

Phillips searched him. There was no gun after all. The bar was dead quiet.

A guy in a porkpie hat came up to me all hot and bothered, like he hadn't been paying attention before, and said, "You can't just attack a, a member of the Congress! That's Congressman Garrett there! I don't care—"

The big talk went right out of him when I slammed a fist into his gut. Porkpie was another lawyer, no real fight in him.

I walked back to the bar and drained my beer. The '56 convention was rolling on, nominations just starting, but you knew that was all bull. Only one man was possible, and when the election came there'd be plenty of guys like me to fix it so he won.

Just then they put on some footage of the president and I stood there a second, just watching him. There was a knot in my throat when I looked at him, a real American. There were damn few of us, even now. We'd gotten in by accident, maybe, but now we were going to make every day count. Clean up the country. And hell, if the work wasn't done by the time his second term ended in 1961, we might have to diddle the Constitution a little, keep him in power until things worked okay.

Cronkite came on then, babbling about letting Adlai Stevenson out of house arrest, and I went to help Phillips get Garrett to his feet. I sure didn't want to have to haul the guy out to our car.

We got him up with his raincoat all twisted around him. Then the porkpie hat guy was there again, but this time with about a dozen of them behind him. They looked mad and jittery. A bunch like that can be trouble. I wondered if this was such a good idea, taking Garrett in his neighborhood bar. But the chief said we had to show these types we'd go anywhere, anytime.

Porkpie said, "You got no warrant."

"Sure I do." I showed them the paper. These types always think paper is God.

"Sit down," Phillips said, being civil. "You people all sit down."

"That's a congressman you got there. We—"

"Traitor, is what you mean," I said.

Peroxide came up then, screeching. "You think you can just take anybody, you lousy sonsabitches—"

Porkpie took a poke at me then. I caught it and gave him a right cross, pretty as you please. He staggered back. Still, I saw we could really get in a fix here if they all came at us.

Peroxide called out, "Come on, we can—"

She stopped when I pulled out the gun. It's a big steel automatic, just about the right size for a guy like me. Some guys use silencers with them, but me, I like the noise.

They all looked at it awhile and their faces changed, closing up, each one of them alone with their thoughts, and then I knew they wouldn't do anything.

"Come on," I said. We carried the traitor out into the night. I was so pumped up he felt light.

Even a year before, we'd have had big trouble bringing in a Commie network type like Garrett. He was a big deal on the House Internal Security Committee and had been giving us a lot of grief. Now nailing him was easy. And all because of one man at the top with real courage.

We don't bother with the formalities anymore. Phillips opened the trunk of the Pontiac and I dumped Garrett in. Easier and faster than cramming him into the front, and I wanted to get out of there.

Garrett was barely conscious and just blinked at

me as I slammed down the trunk. They'd wake him up plenty later.

As I came around to get in the driver's side I looked through the window of the bar. Cronkite was interviewing the president now. Ol' Joe looked like he was in good shape, real statesmanlike, but tough, you could see that.

Cronkite was probably asking him why he'd chosen Nixon for the VP spot, like there was no other choice. Like I'd tried to tell Phillips, Nixon's delivering California on the delegate issue in '52 had paved the way for the Taft ticket. And old Bob Taft, rest his soul, knew what the country needed when the vice presidency nomination came up.

Just like now. Joe, he doesn't forget a debt. So Dick Nixon was a shoo-in. McCarthy and Nixon—good ticket, regional balance, solid anti-Commie values. We could do worse. A lot worse.

I got in and gunned the motor a little, feeling good. The rain had stopped. The meat in the trunk was as good as dead, but we'd deliver it fresh anyway. We took off with a roar into the darkness.

Slices

1.

Even though he has learned it by now, the seeping sensation, the rich tingling comes to him each time: *something more*. No mere bauble, no toy, but the real thing: experience. They will give it to him again. He feels his mind drift to the subject this time and, yes, there it is, something he wants, something—yes, a woman. Again, a woman. Soft and with the by-now-familiar black hair, coming toward him with hips weaving that certain way, eyes intent and flickering with concern (there must always be concern), and the round enveloping fullness, the breasts, all that is there. She swarms over him, without his beckoning, without really even willing it. She is a fog of sensation and he feels her filling him, fluid up his nostrils, clotting in his eyes, piercing his anus *yes she does that* and more, onward, fibers lancing into him, his nerves giving back a smooth chorus of caressing pleasure as he enters her in turn, *yes,* this is it, this is what he wanted, how like them to know it.

2.

In the silent drifting times he wonders. There are
not many such times but, almost pedantically, he times
them by the thumping of his heart—at least he thinks
that it is his heart—and deduces that they allow him
only a few black spots in a day, a mere handful, and
yet in time he has come to treasure them more than
the—

3.

This one is scarlet, flesh aflame, he sees her by a
riveting light that seems to make her face distort,
stretching until he cannot be sure it is an optical
effect—they use those often—or whether in fact the
women are now becoming more distorted, grotesque.
Or is it his taste that is changing?

4.

The jokes go on and on, each one better than the
last and yet strangely all the same. First small quips,
and then one-liners that seem to come from Wilde or
Noel Coward, all good but not gut-busters as his father used to say, and then on to the situation jokes,
even ethnic jokes (how did they know?), odd stories
that seem to mean nothing until the end and then he
finds him rocking back and forth in his chair, when
moments before he did not even know he was sitting,
had no sensation at all, but now feels himself convulse
with laughter and curl up, clenched—

5.

Pressed duck, thick with the burnished sauce; gauzy flavors from Southeast Asia (strange, he thought all that fell long ago); slick fish that goes down easily; cloying scene of garlic in the fat noodles; deeply marbled steaks, glowing red, quick with juice; warm and aromatic sauces slathered over the half-open carapace of the blue-armored thing—it tastes gooey, rich, with a coolness behind the first spicy rush that comes exploding into the mouth, almost drowning the palate; bitter, like old beer, flat but pungent and he cannot get it out of his mouth; the slitted gut of the cow is swarming with maggots but he dips in, choosing carefully among the moving white things, the brown matter coming up on his spoon; dry but light, quenching, quite a nice wine overall when you considered—but he stopped at the thought, did not consider, and ate on; on.

6.

He knows now why they do it, why there are the drifting silent times to let him rest, but he cannot remember from one intense time to the next what the answer is, what they—

7.

The woman is fat and he cannot go on with her. He rolls off her slipperiness, though until this moment there has not been any gravity, feeling her softness yield under him, no this is not it, a failure, he hopes they know that this was not his fault, she was not the right kind.

8.

Yes, that must be it, these are the reward sessions, they are paying him off for some enormous and complex job he does for them. He feels this is right, feels a sudden certainty that burns away all that has happened before, all the gushing stuff that filled him up, all the gut-deep sensations that he thought he could not hold but always finally did. Yes: he cannot remember the job, does not know what it is, and that is precisely why these hammering long sensations, these dreams at last come home, are so effective. These slabs of excess release him. He feels himself set free by them and thus, the logic is immutable, thus he is fully free when his real self goes back to the job, whatever it is, that they press him to do. He must be very valuable and the job must be of that dark kind he has heard whispered about for years, heard mention of across tables in restaurants but never any details, it must be that. And this is his time off, the moments when the psyche is launched so that the upper mind can go on, yes.

9.

It is a man this time. He comes into the booth where the pictures are showing on the big flat screen, the playlet just starting after the quarter has dropped in, clinking in the stillness. There is the usual conversation, a few words, and then the loosening of the belt and he feels himself nod, the hand on him, and the screen seems to fill his eyes. The soft sound comes up to him, the oval into which he is falling, he is becoming harder because they both know that this is what he really wanted all along, as the flesh forms move and slide on each other before him, he feels the strength

and swelling energy of himself about to do what he
always—

10.

Running, sheer empty running, on the beach, the
quick clench of the calves as he digs into the sand and
the air cuts deeply into his lungs, a simple moment
when he hangs suspended at the top of an arc, the
stride tilted forward and forever coming into comple-
tion.

11.

Soft fragrant matting, he glides over it and lets it
fill his nostrils, the silky radiance of it becoming the air
around him, penetrating him, ass and nose and mouth,
streaming, as he slips down a streambed of fur.

12.

He tries to hold on to the information about the
tasks he performs. As the long spaces of sensation get
longer, seeming to stretch out as he enters them and
cannot escape, he struggles for a strand of memory.
The job. Pilot, yes, pilot, on harrowing and lonely mis-
sions, seeking some electronic solace on the long cold
flights between planets which must have some relief or
else he would go mad.

13.

He breathes in the coiling acrid smoke and finds it
good. The long pipe, the oily sensation of fullness, the

cushions under him, yes, it is all very pleasurable, very Asian, he thinks, and he knows this is another way they have of distracting him from the enormity of his tasks, of what destiny calls him to do daily, leaving only these obliterating sessions when he is released of the burden. He thinks of this and has to be distracted again by the smoke.

14.

Water, washing away all the memories, waves breaking over him until he learns to ride them, to match velocities with the looming mountains of toppling water and pick up energy from their headward lunge, struggling to stay on top of the foaming white. It fills him with zest and he lances an arm through the wave to vector left, feeling the wind blow stinging salt into his brimming eyes.

15.

Computer specialist, that is it, it would explain the recurrent dreams of cascading mathematics that he sees at—but no, not dreams, there are no nights, so they must be a memory, something from the job. Unless they were a pleasure in themselves. Could it be that anyone got something out of those lattices of symbols? No, it seems improbable (and he is a believer in probabilities). The busy squiggles of the equations must be part of the job.

16.

This one is fat, conical. He thrusts himself in viciously. A wracking pain fills him, swells into his throat, and brings him to a curious, lurching orgasm.

17.

As he gives the speech beneath the hot, glowing lights he feels the power surge through him, knows that he can turn this crowd any way he likes, senses their need of him, and beneath the immediate sensation the thought comes: this is it, a true memory, the thing they seek to ease him of. This is the task that he must flee, in these dark times. This is the job.

18.

She thrusts it into him and he curls about it, taking it, slippery but welcoming, moist, knowing that this must be part of it, too, as she lunges into him again and he spreads for it, willing.

19.

Falling, cutting through the billowy moist stuff, carving the clouds, he is at last free, knows this will help him when he returns to his rightful place at the center of the vast and complex enterprises which spin about him when he is fully conscious, when he is at his job.

20.

He feels the seeping back of consciousness like burning fog, and then swarming damp sheets, rumpled and
disturbed from a long sleep, and then there comes the
bright cutting light, lamps—*you have a break coming
up*—so he relaxes on the bed, not daring to open his
eyes, because the excitement is welling in him, he knows
that he will come into his real world when he opens the
eyes, he will be at his job and everything will clarify—
might as well take it—and in a burst of energy he opens
them, sees the cheap pasteboard walls and the tangle of
wires and cables like thick ropes, all winding around the
narrow bed—*hey you know you got another coming up
in fifteen minutes, might as well get up an' walk aroun'
a little*—and sees his friend, the other hourly employee
who occupies the next telemetry-studded bed, and knows
that whoever used his body as somofilter for the canned
sensations is gone, the customer is already paying up at
the cashier outside, probably a session caught on a
stopoff during commuter hours, fifty bucks to tap into
someone who can take the shadowy contexts that the
senso tapes provide and transform those one-dimensional
echoes into vivid life, someone who really knows how to
feel and does it by instinct, can give them the intensity
that most of them never know. *Hey you're lookin' kinda
worn down* and he grins wryly. *Well the money's good
anyway,* and indeed it is, far better than he could get otherwise, without this twisted talent. He presses his face
into his hands, not minding any of it, really, because in
earlier days he would have been dismissed as a useless
manic type, blown helpless before whatever emotional
winds prevailed, but still— He had hoped the riveting
moments would release him, as well as the passing customers. He rubs his eyes, feeling the grit in them, and
marvels that the customers can be so easily satisfied by
these mirages, no more lurid than the world he ordinarily

inhabits. What he wants is in the dreams, too, but now he sees that it cannot ever be satisfied, he is transfixed in worlds that others lust for but now imposes on them his own fantasy, and thus has become a customer, too, seeking what is impossible: the pride, the job.

Immortal Night

The man who was going to live forever looked happy.

He came out of the hospital doors into the biting January cold—a burly, tanned figure in a Wertmeiler topcoat with the special cobalt-mist, textured sleeves and black fur ruff.

Walter James Resnick, a walking experiment.

Off to the side, near the curb, Brennan studied the crowd. Their faces jumped into prominence as the big lights went on, welcoming Resnick's exit, pinning him in kilowatts of bold illumination.

Resnick stopped, perfect teeth set against the smooth skin, grinning. There was no sign of the treatments, no washed-out look around the eyes, no thinning of the immaculately combed black hair. He waved with the casualness of habit, looking at the mob without seeing it.

Resnick's advisers flanked him, basking in the spontaneous applause and shouts. The crowd was in a good mood. The media had made Resnick's long battle with bone marrow cancer the stuff of legend—a lonely struggle against apparently impossible odds.

And then— How had that commentator put it last night? "The startling outcome capped one of the most uplifting news events of recent memory."

Sure, if your memory was maybe three weeks long.

Mobs didn't have memories, though, and this one showed it. They called out to him, blew him kisses, clapped their gloved hands wildly, jumped up and down to get a better look.

Resnick gave the two-fingered V sign. They applauded more.

Some shoved and wriggled to get closer to the TV remote crew, mugging for the cameras. The interview was already in the can, shot inside, so the crew was just waiting, bored, for a filler of him leaving.

Important people had crowds outside, you had to splice some of that into the footage, it was part of the business. Otherwise, how would you really be sure who was important? Brennan grinned humorlessly. He had been a minor stringer for the city's second paper, the *Herald,* for thirty years. It had taught him a lot about the chasm between the public and the private.

Resnick made a little speech that the wind caught and tore away. The gusts brought light snow that flared into existence under the glaring lights and then whirled away, darting under the tires of passing traffic, making slush.

A big snowflake stuck on Resnick's cream shirt, right next to the florid Demarcus tie. The speech stopped quickly. It would be ironic if the immortal man got pneumonia leaving the hospital.

Resnick shook hands abruptly with the director of the hospital, and with the head scientist for the research project, getting through the little ceremony for the cameras. Then he ducked toward a black limousine.

The crowd cheered and surged toward him. It was always that way with the big celebs, but this time had a frantic edge to it. A wailing, lost quality.

He's leaving, Brennan could imagine them thinking. *Our brush with immortality, with something big-*

ger than we are. The healthy, well-muscled frame bowed and slipped through the limousine door, not looking back. *Don't go, not yet.*

Resnick went. The limousine pulled out, edging by some of the crowd in the street. Faceless assistants had slipped into the front seats. The darkened windows showed nothing. Brennan couldn't even tell where Resnick was sitting.

Brennan brushed by a man who was saying to a woman, "I'll be able to say I saw the first one, right when he came out."

The woman said, "Did you see the way he *looked*? Like he'd been to Florida or somethin'."

"Yeah, instead of lyin' in a bottle for three months."

"News said he didn't even know it. Thought he'd been asleep overnight or somethin'." They both laughed.

Brennan was parked illegally halfway down the block. The sudden snow flurry had predictably jammed up traffic, so he kept pace with the limo. He tucked his hands into the pockets of his cloth overcoat and studied the building on his left. The driver never looked his way.

There was a ticket under his wiper. He crumpled it up and threw it into the gutter.

He slid behind the wheel of his anonymous green sedan as the traffic light changed down the block. Brennan edged out into traffic and gunned it to get across in time. The light went yellow before he reached the corner.

His stomach knotted. He tromped down, hunching over the wheel. The sedan had no pickup at all. It bucked once and sluggishly accelerated into the intersection.

Red light. A horn blared to his left, frighteningly close. Then he was through and the lanes were clear in front. He kept his speed, peering ahead through the water-speckled windshield.

He closed his eyes and felt nausea, fear. His stomach wouldn't unknot. Ruby taillights coasted by ahead of him but he could not tell which was the limo.

One block. Two.

Had they turned off? The papers said Resnick would go to the Hilton. Some movie and TV people were putting on a party for him, welcoming him back, like he'd been away on a long trip or something. Resnick hadn't made his money in the media but he had friends in it, like all of them these days.

But if he was going to the Hilton he should be right ahead, on Park Drive. That was the direct route.

Another block. He was getting worried. His stomach started tightening up again. The tension always brought that on. That and the hot sensation lower down, like he had to take a crap all of a sudden. Only he never did, it just felt that way. Humiliating. He had gotten used to it but it still made his face burn.

He came to a big glowing department store, closed but with the lights all on. An ivory glow poured onto the street ahead.

A grocery truck slid into the left turn lane, clearing his view, and he suddenly saw the limo. He sped up. The limo pulled into the slow lane.

Brennan was going too fast. He had to pass them, looking straight ahead. They turned right.

Not going to the Hilton, not unless the chauffeur was a moron. So much for the papers.

Then again, maybe Resnick wasn't in any hurry. He had all the time in the world.

Brennan turned into the next driveway. It was a big steel and glass bank, with a sprawling parking lot. He gunned the engine crossing it. There was a wooden pass barrier at the far end and a ticket-taking machine.

He went through it. The wood snapped off and a hooter started blaring behind him. He turned right again into a side street. Down a half block, tires hissing on the glossy black. The warm musty smell of the sedan's heater seeped into the air.

A red light here, coming up. He slowed, looked both ways. Nobody to the right. This one looked like a long light. As he went into the turn he spotted ruby taillights a block away on the left. Nobody else on the street. He went through the red light and swerved left, tires screeching.

He hit the gas hard. The ruby lights ahead got closer and then they turned off into a driveway. It was the limo.

He stopped fifty yards from the driveway. The tightness in his belly rode like a stone as he walked down the driveway and into a big turnaround for the entrance of an apartment building. There was a parking attendant driving a Mercedes away and the limo was empty.

Beyond it was a big well-lit foyer. Brennan could see Resnick leaving the foyer through some revolving doors.

He followed, going past the attendant without a glance. It worked. Beyond the revolving door was a sprawling inner garden, taking up half the ground floor. It gave the impression of passing through a stand of trees, with a gaily tinkling fountain halfway through. Brennan stopped just before the stone path reached large glass doors, because through them he could see a house guard in uniform. An elevator door was closing on Resnick's party.

Damn. He might be in there for days.

There was probably some smart way to get past that guard, but Brennan couldn't think of any. But the guard had seen him now.

He kept walking, right up to the elevator. "When's he coming down?" he asked the guard.

"He doesn't tell me, bud." The eyes narrowed. "What you want?"

"I'm Herb Brennan, a reporter for the *Herald*." People never knew what a stringer was, that he just sent in occasional pieces and didn't have steady newspaper work, so "reporter" went down better with them.

"You got ID?"

Brennan took out the little leather packet and unfolded to the *Herald* card.

The man nodded. "No reporters inside, that's the word."

Brennan sighed realistically. "Yeah, print media are always the last."

"Hell, Resnick wouldn't let CBS follow him around even, that's what I heard. You got no reason to bitch."

Brennan shrugged. "Yeah, maybe you're right. Can I wait here?"

"No way, man." The guard sucked on his teeth. "Resnick's security people say nobody should be waiting outside the building."

"They afraid I'm going to breathe on him?"

The guard laughed. "Guess so. They even had their men outside in those trees, earlier. Waiting for him."

"Careful man."

"You bet."

"Okay if I wait outside?"

He nodded. "I guess so. Stay off the pathway though. Management don't like blocking the way."

"Sure."

He went out. It had gone pretty well. Once people knew who you were they looked right through you and you could get your job done.

He stepped back into the trees and watched the guard for a while. The man didn't look out into the garden often, just sat at a desk and watched a television. Brennan could see a fraction of the screen reflected in one of the doors.

It took him several minutes to realize the guard wasn't watching a TV program. It was a security snooper, fed by cameras in the building. He glanced nervously around. There—two inconspicuous snouts near the foyer. And one nearer, just outside the doors. But none in the trees, as far as he could see.

But there was something over beside the wall. A bulge in the shadows that moved now and then, not swaying in the slight breeze. A man, moving from one foot to the other.

An external guard, then. One of Resnick's men. Or a commercial cop hired by the building itself. The guard would have seen Brennan, then. Seen him shoot the breeze with the elevator guard inside. Write him off as a persistent nobody.

The hotness flooded through his guts again. Burning coils crawled up through him, adding to the weight in his belly.

He bit his lip. He was scared—sure. But he had thought it over and and he couldn't hold on to any more of his self-respect if he didn't go through with this, do it now.

He shivered and thrust his hands deep into his coat pockets. *Should have remembered to wear gloves. On the other hand, they'd get in the way.*

He could hear his own wristwatch ticking, it was that quiet. Seconds dropping away, gone forever. Light snowflakes fell from the hard blackness above.

That was how the TV guy had said it was for Resnick. Spinning slowly in a tank in a drifting aimless dream, the fluids filling his lungs, invading his tissues, finding the cancerous cells and renegade chemicals, devouring them, scraping away the cellular grime of a lifetime, subtracting years from Resnick's body while he swam—erasing, healing, curing, his skin silently shedding like snowflakes in a night of spongy sleep.

At first the story had been that this was a radical new treatment for advanced cancer. That Resnick was a hero because he put a lot of his own money into the research, year after year, while his own cancer was chewing at him.

They held it off with chemotherapy and burned it out with radioactivity and all the time tried this new method—a cancer-seeking molecule that would go for mutated cells, comparing them with the body's own healthy cells and killing them off if they didn't match. High risk. High cost.

And it worked. It aced out the bone marrow cancer and it erased a lot of other diseases Resnick might have, or was about to get, lying in wait down there in the cells. If he caught anything, developed more cancers, they'd pop him back in the tank, clean him out, put him back on the street.

Change the oil, fella. And lube it. Ten million bucks? Put it on the card.

Resnick volunteered for it, same as the guys who volunteered for artificial hearts and kidneys and lungs. Only Resnick had bought his way in, spent hundreds of millions—because otherwise nobody, not even the government, was going to buy a cure at that price.

And it would stay that way. The process took dozens of specialists working three shifts a day, month after month. Nothing you could make copies of, like an artificial heart. Labor. Expensive labor. So the Resnicks of the world could buy it.

And nobody else.

Brennan's fist squeezed the revolver in his pocket.

Across the garden, under a tree, another shadow faded and then reappeared. *Another.* They had guards everywhere.

He realized he had been standing still for a long time, like he was hiding. Exactly the wrong thing to do.

He paced out to the walkway, around some bushes, and back to some nearby trees. He tried to look impatient and stamped his feet to keep warm.

The guard inside was just hired help, a rent-a-cop. He didn't have the checklist of newsmen, probably didn't know there was one. If Resnick's main party had braced Brennan, or the men in the shadows had stopped him, they'd have known the *Herald* wouldn't send a stringer on this job. Brennan had already seen Watkins, one of the *Herald*'s best front-page men, back at the hospital.

So until somebody in the know saw Brennan and recognized him, he was okay. The men in the garden had taken the elevator guard's acceptance as good enough.

Brennan hadn't known enough about the layout to anticipate that, but he'd gotten by anyway. Luck, and a little fast thinking.

They'd still see something was wrong if Brennan got excited, went for Resnick, tried to get in close. So it would have to be a long shot and a good one.

He hadn't fired the .32 in ten years at least, had forgotten he had it until he was lying up in that hospital, watching the news, trying not to think about the tubes they had up his ass and down his throat, plastic and wires and barium enemas and endless X rays, trying to find the bowel cancer, track it down so they could cut him open again and again, run up the bills, shoot him full of dope so he couldn't think straight, so he'd wake up sweating at night, the red fever dreams swarming in his head, and next morning they'd make him collect his shit in a bag—

The elevator door opened.

Resnick was looking straight out at him, smiling broadly.

Brennan felt hot oil sliding through his guts.

Resnick stepped out of the elevator, talking to the bland-faced man next to him, nodding to the guard.

Smoking a cigarette. Grinning. Looking forward to the Hilton.

The two shadows in the garden were moving. Silhouettes melted from one tree to the next. Converging on the path, to cover Resnick when he came out.

Well, Brennan wasn't going to give them an easy target. He would stay where he was, fire from the darkness.

He had been a pretty good shot once. He could get in two, maybe three before they knew who the hell he was. All the cancer baths in the world couldn't fix up bullet holes.

Resnick pushed open the door himself, beaming, coming out, on his way to the Hilton and all his famous friends.

There was a tall, leggy woman with him, twenty years younger than Resnick, brunette, her full red lips set in an easy, superior smile. High heel shoes and a white gown under the fur coat. She said something light and airy and a murmur of conversation came across the chilled air.

Two guards walked in front. Brennan sucked in a breath and held it, leveling the pistol on Resnick's outline, squeezing a little on the trigger already. Two-handed, hands in front, professional style. Waiting until there was a clear space between trees, enough angle for a clean—

A shot boomed. A man in front shouted something and an orange flash came from across the garden. Two quick explosions.

Screaming. A muzzle flash, then another.

Brennan froze, his finger rigid. He hadn't fired.

Two figures were down on the walkway and the tall woman was stumbling back toward the elevators, a high ragged screaming coming from her.

A man ran into the trees, away from Brennan, and fired three times at a shadow. It fell.

"Get a doctor! Get a doctor!" someone shouted. A figure bent over the walkway, and then jumped up and pounded into the foyer.

Brennan walked silently past Resnick's sprawled

form. The eyes stared blankly up at the falling white flakes.

Two men were bent over him, trying to get some signs of life out of the body, but there was a big hole in the chest. A dark stain spread over the Wertmeiler topcoat.

Nobody noticed Brennan. He reached the first body under the trees and rolled it over. It was a man, emaciated, skin mottled. A pistol lay on the snow.

The second was a woman, still alive. She was about sixty and a sour ragged breath came out of her, a smell he knew was not right and would not get right. She had one shoulder wound.

No weapon visible. He felt in her coat pocket. A kitchen knife.

She blinked up at the night above, not seeing him. Her lips moved but nothing came out.

Brennan didn't say anything to her. He walked away through the trees.

Nobody tried to stop him. They were all running around and yelling.

His gut didn't burn anymore but he knew it would tomorrow. That didn't matter. What made him feel good, really good, as he hit the cold slick street, was that there were other sick people in the world, millions of them, a lot more there would ever be Resnicks.

The Bigger One

ANNOUNCER: That finishes the roundup on damage in the Los Angeles area from the Big One—an 8.1 Richter scale earthquake!

To recap, devastation in Los Angeles and San Diego counties is widespread, with fires raging. There is mercifully little loss of life because the Big One was centered somewhere to the southeast of Southern California.

We have a report now from Herb Walker, on the scene near the border town of Mexicali.

WALKER: Thanks, Todd. The quake center lay somewhere south of here and big aftershocks are continuing! I'm standing at a desert highway intersection, where people have stopped to wait out the aftermath, obviously unsure of where to go.

Distant trembling. Heavy howling winds. A car door slams.

WALKER: Excuse me, what was it like for you, sir?

FIRST MAN: Awful. And these aftershocks, they're worse than the earthquake was.

WOMAN: We're okay, out here in the desert. Nothing to fall on us.

WALKER: Aftershocks are lessening, but we can't get through to Mexicali. Have you seen anyone from that direction? What were your emotions as—

FIRST MAN: Hey, what's that sound?

Faint rumble in the distance.

WOMAN: I can't see anything in all this damned dust.

A growing growl, deep bass. Winds howl louder.

WOMAN: Something's coming. Like a big truck or—

FIRST MAN: No truck is *that* big. Feel that? The ground's trembling.

Growling turns to a heavy rumble.

ANNOUNCER: Herb, can you hear me? We have reports of a breakthrough of the Pacific Ocean along the new openings in the San Andreas fault. Satellite photos show water rushing through the break from the Gulf of California. Can you see any evidence of this?

Rumble grows. Worried shouts.

WALKER (shaken): You mean that sound, that's the *ocean*?

WOMAN: Coming at us from the south!

FIRST MAN (dryly): Solves our problem of where to go. Mexicali isn't there anymore.

WOMAN: It's *loud*.

FIRST MAN: But why should it come here? This is desert, way far inland.

WOMAN: We're maybe fifty miles from the Gulf of California. The fault must've unzipped all along that north-south line.

ANNOUNCER: Herb? Can you see any—

A deep bass roar, like rolling thunder. Hoarse yells. Screams.

FIRST MAN: Hey, your radio guy just ran off. Hope this headset works. Hear me? Get some helicopters here right away! I can see a dark line south of here, might be the ocean. Please, helicopters, they could pick us up—

Sudden silence.

ANNOUNCER: We seem to have lost contact with our unit near Mexicali. Let's go to Pamela Merkle, some-where to the north in a mobile unit. Pamela, can you—

MERKLE: I'm in a van speeding up along Route 111, with my driver, Doug Aron. Traffic is all around us, panicked. We just passed a burning shopping mall.

Tires howl. Wind roars. Snapping flames. Distant si-rens.

MERKLE: My God, this dust, I can't see anything. We're going so fast!

ARON: That water, it'll be moving hard. We got to run.

MERKLE: But we'll hit somebody!

ARON: Just be glad more people didn't get out of Mexicali, or there'd be a jam.

MERKLE: If you keep driving like this—

Horn blares. Distant angry shouts.

ARON: Damn fools! Packing a pickup truck full like that, and they're not even going fifty.

MERKLE: Look, there's a boy. We should pick him up.

ARON: We don't dare stop. Somebody'll rear-end us.

Van thrums louder, but an ominous rumble overwhelms it.

MERKLE: We're hitting ninety here, heading north, but the noise behind us keeps getting louder. I'm trying to see out the back.

ANNOUNCER: Pamela, we have reports that Mexicali is completely inundated by water. I'd advise you—

MERKLE: My God. A wall. A black wall.

ARON: How far away? How big?

MERKLE: It's hard to tell. A mile? Tall as an office building, maybe more. It's so broad, like a barrier.

ARON: It's chasing us. Question is, how far will it go?

MERKLE: The guidebook, it said this whole place, the

Imperial Valley, it's more than two hundred feet below sea level.

ARON: Damn—like Death Valley. A deep-dish frying pan.

ANNOUNCER: Pamela, the water is reportedly moving at seventy miles per hour. Make every effort—

MERKLE: We're running for our lives! Hey—there's the exit sign for Brawley.

ARON: The town's dead meat. God, look at the traffic ahead. Big interchange here.

MERKLE: We'll never get through.

ARON: We've got to. Where's the water now?

MERKLE: Closer. So *big*.

ARON: It'll fill this whole valley. If we can just get—

MERKLE: Wait, even if we get through the traffic, we'll be heading toward the Salton Sea.

ARON: Yeah, so?

MERKLE: That's the lowest part of the valley!

ARON: Jesus, you're right. Where can we go?

MERKLE: East—go east. The Chocolate Mountains.

ARON: Yeah, right, get some altitude.

MERKLE: I hope to God that'll slow it down. It's so—

ARON: There's the turnoff—Route 78, right?

Engine strains, roars. The rumble gathers force.

ANNOUNCER: We have dispatched a rescue helicopter for you, Pamela. If you could just—

MERKLE: No time for that!

ARON: It's gaining on us.

MERKLE: Of course—now we're running parallel to the water. I can see it better—it's so tall!

ARON: Yeah, but we're getting higher. Hope this Chevy holds up. We're doing a hundred, going uphill.

MERKLE: These hills—they're high. Maybe—

ARON: These aren't hills, they're sand. Sand dunes.

MERKLE: The water—it's catching up!

ARON: I'll run us up this dune. If it's tall enough—

A thunderous, watery roar.

MERKLE: It's all around us!

Engine flags, sputters. Rushing water. Engine chokes off. Ignition whines, fails.

ARON: Water's rising. Try the door.

MERKLE: God, it's everywhere.

ARON: Get out, hold on to the door. Here—

Pamela screams. Door wrenches open. Cascading water.

ARON: Climb up. That's it—onto the roof. Here—

MERKLE: Take my hand. Hurry!

ARON: Ah! Current almost got me. Stand here, hold on to me.

MERKLE: Is it still rising?

ARON: I can't tell. The big splash is past, though.

MERKLE: I've still got my mobile transmitter. Can you hear me? We're standing on top of the van. Water everywhere, muddy, salty. It's coming over the windshield.

ARON: Hold on! It's over the top.

MERKLE: Look, it's going on toward the Salton Sea. Maybe that'll draw it away from us.

ARON: Hope so. Hey, you feel that?

MERKLE: The van's moving.

ARON: These currents are eroding the sand. If this dune gives—

MERKLE: It's creeping up my legs. Hold me!

ARON: No place nearby to swim to, even if we could make it against the flow.

ANNOUNCER: Pamela, our chopper pilot reports

thick clouds, apparently from seawater evaporating as it strikes the hot desert. He can't see through them.

MERKLE: Oh, great. I hope this dune is as high as sea level. That'll save us, won't it?

ARON: The water's still going like crazy, see? It'll run north of the Salton Sea for sure, maybe to Indio.

MERKLE: What'll we do if this sand gives way?

ARON: Find something that floats. But I don't think it's getting any higher.

MERKLE: It's up to my knees! At least it's warm.

ARON: And salty. I was thinking . . .

MERKLE: Hold me tight. Did the van move just now?

ARON: No, I did. Trying to see up toward the north. The dust is thinning out. Y'know, this water will reach pretty far.

MERKLE: I, I think it's slacking.

ARON: After things calm down, maybe we can swim to one of those hills over there.

MERKLE: Let's survive first. Just survive.

Watery sounds fade.

ANNOUNCER (somber): What a tragedy, a genuine tragedy . . . vast loss of life . . . awful . . .

　　　(switching to crisp, factual)

We'll return to the site in a moment. Meanwhile, speculation has already begun that the ocean flooding will cover several hundred square miles, killing more people than the earthquake itself.

However, experts point out that formation of a new bay extending as far north as Indio will produce several hundred miles of fresh California coastline. An inland sea!

The prospect of such an economic bonanza may help overcome the grief this monstrous event has brought. Tragic, yes—but part of nature's plan, perhaps, for our great land.

    (brisk tone)

What will this mean for our economy? New opportunities, to be sure. Less agriculture, but greater tourism. Sunny beaches, sailing, and—as soon as the water settles down—no doubt some terrific sport fishing.

    (chuckles warmly)

We now go to our real estate correspondent, always first with the fresh point of view, standing in the hills above the flooding . . .

Cadenza

When she wakes up that morning she is officially dead. She rolls over in the crisp hospital sheets and reads the monitor.

MORT 17:36

The visual display is on the other side of the monitor, where the patient cannot see it. Two nights ago she had slipped out of bed and walked, teetering, over to the little personal effects table where her cosmetics are scattered. She had moved the standup mirror so it reflected the visual readout toward the bed.

Now, by lying flat, she can read the reversed image.

So this is it. MORT 17:36. And the diagnostics are reliable down to the third decimal place, for her particular kind of interferon screwup. The chemsampler sucks on her arm, reading the delicate swarm of alphas and gamma-primes. These soft probings tell the medmon how to counteract the cascade effect. But eventually the gammas will go into systemic oscillation, and down deep in her nerve cells the neurotransmitters will begin to go gray and numb, falling silent. She will blank out, the system will go into electromotive spasm.

The medmon knows this. It sits there, white and

223

large and impassive, a hulking weight. It knows. Only the minor deception of the concealed visual display gives away the news. Of course, the magnetic bubble memory of the hospital has by now stored the fact. It has digested her terminal stage into its ongoing study of this new and fascinating disease. And it will do its best to counteract the spasms and pain and wild, rolling delirium. It will try to play out her hours.

Lydia glances at the wall clock. It is 6:24. Morning. MORT 17:36. So she has eleven hours, twelve minutes. The medmon will probably turn out to be correct to within a few minutes. Maybe the cascade will get her at 17:40 or 17:20, but that is just about all the error she can expect.

Lydia rings for the nurse.

When the horse-faced woman appears, Lydia says, "I'm leaving."

"Why, whatever do you—"

"I know my rights. I'm a walking zombie and I want to walk." She keeps her voice flat and distant.

"The doctor—"

"Get him." She dismisses the nurse with a wave.

She crosses the room with uncertain steps. She is panting slightly, but not from exertion. She avoids the cool enamel skin of the medmon, circling around until she finds the bright yellow and red and blue tangle of connectors.

Lydia carefully unpatches the chemsampler from her arm. There are other tubes and wires; they all come off pretty easily. The medmon lights up with warnings: violet, red, orange, oscillating pink. *Rather pretty*, Lydia thinks. She lets a tremor of excitement almost like lust sweep through her with a heady energy.

She is getting together her personal effects when Dr. Reiss comes bustling in. "Hey, hey. What's this I hear?" he says with a compressed kind of joviality.

"Frank, no, Just no," she says flatly. And leaves it at that. They have gone through all the stages already and she thinks he owes her something better than this false buoyancy.

Death therapy. She has been through the stages with Frank, and with Rita, the therapist. Rejection of the news, followed by an apparent acceptance. Then a sudden point where the bottom dropped out of that and she fell into the first real depression. Afterward, a slow working uphill until a calmness returned. She had felt expansive. She had wanted to gobble up the world, travel everywhere and read everything, and see everyone she had ever known, and relive what she could. But the interferon therapy required that she stay nearby, and by then her energy was trickling away. So she had entered the last predictable depression with a glacial slowness. Rita had seen it and authorized some of the mild euphorics. The tunable hallucinations helped. By then Lydia had reached a kind of plateau, the one the books said was a last secure emotional base, a launching platform to—

"Don't bullshit me, Frank," she says to break the silence between them.

"Lydia, we're at the crucial point now."

"No, Frank. *I* am."

"Of course, I didn't mean— Look, Rita won't be in for two more hours, I think you should see her and—"

"I haven't *got* two hours. Not to spare."

"These diagnostics can be wrong."

"Not by much. Frank, I know my rights. I know you want to study the last stages of the process. I agreed to play good guinea pig for you. But now I'm leaving."

"We can damp the last oscillations in the cascade. Without that, away from the equipment, the pain—"

"I can take it." She nods toward the medmon. "I just want to get away from that. And I know my legal rights. Once that thing says I'm a certain case, I'm free. My contract is void and the fee goes to my estate."

"Well, I know Rita will be—Lydia, she *cares* about you."

She looks at him. A betraying tremor of weakness sweeps through her. It would be so easy to stay . . . She blinks. No. Just *no*. She has come to a place that wasn't talked about in the books she has read. He doesn't know about it, Lydia sees that. And neither does Rita.

"I'm going to make a call now," she says. "Then I'm getting dressed and I'm walking out of here." She turns away from him.

She punches in Michael's number without having to look it up. She smiles without humor. Two years, and she still remembers. He has an override number that will get through his Sec. She uses it. Five rings, six—he answers. A groggy voice.

She speaks quickly and precisely. He knows about her, of course. She has made sure word got to him through mutual friends. She had sworn she would never speak to him again, but now— She tells him what she wants. A walk, a few hours.

His voice wavers. He is awake now but he is slow to react. He is puzzled and then, suddenly, sensing something in her voice, flustered. He tries to reason with her. She cuts him off, not letting him finish a sentence.

"Look, there's got to be somebody else . . ." he says, not wanting this burden.

She smiles at his weakness, his habitual slippery way. "No, there isn't anybody else. You left me like that. That's what you did to me."

"Well, Christ, I can't—"

"I'm not concerned with the past anymore, Michael." She smiles again as she lies.

Finally he agrees to come and get her. He is still trying to say something more when she hangs up.

Dr. Reiss himself brings in her suitcase. She takes

it without a word. She begins packing her clothes and books and odd items. She throws her copy of *Death: The Last Stage of Growth* into the trash. Her shoulder bag is still there where she left it, tucked in among the street clothes she had abandoned months ago. They look like rumpled, discarded rags. She puts them on.

Dr. Reiss tries to talk to her. She ignores him. She has to concentrate her energies, she tells herself. She has learned that in the months spent here. She has to ignore everything and everybody else. She has to focus to bring this off at all.

"Lydia, you could talk more. I think you need—"

So Reiss is going to try one last time. "No point in talking about what you're dead sure of, is there?"

Dr. Reiss blinks at her choice of words. "I don't get it."

"Let's say I have to finish something."

"What? What do you have left to—"

"Something *I* must be sure of. *Me*, Frank."

Dr. Reiss gives up and walks stiffly out into the corridor to speak to the section head. Lydia takes her shoulder bag out of the suitcase. She feels the extra weight in it. She slips a hand inside. It is still there; the hospital has not gone through her things; good. The smooth, cool metal of the small pistol has a reassuring solidity.

Dr. Reiss returns. He insists on giving her an emergency hailer, in case she changes her mind and—

She shakes her head, no. She won't be using it. But she drops it into her bag to avoid arguing. And she lets him attach sterotabs to her arms and legs, where the medmon had sucked its information from her and given in return the blood stabilizers.

The section head and some others come in. When they see she will not talk about it, they quietly move aside. A nurse brings in a wheelchair. They insist that she ride down to the outpatient clinic in it. She gets in and holds her bag in her lap, not letting anyone touch it.

When they reach the ground floor Michael is coming through the glass doors. He wears a brown suit, one she has always liked. She knows it is not for her; there hasn't been time for him to do more than throw on some clothes and get here. And the familiar knotted lines around his eyes tell her he is too off balance to have thought of a thing like that, anyway.

They decide to take the planetran. She has always enjoyed the soft glide over magnetic fields. The tube outside is dark as they fall through vacuum, listening to the muffled clacking of the pressure irises as they fly by. Michael takes refuge in talking about himself. He has always been like that. She knows it is the best way to avoid the choking silences between them.

Within fifteen minutes they are thirty klicks out from the city. He ushers her off the planetran platform and into a rental car. She has asked for someplace wooded and relaxing. He drives her away from the solemn granite buildings and out, away.

They drive through fields which are spotted with microstrain blight. The patches are gray and dry. *Appropriate setting*, Lydia thinks. Her nervous system is developing the same spotty deadness as she sits there; the cascade is building.

They stop in a thick patch of woods that has withstood autumn's heavy hand. Fog shrouds the low dips in an otherwise smoothly curving hillside. They climb out. Her knees tremble with the weight of what lies ahead.

She puts a lilt into her voice. Long ago, she recalls, she knew how to do it without thinking. "What makes it like this? It's beautiful."

"Something about the wind and humidity getting trapped here. It blows in from the sea and then eddies form, when it hits the hills." He gestures at the steep slopes in the distance. She studies him. He has filled in at the waist slightly. His smile is tilted slightly askew in that wry way of his. The gray eyes question her.

Blades of sunlight lance through the trees. She feels the pressure building in him and cuts it off with, "Let's go down that way," pointing to a country lane through thickening woodland.

"Well, I . . . Why don't we go the other way. It's just as—"

"That looks better." She strides off energetically. She has to draw in deep, ragged breaths to find the energy. He hesitates, and then follows, as she knew he would.

This is what she wants. To be alone with him. In the hospital it could not have worked. She hefts the tugging mass of the pistol in her shoulder bag and it feels good.

"Lydia, I . . ." Michael begins, trying to break through. But she turns and walks toward a dense thicket. Then she sees wrought-iron fencing through the trees. The fencing is so rickety it sags to the ground at spots. She knows why he was reluctant to come this way.

"Say, we could go down to the left. There's a stream . . ."

"No," she says with a knife-edge merriment. "No, this is what I want."

They find the creaky gate that opens into the cemetery. The gravel footpaths are choked with brambles and undergrowth. Nobody seems to come here anymore. The thinned trees let in more of autumn's pale, lancing light. The land opens as they walk, yielding itself to the patchy blue sky. Fog nestles around the streaked marble headstones. Long rows of boxy tombs seem like small tiny houses. This is a very old place. The vault doors have keyholes, lintels, doorknobs, even working knockers. Bleached white stonework, ornamental gratings. She stops to read the inscription on a browning limestone tomb. " 'Feldsworth. Captain in the Service of His Country. Interred this day' et cetera. Look here."

She gestures at a smashed grating. Michael peers in through the narrow slit. "See that? The pile of sawdust on the floor. A rat or something's gnawed into the coffin."

"Oh. Yes."

"Michael, you've got to tell me now." She turns and gazes at him directly.

"Tell . . ."

"Why you left, for chrissake."

"I didn't leave. I just went on a trip."

"Yeah, and when you came back I was already in for treatment. Only you didn't come around."

"I visited you."

"Three times. That was all."

"I . . ."

"We loved each other, you bastard."

"Yes. Yes, we did."

"Past tense, huh?"

He nods, resigned. "I suppose so." The lines in his face twist. She can see he is under some inner pressure.

"*Why*, Michael?" She cannot keep the pleading out of her voice.

"I . . . I knew what was coming. I couldn't take it. I . . ."

"You knew the treatments wouldn't work?"

"Yes."

"How could you? This is a new disease. Stimulated by this crapped-out environment, they keep telling me. How could *you* know?"

"I did. I just did. And I didn't want to—"

"To go through it all with me? You're a coward, Michael." She reaches into her shoulder bag and feels the smooth metal. "I cried, Michael. I cried and begged and pleaded with you. Remember? But you wouldn't come see me, wouldn't answer—"

He holds up his hands. "I know. I know."

"It wasn't that you had somebody else?"

"No."

"You really are a coward." She grits her teeth and feels a sudden wave of nausea. At him? Or from the damned cascade? She will have to get this done faster than she thought. This is one thing she wants to be sure of.

Abruptly, before she can do anything more, Michael swerves and walks up the gravel path. "This one's nice," he calls. In the chill his breath fogs the air. "It says, 'Together now at last.' I should say so. Ha."

His laugh has a shrill edge. She frowns.

He turns jerkily away, his shoes spattering gravel against a headstone. "Pious shits, weren't they?" he calls loudly. "Look at this. 'From strength to strength in the everlasting.' Jesus. Self-serving dreams."

"Who else should a person's dreams serve?" Lydia says mildly.

Michael does not seem to have heard her. He walks stiffly on to the next vault. He rattles the iron grating. Rust scrapes off onto his palms, staining them a brownish-red. He savagely claps his hands together to brush it away. "Damn! Look at this. 'Honor perisheth never.' Well, Mister John Bradley, Esquire, it sure as hell has."

"Michael—"

"So his bones are used as a nest by rats. His flesh is powder." He laughs raggedly. He lurches on to the next mausoleum. Lydia hesitates, frowns, then follows. The bulky thing rears up at the crest of the hillside, streaked with brown. Lime stains smear its corners. Cracks in the cupola, thick with lime, show where pigeons have made their way inside. From behind Michael, Lydia can see through the grating. The marble interior is spattered with droppings. There are religious murals on the walls, once probably garish but now faded. The coffin is crusted with bird lime, its brass clouded and pitted.

Michael stops and points. "It says, 'We shall meet together in Life Eternal, with Saving Grace.' A married couple. Yea, verily. Shit!"

He smacks a palm against the stained stone. He whirls toward her. "God, Lydia! They were so smug! They lost someone, but they *knew* they'd never really lose them. They'd all meet again."

She studies him closely. His reaction is still self-involved, even now. Nothing has changed. He feels and thinks about this from one pivot: how does it affect Michael? He can't get away from that.

She looks at him and suddenly sees him clearly, really clearly, for the first time. He is afraid of death as an *ending*. Sweat glistens on his forehead. He feels the knife of time in his guts.

Numbly, automatically, she takes out the pistol. He stares at it. Sudden comprehension flickers in his face. "What . . ."

"Wait."

She knows what she intends to do, she has planned it so often. Felt the savage pleasure it would give her. Though of the blunt bullets plowing through him, paying back all the pain—

"Wait." Now, suddenly, she wants time. There is something . . .

She caresses the pistol with her left hand, feeling the sullen weight of the five bullets, cylindrical and sure, sluglike in their hard shells.

"Lydia . . . You did mean a lot . . . we . . . But I couldn't take it. Not, not the having you and then losing you again, so fast, so . . ."

"Quiet. Quiet." The cold seems to rise up out of the autumn earth. Fog gathers among the hummocks of the graveyard. She sees now that a vast and silent pane of glass has descended between them, these last months. Death to her is a mere stopping. To him . . .

He does not even know what he has. Until she pulled the blunt logic of the pistol from her bag, he saw his future as hazy and infinite. Now, in the first moment of seeing it fresh and final, his reaction is fear, panic. What he has lost is the sense of opening possibilities, though he does not know that. In the end . . . She shakes her head, closing her eyes. The world spins. The pistol—her hand dips beneath the weight of inert, passive metal. But Michael does not move. He is petrified. She gazes at him through a numb sheet of air between them. In the end, she will miss not life, but the uncertainty of it. To walk among woods and open fields and the tangle of life, and then, at the end, simply to have something come out of the sky at you, casual and natural. Not MORT 17:36, but the world itself, pressing close to you, through the pane of silence.

She says conversationally, "Do you know what I was going to do with this?"

"I . . . I thought . . ."

"You were right." She hefts it in her hand. It feels lighter. "Come on. Let's go for a walk. Get away from this damned place."

In the hush of the forest the sudden loud clap comes sharp and clean. It reflects off the stone slabs of the tombs. The carpet of fall leaves dampens the waves. Gray dead winter grass absorbs the last echoes from the distant hills.

A team answered the emergency hailer she had in her bag. The ambulance hummed and rattled as it came down the country road. The land seemed to glow beneath the light of late afternoon. They saw the body at the edge of a grove of walnut trees. The figure near it was pacing, hands in pockets, self-absorbed. They trotted over and stood around the body, a circle of men in white coveralls. There was obviously no chance; the head wound was massive. The blood had already turned dark brown.

"Christ," the team leader said bitterly. "Inflicted at close range, I'd say."

"Yes."

The team leader looked at the man's jacket. It was spattered with blood. "Say, you . . ."

Michael looked down at himself. "I was holding her in my arms," he said simply.

"Ah . . . where's the weapon?"

"Here." Michael took the pistol out of his jacket pocket and handed it to the man.

"Huh. You pick it up after . . . ?"

"No. I did it myself."

"You . . . ?" The man frowned.

"I've got a statement. Signed."

"I hope you know that—"

"I'm a lawyer. It's a simple document. She had her contract with her, and the consensual assisted suicide part is in there, too. I filled it out for her. She had it notarized by remote Sec, from my car."

"You got it all under control, don't you?"

Michael refused to rise to the challenge in the man's voice. He handed the team leader some papers. The man grunted disagreeably. He paged through the forms. "All made out nice and clear."

"Yes."

"There's going to have to be a hearing. There's always a hearing, even if everything's okay."

"Right."

"I got a readout on her case on the way over here. You arrange all this with her?"

Michael turned away. "No. She had . . . something else . . . planned. But we talked and . . ." He let the sentence die.

"I don't get it. She could've stayed right there, in the hospital, had no pain—"

"Sure."

Michael walked a few steps away. He peered upward. On the wooded slope above the trees thinned. He could see the pale slabs, embedded like bleached bones in the autumn earth.

"Well, shit, why'd she do this—have *you* do this—when—"

Michael turned back toward the group of men. For a moment he could not tell which of the white figures had spoken.

"Because I'm not a machine," he said.

Matter's End

When Dr. Samuel Johnson felt himself getting
tied up in an argument over Bishop Berkeley's
ingenious sophistry to prove the nonexistence
of matter, and that everything in the universe
is merely ideal, he kicked a large stone and
answered, "I refute it *thus*." Just what that
action assured him of is not very obvious, but
apparently he found it comforting.

—Sir Arthur Eddington

1.

 India came to him first as a breeze like
soured buttermilk, rich yet tainted. A door
banged somewhere, sending gusts sweeping
through the Bangalore airport, slicing
through the four A.M silences.

Since the Free State of Bombay had left India, Bangalore had become an international airport. Yet the
damp caress seemed to erase the sterile signatures that
made all big airports alike, even giving a stippled texture
to the cool enamel glow of the fluorescents.

The moist air clasped Robert Clay like a stranger's
sweaty palm. The ripe, fleshy aroma of a continent en-

folded him, swarming up his nostrils and soaking his lungs with sullen spice. He put down his carryon bag and showed the immigration clerk his passport. The man gave him a piercing, ferocious stare—then mutely slammed a rubber stamp onto the pages and handed it back.

A hand snagged him as he headed toward Baggage Claim.

"Professor Clay?" The face was dark olive with intelligent eyes riding above sharp cheekbones. A sudden white grin flashed as Clay nodded. "Ah, *good*. I am Dr. Sudarshan Patil. Please come this way."

Dr. Patil's tone was polite, but his hands impatiently pulled Clay away from the sluggish lines, through a battered wooden side door. The heavy-lidded immigration guards were carefully looking in other directions, hands held behind their backs. Apparently they had been paid off and would ignore this odd exit. Clay was still groggy from trying to sleep on the flight from London. He shook his head as Patil led him into the gloom of a baggage storeroom.

"Your clothes," Patil said abruptly.

"What?"

"They mark you as a Westerner. Quickly!"

Patil's hands, light as birds in the quilted soft light, were already plucking at his coat, his shirt. Clay was taken aback at this abruptness. He hesitated, then struggled out of the dirty garments, pulling his loose slacks down over his shoes. He handed his bundled clothes to Patil, who snatched them away without a word.

"You're welcome," Clay said. Patil took no notice, just thrust a wad of tan cotton at him. The man's eyes jumped at each distant sound in the storage room, darting, suspecting every pile of dusty bags.

Clay struggled into the pants and rough shirt. They looked dingy in the wan yellow glow of a single distant fluorescent tube.

"Not the reception I'd expected," Clay said, straightening the baggy pants and pulling at the rough drawstring.

"These are not good times for scientists in my country, Dr. Clay," Patil said bitingly. His voice carried that odd lilt that echoed both the Raj and Cambridge.

"Who're you afraid of?"

"Those who hate Westerners and their science."

"They said in Washington—"

"We are about great matters, Professor Clay. Please cooperate, please."

Patil's lean face showed its bones starkly, as though energies pressed outward. Promontories of bunched muscle stretched a mottled canvas skin. He started toward a far door without another word, carrying Clay's overnight bag and jacket.

"Say, where're we—"

Patil swung open a sheet-metal door and beckoned. Clay slipped through it and into the moist wealth of night. His feet scraped on a dirty sidewalk beside a black tar road. The door hinge squealed behind them, attracting the attention of a knot of men beneath a vibrant yellow streetlight nearby.

The bleached fluorescence of the airport terminal was now a continent away. Beneath a line of quarter-ton trucks huddled figures slept. In the astringent street-lamp glow he saw a decrepit green Korean Tochat van parked at the curb.

"In!" Patil whispered.

The men under the streetlight started walking toward them, calling out hoarse questions.

Clay yanked open the van's sliding door and crawled into the second row of seats. A fog of unknown pungent smells engulfed him. The driver was a short man hunched over the wheel. Patil sprang into the front seat and the van ground away, its low gear whining.

Shouts. A stone thumped against the van roof. Pebbles rattled at the back.

They accelerated, the engine clattering. A figure loomed up from the shifting shadows and flung muck against the window near Clay's face. He jerked back at the slap of it. "Damn!"

They plowed through a wide puddle of dirty rainwater. The engine sputtered and for a moment Clay was sure it would die. He looked out the rear window and saw vague forms running after them. Then the engine surged again and they shot away.

They went two blocks through hectic traffic. Clay tried to get a clear look at India outside, but all he could see in the starkly shadowed street were the crisscrossings of three-wheeled taxis and human-drawn rickshaws. He got an impression of incessant activity, even in this desolate hour. Vehicles leaped out of the murk as headlights swept across them and then vanished utterly into the moist shadows again.

They suddenly swerved around a corner beneath spreading, gloomy trees. The van jolted into deep potholes and jerked to a stop. "Out!" Patil called.

Clay could barely make out a second van at the curb ahead. It was blue and caked with mud, but even in the dim light would not be confused with their green one. A rotting fetid reek filled his nose as he got out the side door, as if masses of overripe vegetation loomed in the shadows. Patil tugged him into the second van. In a few seconds they went surging out through a narrow, brick-lined alley.

"Look, what—"

"Please, quiet," Patil said primly. "I am watching carefully now to be certain that we are not being followed."

They wound through a shantytown warren for several minutes. Their headlights picked up startled eyes that blinked from what Clay at first had taken to be bundles of rags lying against the shacks. They seemed impossibly small even to be children. Huddled against decaying tin lean-tos, the dim forms often did not stir even as the van splashed dirty water on them from potholes.

Clay began, "Look, I understand the need for—"

"I apologize for our rude methods, Dr. Clay," Patil said. He gestured at the driver. "May I introduce Dr. Singh?"

Singh was similarly gaunt and intent, but with bushy hair and a thin, pointed nose. He jerked his head aside to peer at Clay, nodded twice like a puppet on strings, and then quickly stared back at the narrow lane ahead. Singh kept the van at a steady growl, abruptly yanking it around corners. A wooden cart lurched out of their way, its driver swearing in a strident singsong. "Welcome to India," Singh said with reedy solemnity. "I am afraid circumstances are not the best."

"Uh, right. You two are heads of the project, they told me at the NSF."

"Yes," Patil said archly, "the project which officially no longer exists and unofficially is a brilliant success. It is amusing!"

"Yeah," Clay said cautiously, "we'll see."

"Oh, you will see," Singh said excitedly. "We have the events! More all the time."

Patil said precisely, "We would not have suggested that your National Science Foundation send an observer to confirm our findings unless we believed them to be of the highest importance."

"You've seen proton decay?"

Patil beamed. "Without doubt."

"Damn."

"Exactly."

"What mode?"

"The straightforward pion and positron decay products."

Clay smiled, reserving judgment. Something about Patil's almost prissy precision made him wonder if this small, beleaguered team of Indian physicists might actually have brought it off. An immense long shot, of course, but possible. There were much bigger groups of particle physicists in Europe and the USA who had tried to detect proton decay using underground swimming pools of pure water. Those experiments had enjoyed all the benefits of the latest electronics. Clay had worked on the big American project in a Utah salt mine, before lean budgets and lack of results closed it down. It would be galling if this lone, underfunded Indian scheme had finally done it. Nobody at the NSF believed the story coming out of India.

Patil smiled at Clay's silence, a brilliant slash of white in the murk. Their headlights picked out small panes of glass stuck seemingly at random in nearby hovels, reflecting quick glints of yellow back into the van. The night seemed misty; their headlights forked ahead. Clay thought a soft rain had started outside, but then he saw that thousands of tiny insects darted into their headlights. Occasionally big ones smacked against the windshield.

Patil carefully changed the subject. "I . . . believe you will pass unnoticed, for the most part."

"I look Indian?"

"I hope you will not take offense if I remark that you do not. We requested an Indian, but your NSF said they did not have anyone qualified."

"Right. Nobody who could hop on a plane, anyway." *Or would,* he added to himself.

"I understand. You are a compromise. If you will put this on . . ." Patil handed Clay a floppy khaki hat. "It will cover your curly hair. Luckily, your nose is rather more narrow than I had expected when the NSF cable announced they were sending a Negro."

"Got a lot of white genes in it, this nose," Clay said evenly.

"Please, do not think I am being racist. I simply wished to diminish the chances of you being recognized as a Westerner in the countryside."

"Think I can pass?"

"At a distance, yes."

"Be tougher at the site?"

"Yes. There are 'celebrants,' as they term themselves, at the mine."

"How'll we get in?"

"A ruse we have devised."

"Like that getaway back there? That was pretty slick."

Singh sent them jouncing along a rutted lane. Withered trees leaned against the pale stucco two-story buildings that lined the lane like children's blocks lined up not quite correctly. "Men in Customs, they would give word to people outside. If you had gone through with the others, a different reception party would have been waiting for you."

"I see. But what about my bags?"

Patil had been peering forward at the gloomy jumble of buildings. His head jerked around to glare at Clay. "You were not to bring more than your carryon bag!"

"Look, I can't get by on that. Chrissake, that'd give me just one change of clothes—"

"You left bags there?"

"Well, yeah, I had just one—"

Clay stopped when he saw the look on the two men's faces.

Patil said with strained clarity, "Your bags, they had identification tags?"

"Sure, airlines make you—"

"They will bring attention to you. There will be inquiries. The devotees will hear of it, inevitably, and know you have entered the country."

Clay licked his lips. "Hell, I didn't think it was so important."

The two lean Indians glanced at each other, their faces taking on a narrowing, leaden cast. "Dr. Clay," Patil said stiffly, "the 'celebrants' believe, as do many, that Westerners deliberately destroyed our crops with their biotechnology."

"Japanese companies' biologists did that, I thought," Clay said diplomatically.

"Perhaps. Those who disturb us at the Kolar gold mine make no fine distinctions between biologists and physicists. They believe that we are disturbing the very bowels of the earth, helping to further the destruction, bringing on the very end of the world itself. Surely you can see that in India, the mother country of religious philosophy, such matters are important."

"But your work, hell, it's not a matter of life or death or anything."

"On the contrary, the decay of the proton is precisely an issue of death."

Clay settled back in his seat, puzzled, watching the silky night stream by, cloaking vague forms in its shadowed mysteries.

2.

Clay insisted on the telephone call. A wan winter sun had already crawled partway up the sky before he awoke, and the two Indian physicists wanted to leave immediately. They had stopped while still in Bangalore, holing up in the cramped apartment of one of Patil's graduate students. As Clay took his first sip of tea, two other students had turned up with his bag, retrieved at a cost he never knew.

Clay said, "I promised I'd call home. Look, my family's worried. They read the papers, they know the trouble here."

Shaking his head slowly, Patil finished a scrap of

curled brown bread that appeared to be his only breakfast. His movements had a smooth liquid inertia, as if the sultry morning air oozed like jelly around him. They were sitting at a low table which had one leg too short; the already rickety table kept lurching, slopping tea into their saucers. Clay had looked for something to prop up the leg, but the apartment was bare, as though no one lived here. They had slept on pallets beneath a single bare bulb. Through the open windows, bare of frames or glass, Clay had gotten fleeting glimpses of the neighborhood—rooms of random clutter, plaster peeling off slumped walls, revealing the thin steel cross-ribs of the buildings, stained windows adorned with gaudy pictures of many-armed gods, already sun-bleached and frayed. Children yelped and cried below, their voices reflected among the odd angles and apertures of the tangled streets, while carts rattled by and bare feet slapped the stones. Students had apparently stood guard last night, though Clay had never seen more than a quick motion in the shadows below as they arrived.

"You ask much of us," Patil said. By morning light his walnut-brown face seemed gullied and worn. Lines radiated from his mouth toward intense eyes.

Clay sipped his tea before answering. A soft, strangely sweet smell wafted through the open window. They sat well back in the room so nobody could see in from the nearby buildings. He heard Singh tinkering downstairs with the van's engine.

"Okay, it's maybe slightly risky. But I want my people to know I got here all right."

"There are few telephones here."

"I only need one."

"The system, often it does not work at all."

"Gotta try."

"Perhaps you do not understand—"

"I understand damn well that if I can't even reach

my people, I'm not going to hang out here for long. And if I don't see that your experiment works right, nobody'll believe you."

"And your opinion depends upon . . . ?"

Clay ticked off points on his fingers. "On seeing the apparatus. Checking your raw data. Running a trial case to see your system response. Then a null experiment—to verify your threshold level on each detector." He held up five fingers. "The works."

Patil said gravely, "Very good. We relish the opportunity to prove ourselves."

"You'll get it." Clay hoped to himself that they were wrong, but he suppressed that. He represented the faltering forefront of particle physics, and it would be embarrassing if a backwater research team had beaten the world. Still, either way, he would end up being the expert on the Kolar program, and that was a smart career move in itself.

"Very well. I must make arrangements for the call, then. But I truly—"

"Just do it. Then we get down to business."

The telephone was behind two counters and three doors at a Ministry for Controls office. Patil did the bribing and cajoling inside and then brought Clay in from the back of the van. He had been lying down on the back seat so he could not be seen easily from the street.

The telephone itself was a heavy black plastic thing with a rotary dial that clicked like a sluggish insect as it whirled. Patil had been on it twice already, clearing international lines through Bombay. Clay got two false rings and a dead line. On the fourth try he heard a faint, somehow familiar buzzing. Then a hollow, distant click.

"Angy?"

"Daddy, is that you?" Faint rock music in the background.

"Sure, I just wanted to let you know I got to India okay."

"Oh, Mommy will be so glad! We heard on the TV last night that there's trouble over there."

Startled, Clay asked, "What? Where's your mother?"

"Getting groceries. She'll be *so* mad she missed your call!"

"You tell her I'm fine, okay? But what trouble?"

"Something about a state leaving India. Lots of fighting, John Trimble said on the news."

Clay never remembered the names of news announcers; he regarded them as faceless nobodies reading prepared scripts, but for his daughter they were the voice of authority. "Where?"

"Uh, the lower part."

"There's nothing like that happening here, honey. I'm safe. Tell Mommy."

"People have ice cream there?"

"Yeah, but I haven't seen any. You tell your mother what I said, remember? About being safe?"

"Yes, she's been worried."

"Don't worry, Angy. Look, I got to go." The line popped and hissed ominously.

"I miss you, Daddy."

"I miss you double that. No, squared."

She laughed merrily. "I skinned my knee today at recess. It bled so much I had to go to the nurse."

"Keep it clean, honey. And give your mother my love."

"She'll be *so* mad."

"I'll be home soon."

She giggled and ended with the joke she had been using lately. "G'bye, Daddy. It's been real."

Her light laugh trickled into the static, a grace note from a bright land worlds away. Clay chuckled as he replaced the receiver. She cut the last word of "real nice" to make her good-byes hip and sardonic, a mannerism she had heard on television somewhere. An old joke; he had heard that even "groovy" was coming back in.

Clay smiled and pulled his hat down farther and went quickly out into the street where Patil was waiting. India flickered at the edge of his vision, the crowds a hovering presence.

3.

They left Bangalore in two vans. Graduate students drove the green Tochat from the previous night. He and Patil and Singh took the blue one, Clay again keeping out of sight by lying on the back seat. The day's raw heat rose around them like a shimmering lake of light.

They passed through lands leached of color. Only gray stubble grew in the fields. Trees hung limply, their limbs bowing as though exhausted. Figures in rags huddled for shade. A few stirred, eyes white in the shadows, as the vans ground past. Clay saw that large boles sat on the branches like gnarled knots with brows sheaths wrapped around the underside.

"Those some of the plant diseases I heard about?" he asked.

Singh pursed his lips. "I fear those are the pouches like those of wasps, as reported in the press." His watery eyes regarded the withered, graying trees as Patil slowed the van.

"Are they dangerous?" Clay could see yellow sap dripping from the underside of each.

"Not until they ripen," Singh said. "Then the assassins emerge."

"They look pretty big already."

"They are said to be large creatures, but of course there is little experience."

Patil downshifted and they accelerated away with

an occasional sputtering misfire. Clay wondered whether they had any spare spark plugs along. The fields on each side of the road took on a dissolute and shredded look. "Did the genetech experiments cause this?" he asked.

Singh nodded. "I believe this emerged from the European programs. First we had their designed plants, but then pests found vulnerability. They sought strains which could protect crops from the new pests. So we got these wasps. I gather that now some error or mutation has made them equally excellent at preying on people and even cows."

Clay frowned. "The wasps came from the Japanese aid, didn't they?"

Patil smiled mysteriously. "You know a good deal about our troubles, sir."

Neither said anything more. Clay was acutely conscious that his briefing in Washington had been detailed technical assessments, without the slightest mention of how the Indians themselves saw their problems. Singh and Patil seemed either resigned or unconcerned; he could not tell which. Their sentences refracted from some unseen nugget, like seismic waves warping around the Earth's core.

"I would not worry greatly about these pouches," Singh said after they had ridden in silence for a while. "They should not ripen before we are done with our task. In any case, the Kolar fields are quite barren, and afford few sites where the pouches can grow."

Clay pointed out the front window. "Those round things on the walls—more pouches?"

To his surprise, both men burst into merry laughter. Gasping, Patil said, "Examine them closely, Dr. Clay. Notice the marks of the species which made them."

Patil slowed the car and Clay studied the round, circular pads on the whitewashed vertical walls along the road. They were brown and matted and marked in a pattern of radial lines. Clay frowned and then felt enormously stupid: the thick lines were handprints.

"Drying cakes, they are," Patil said, still chuckling.

"Of what?"

"Dung, my colleague. We use the cow here, not merely slaughter it."

"What for?"

"Fuel. After the cakes dry, we stack them—see?" They passed a plastic-wrapped tower. A woman was adding a circular, annular tier of thick dung disks to the top, then carefully folding the plastic over it. "In winter they burn nicely."

"For heating?"

"And cooking, yes."

Seeing the look on Clay's face, Singh's eyes narrowed and his lips drew back so that his teeth were bright stubs. His eyebrows were long brush strokes that met the deep furrows of his frown. "Old ways are still often preferable to the new."

Sure, Clay thought, the past of cholera, plague, infanticide. But he asked with neutral politeness, "Such as?"

"Some large fish from the Amazon were introduced into our principal river three years ago to improve fishing yields."

"The Ganges? I thought it was holy."

"What is more holy than to feed the hungry?"

"True enough. Did it work?"

"The big fish, yes. They are delicious. A great delicacy."

"I'll have to try some," Clay said, remembering the thin vegetarian curry he had eaten at breakfast.

Singh said, "But the Amazon sample contained some minute eggs which none of the proper procedures eliminated. They were of a small species—the candiru, is that not the name?" he inquired politely of Patil.

"Yes," Patil said, "a little being who thrives

mostly on the urine of larger fish. Specialists now believe that perhaps the eggs were inside the large species, and so escaped detection."

Patil's voice remained calm and factual, although while he spoke he abruptly swerved to avoid a goat that spontaneously ambled onto the rough road. Clay rocked hard against the van's door, and Patil then corrected further to stay out of a gratuitous mud hole that seemed to leap at them from the rushing foreground. They bumped noisily over ruts at the road's edge and bounced back onto the tarmac without losing speed. Patil sat ramrod straight, hands turning the steering wheel lightly, oblivious to the wrenching effects of his driving.

"Suppose, Professor Clay, that you are a devotee," Singh said. "You have saved to come to the Ganges for a decade, for two. Perhaps you can even plan to die there."

"Yeah, okay." Clay could not see where this was leading.

"You are enthused as you enter the river to bathe. You are perhaps profoundly affected. An intense spiritual moment. It is not uncommon to merge with the river, to inadvertently urinate into it."

Singh spread his hands as if to say that such things went without saying.

"Then the candiru will be attracted by the smell. It mistakes this great bountiful largess, the food it needs, as coming from a very great fish indeed. It excitedly swims up the stream of uric acid. Coming to your urethra, it swims like a snake into its burrow, as far up as it can go. You will see that the uric flow velocity will increase as the candiru makes its way upstream, inside you. When this tiny fish can make no further progress, some trick of evolution tells it to protrude a set of sidewise spines. So intricate!"

Singh paused a moment in smiling tribute to this intriguing facet of nature. Clay nodded, his mouth dry.

"These embed deeply in the walls and keep the candiru close to the source of what it so desires." Singh made short, delicate movements, his fingers jutting in the air. Clay opened his mouth, but said nothing.

Patil took them around a team of bullocks towing a wooden wagon and put in, "The pain is intense. Apparently there is no good treatment. Women—forgive this indelicacy—must be opened to get the offending tiny fish before it swells and blocks the passage completely, having gorged itself insensate. Some men have an even worse choice. Their bladders are already engorged, having typically not been much emptied by the time the candiru enters. They must decide whether to attempt the slow procedure of poisoning the small thing and waiting for it to shrivel and withdraw its spines. However, their bladders might burst before that, flooding their abdomens with urine and of course killing them. If there is not sufficient time . . ."

"Yes?" Clay asked tensely.

"Then the penis must be chopped off," Singh said, "with the candiru inside."

Through a long silence Clay rode, swaying as the car wove through limitless flat spaces of parched fields and ruined brick walls and slumped whitewashed huts. Finally he said hoarsely, "I . . . don't blame you for resenting the . . . well, the people who brought all this on you. The devotees—"

"They believe this apocalyptic evil comes from the philosophy which gave us modern science."

"Well, look, whoever brought over those fish—"

Singh's eyes widened with surprise. A startled grin lit his face like a sunrise. "Oh no, Professor Clay! We do not blame the errors, or else we would have to blame equally the successes!"

To Clay's consternation, Patil nodded sagely.

He decided to say nothing more. Washington had warned him to stay out of political discussions, and though he was not sure if this was such, or if the light-hearted way Singh and Patil had related their story told their true attitude, it seemed best to just shut up. Again Clay had the odd sensation that here the cool certainties of Western biology had become diffused, blunted, crisp distinctions rendered into something beyond the constraints of the world outside, all blurred by the swarming, dissolving currents of India. The tin-gray sky loomed over a plain of ripe rot. The urgency of decay here was far more powerful than the abstractions that so often filled his head, the digitized iconography of sputtering, splitting protons.

4.

The Kolar gold fields were a long, dusty drive from Bangalore. The sway of the van made Clay sleepy in the back, jet lag pulling him down into fitful, shallow dreams of muted voices, shadowy faces, and obscure purpose. He awoke frequently amid the dry smells, lurched up to see dry farmland stretching to the horizon, and collapsed again to bury his face in the pillow he had made by wadding up a shirt.

They passed through innumerable villages that, after the first few, all seemed alike with their scrawny children, ramshackle sheds, tin roofs, and general air of sleepy dilapidation. Once, in a narrow town, they stopped as rickshaws and carts backed up. An emaciated cow with pink paper tassels on its horns stood square in the middle of the road, trembling. Shouts and honks failed to move it, but no one ahead made the slightest effort to prod it aside.

Clay got out of the van to stretch his legs, ignoring Patil's warning to stay hidden, and watched. A crowd collected, shouting and chanting at the cow but not touching it. The cow shook its head, peering at the road as if searching for grass, and urinated powerfully.

A woman in a red sari rushed into the road, knelt, and thrust her hand into the full stream. She made a formal motion with her other hand and splashed some urine on her forehead and cheeks. Three other women had already lined up behind her, and each did the same. Disturbed, the cow waggled its head and shakily walked away. Traffic started up and Clay climbed back into the van. As they ground out of the dusty town, Singh explained that holy bovine urine was widely held to have positive health effects.

"Many believe it settles stomach troubles, banishes headaches, even improves fertility," Singh said.

"Yeah, you could sure use more fertility." Clay gestured at the throngs that filled the narrow clay sidewalks.

"I am not so Indian that I cannot find it within myself to agree with you, Professor Clay," Singh said.

"Sorry for the sarcasm. I'm tired."

"Patil and I are already under a cloud simply because we are scientists, and therefore polluted with Western ideas."

"Can't blame Indians for being down on us. Things're getting rough."

"But you are a black man. You yourself were persecuted by Western societies."

"That was a while back."

"And despite it you have risen to a professorship."

"You do the work, you get the job." Clay took off his hat and wiped his brow. The midday heat pressed sweat from him.

"Then you do not feel alienated from Western ideals?" Patil put in.

"Hell no. Look, I'm not some sharecropper who pulled himself up from poverty. I grew up in Falls Church, Virginia. Father's a federal bureaucrat. Middle class all the way."

"I see," Patil said, eyes never leaving the rutted road. "Your race bespeaks an entirely different culture, but you subscribe to the program of modern rationalism."

Clay looked at them quizzically. "Don't you?"

"As scientists, of course. But that is not all of life."

"Um," Clay said.

A thousand times before he had endured the affably condescending attention of whites, their curious eyes searching his face. No matter what the topic, they somehow found a way to inquire indirectly after his *true* feelings, his *natural* emotions. And if he waved away these intrusions, there remained in their heavy-lidded eyes a subtle skepticism, doubts about his authenticity. Few gave him space to simply be a suburban man with darker skin, a man whose interior landscape was populated with the same icons of middle America as their own. Hell, his family name came from slaves, given as a tribute to Henry Clay, a nineteenth-century legislator. He had never expected to run into stereotyping in India, for chrissakes.

Still, he was savvy enough to lard his talk with some homey touches, jimmy things up with collard greens and black-eyed peas and street jive. It might put them at ease.

"I believe a li'l rationality could help," he said.

"Um." Singh's thin mouth twisted doubtfully. "Perhaps you should regard India as the great chessboard of our times, Professor. Here we have arisen from the great primordial agrarian times, fashioned our gods from our soil and age. Then we had orderly thinking, with all its assumptions, thrust upon us by the British. Now they are all gone, and we are suspended between the miasmic truths of the past and the failed strictures of the present."

Clay looked out the dirty window and suppressed a smile. Even the physicists here spouted mumbo jumbo. They even appeared solemnly respectful of the devotees, who were just crazies like the women by the cow. How could anything solid come out of such a swamp? The chances that their experiment was right dwindled with each lurching, damp mile.

They climbed into the long range of hills before the Kolar fields. Burnt-tan grass shimmered in the prickly heat. Sugarcane fields and rice paddies stood bone dry. In the villages thin figures watched them pass from beneath the shade of awnings, canvas tents, lean-tos. Lean faces betrayed only dim, momentary interest and Clay wondered if his uncomfortable disguise was necessary outside Bangalore.

Without stopping they ate their lunch of dried fruit and thin brown bread. In a high hill town Patil stopped to refill his water bottle at a well. Clay peered out and saw down an alley a gang of stick-figure boys chasing a scrawny dog. They hemmed it in and the bedraggled hound fled yapping from one side of their circle to the other. The animal whined at each rebuff and twice lost its footing on the cobblestones, sprawling, only to scramble up again and rush on. It was a cruel game, and the boys were strangely silent, playing without laughter. The dog was tiring; they drew in their circle.

A harsh edge to the boys' shouts made Clay slide open the van door. Several men were standing beneath a rust-scabbed sheet metal awning nearby, and their eyes widened when they saw his face. They talked rapidly among themselves. Clay hesitated. The boys down the alley rushed the dog. They grabbed it as it yapped futilely and tried to bite them. They slipped twine around its jaws and silenced it. Shouting, they hoisted it into the air and marched off.

Clay gave up and slammed the door. The men came from under the awning. One rapped on the window. Clay just stared at them. One thumped on the door. Gestures, loud talk.

Patil and Singh came running, shouted something.

Singh pushed the men away, chattering at them while Patil got the van started. Singh slammed the door in the face of a man with wild eyes. Patil gunned the engine and they ground away.

"They saw me and—"

"Distrust of outsiders is great here," Singh said. "They may be connected with the devotees, too."

"Guess I better keep my hat on."

"It would be advisable."

"I don't know, those boys—I was going to stop them pestering that dog. Stupid, I guess, but—"

"You will have to avoid being sentimental about such matters," Patil said severely.

"Uh—sentimental?"

"The boys were not playing."

"I don't—"

"They will devour it," Singh said.

Clay blinked. "Hindus eating meat?"

"Hard times. I am really quite surprised that such an animal has survived this long," Patil said judiciously. "Dogs are uncommon. I imagine it was wild, living in the countryside, and ventured into town in search of garbage scraps."

The land rose as Clay watched the shimmering heat bend and flex the seemingly solid hills.

5.

They pulled another dodge at the mine. The lead green van veered off toward the main entrance, a cluster of concrete buildings and conveyer assemblies. From a distance the physicists in the blue van watched a ragtag group envelop the van before it had fully stopped.

"Devotees," Singh said abstractedly. "They search each vehicle for evidence of our research."

"Your graduate students, the mob'll let them pass?"

Patil peered through binoculars. "The crowd is administering a bit of a pushing about," he said in his oddly cadenced accent, combining lofty British diction with a singsong lilt.

"Damn, won't the mine people get rid—"

"Some mine workers are among the crowd, I should imagine," Patil said. "They are beating the students."

"Well, can't we—"

"No time to waste." Singh waved them back into the blue van. "Let us make use of this diversion."

"But we could—"

"The students made their sacrifice for you. Do not devalue it, please."

Clay did not take his eyes from the nasty knot of confusion until they lurched over the ridge line. Patil explained that they had been making regular runs to the main entrance for months now, to establish a pattern that drew devotees away from the secondary entrance.

"All this was necessary, and insured that we could bring in a foreign inspector," Patil concluded. Clay awkwardly thanked him for the attention to detail. He wanted to voice his embarrassment at having students roughed up simply to provide him cover, but something in the offhand manner of the two Indians made him hold his tongue.

The secondary entrance to the Kolar mine was a wide, tin-roofed shed like a low aircraft hangar. Girders crisscrossed it at angles that seemed to Clay dictated less by the constraints of mechanics than by the whims of the construction team. Cables looped among the already rusting steel struts and sang low notes in the rot-tinged wind that brushed his hair.

Monkeys chattered and scampered high in the struts. The three men walked into the shed, carrying cases. The cables began humming softly. The weave above their heads tightened with pops and sharp cracks. Clay realized that the seemingly random array was a complicated hoist that had started to pull the elevator up from miles beneath their feet. The steel lattice groaned as if it already knew how much work it had to do.

When it arrived, the elevator was a huge rattling box that reeked of machine oil. Clay lugged his cases in. The walls were broad wooden slats covered with chicken wire. Heat radiated from them. Patil stabbed a button on the big control board, and they dropped quickly. The numbers of the levels zipped by on an amber digital display. A single dim yellow bulb cast shadows onto the wire. At the fifty-third level the bulb went out. The elevator did not stop.

In the enveloping blackness Clay felt himself lighten, as if the elevator was speeding up.

"Do not be alarmed," Patil called. "This frequently occurs."

Clay wondered if he meant the faster fall or the light bulb. In the complete dark he began to see blue phantoms leaping out from nowhere.

Abruptly he became heavy—and thought of Einstein's *gedanken* experiment, which equated a man in an accelerating elevator to one standing on a planet. Unless Clay could see outside, check that the massive earth raced by beyond as it clasped him further into its depths, in principle he could be in either situation. He tried to recall how Einstein had reasoned from an imaginary elevator to deduce that matter curved space-time, and could not.

Einstein's elegant proof was impossibly far from the pressing truth of *this* elevator. Here Clay plunged in thick murk, a weight of tortured air prickling his nose, making sweat pop from his face. Oily, moist heat climbed into Clay's sinuses.

And he was not being carried aloft by this elevator, but allowed to plunge into heavy, primordial darkness—Einstein's vision in reverse. No classical coolness separated him from the press of a raw, random world. That European mindscape—Galileo's crisp cylinders rolling obediently down inclined planes, Einstein's dispassionate observers surveying their smooth geometries like scrupulous bank clerks—evaporated here like yesterday's stale champagne. Sudden anxiety filled his throat. His stomach tightened and he tasted acrid gorge. He opened his mouth to shout, and as if to stop him his own knees sagged with suddenly returning weight, physics regained.

A rattling thump—and they stopped. He felt Patil slam aside the rattling gate. A sullen glow beyond bathed an ornate brass shrine to a Hindu god. They came out into a steepled room of carved rock. Clay felt a breath of slightly cooler air from a cardboard-mouthed conduit nearby.

"We must force the air down from above." Patil gestured. "Otherwise this would read well over a hundred and ten Fahrenheit." He proudly pointed to an ancient battered British thermometer, whose mercury stood at ninety-eight.

They trudged through several tunnels, descended another few hundred feet on a ramp, and then followed gleaming railroad tracks. A white bulb every ten meters threw everything into exaggerated relief, shadows stabbing everywhere. A brown cardboard sign proclaimed from the ceiling:

FIRST EVER COSMIC RAY NEUTRINO
INTERACTION
RECORDED HERE IN APRIL 1965.

For over forty years teams of devoted Indian physicists had labored patiently inside the Kolar Gold Fields. For half a century India's high mountains and deep mines had made important cosmic ray experiments possible with inexpensive instruments. Clay recalled how a joint Anglo-Indian-Japanese team had detected that first neutrino, scooped it from the unending cosmic sleet that penetrated even to this depth. He thought of unsung Indian physicists sweating here, tending the instruments, and tracing the myriad sources of background error. Yet they themselves were background for the original purpose of the deep holes: two narrow cars clunked past, full of chopped stone.

"Some still work this portion." Patil's clear voice cut through the muffled air. "Though I suspect they harvest little."

Pushing the rusty cars were four wiry men, so sweaty that the glaring bulbs gave their sliding muscles a hard sheen like living stone. They wore filthy cloths wrapped around their heads, as if they needed protection against the low ceiling rather than the heat. As Clay stumbled on he felt that there might be truth to this, because he sensed the mass above as a precarious judgment over them all, a sullen presence. Einstein's crisp distinctions, the clean certainty of the *gedanken* experiments, meant nothing in this blurred air.

They rounded an irregular curve and met a niche neatly cut off by a chain-link fence.

PROTON STABILITY EXPERIMENT
TATA INSTITUTE OF FUNDAMENTAL
RESEARCH, BOMBAY
80th Level Heathcote Shaft, KFG
2300 meters depth

These preliminaries done, the experiment itself began abruptly. Clay had expected some assembly rooms, an office, refrigerated 'scope cages. Instead, a few meters ahead the tunnel opened in all directions. They stood before a huge bay roughly cleaved from the brown rock.

And filling the vast volume was what seemed to be

a wall as substantial as the rock itself. It was an iron grid of rusted pipe. The pipes were square, not round, and dwindled into the distance. Each had a dusty seal, a pressure dial, and a number painted in white. Clay estimated them to be at least a hundred feet long. They were stacked Lincoln Logs fashion. He walked to the edge of the bay and looked down. Layers of pipe tapered away below to a distant floodlit floor and soared to meet the gray ceiling above.

"Enormous," he said.

"We expended great effort in scaling up our earlier apparatus," Singh said enthusiastically.

"As big as a house."

Patil said merrily, "An American house, perhaps. Ours are smaller."

A woman's voice nearby said, "And nothing lives in this iron house, Professor Clay."

Clay turned to see a willowy Indian woman regarding him with a wry smile. She seemed to have come out of the shadows, a brown apparition appearing full-blown in shorts and a scrupulously white blouse, where a moment before there had been nothing. Her heavy eyebrows rose in amusement.

"Ah, this is Mrs. Buli," Patil said.

"I keep matters running here, while my colleagues venture into the world," she said.

Clay accepted her coolly offered hand. She gave him one quick, well-defined shake and stepped back. "I can assist your assessment, perhaps."

"I'll need all your help," he said sincerely. The skimpy surroundings already made him wonder if he could do his job at all.

"Labor we have," she said. "Equipment, little."

"I brought some cross-check programs with me," he said.

"Excellent," Mrs. Buli said. "I shall have several of my graduate students assist you, and of course I offer my full devotion as well."

Clay smiled at her antique formality. She led him down a passage into the soft fluorescent glow of a large data-taking room. It was crammed with terminals and a bank of disk drives, all meshed by the usual cable spaghetti. "We keep our computers cooler than our staff, you see," Mrs. Buli said with a small smile.

They went down a ramp, and Clay could feel the rock's steady heat. They came out onto the floor of the cavern. Thick I-beams roofed the stone box.

"Over a dozen lives, that was the cost of this excavation," Singh said.

"That many?"

"They attempted to save on the cost of explosives," Patil said with a stern look.

"Not that such will matter in the long run," Singh said mildly. Clay chose not to pursue the point.

Protective bolts studded the sheer rock, anchoring cross-beams that stabilized the tower of pipes. Scaffolding covered some sections of the blocky, rusty pile. Blasts of compressed air from the surface a mile above swept down on them from the ceiling, flapping Clay's shirt.

Mrs. Buli had to shout, the effort contorting her smooth face. "We obtained the pipes from a government program that attempted to improve the quality of plumbing in the cities. A failure, I fear. But a godsend for us."

Patil was pointing out electrical details when the air conduits wheezed into silence. "Hope that's temporary," Clay said in the sudden quiet.

"A minor repair, I am sure," Patil said.

"These occur often," Singh agreed earnestly.

Clay could already feel prickly sweat oozing from him. He wondered how often they had glitches in the circuitry down here, awash in pressing heat, and how much that could screw up even the best diagnostics.

Mrs. Buli went on in a lecturer's singsong. "We hired engineering students—there are many such, an oversupply—to thread a single wire down the bore of each pipe. We sealed each, then welded them together to make lengths of a hundred feet. Then we filled them with argon and linked them with a high-voltage line. We have found that a voltage of 280 keV . . ."

Clay nodded, filing away details, noting where her description differed from that of the NSF. The Kolar group had continuously modified their experiment for decades, and this latest enormous expansion was badly documented. Still, the principle was simple. Each pipe was held at high voltage, so that when a charged particle passed through, a spark leaped. A particle's path was followed by counting the segments of triggered pipes. This mammoth stack of iron was a huge Geiger counter.

He leaned back, nodding at Buli's lecture, watching a team of men at the very top. A loud clang rang through the chasm. Sparks showered, burnt orange and blue. The garish plumes silhouetted the welders and sent cascades of sparks down through the lattice of pipes. For an instant Clay imagined he was witnessing cosmic rays sleeting down through the towering house of iron, illuminating it with their short, sputtering lives.

"—and I am confident that we have seen well over fifty true events," Mrs. Buli concluded with a jaunty upward tilt of her chin.

"What?" Clay struggled back from his daydreaming. "That many?"

She laughed, a high tinkling. "You do not believe!"

"Well, that is a lot."

"Our detecting mass is now larger," Mrs. Buli said.

"Last we heard it was five hundred tons," Clay said carefully. The claims wired to the NSF and the Royal Society had been skimpy on details.

"That was years ago," Patil said. "We have redoubled our efforts, as you can see."

"Well, to see that many decays, you'd have to have a hell of a lot of observing volume," Clay said doubtfully.

"We can boast of five *thousand* tons, Professor Clay," Mrs. Buli said.

"Looks it," Clay said laconically to cover his surprise. It would not do to let them think they could overwhelm him with magnitudes. Question was, did they have the telltale events?

The cooling air came on with a thump and *whoosh*. Clay breathed it in deeply, face turned up to the iron house where protons might be dying, and sucked in swarming scents of the parched countryside miles above.

6.

He knew from the start that there would be no eureka moment. Certainty was the child of tedium.

He traced the tangled circuitry for two days before he trusted it. "You got to open the sack 'fore I'll believe there's a cat in there," he told Mrs. Buli, and then had to explain that he was joking.

Then came a three-day trial run, measuring the exact sputter of decay from a known radioactive source. System response was surprisingly good. He found their techniques needlessly byzantine, but workable. His null checks of the detectors inside the pipes came up goose-egg clean.

Care was essential. Proton decay was rare. The Grand Unified Theories which had enjoyed such success in predicting new particles had also sounded a somber note through all of physics. Matter was mortal. But not very mortal, compared with the passing flicker of a human lifetime.

The human body had about 10^{29} neutrons and protons in it. If only a tiny fraction of them decayed in a human lifetime, the radiation from the disintegration would quickly kill everyone of cancer. The survival of even small life-forms implied that the protons inside each nucleus had to survive an average of nearly a billion billion years.

So even before the Grand Unified Theories, physicists knew that protons lived long. The acronym for the theories was GUTs, and a decade earlier graduate students like Clay had worn T-shirts with insider jokes like IT TAKES GUTS TO DO PARTICLE PHYSICS. But proving that there was some truth to the lame nerd jests took enormous effort.

The simplest of the GUTs predicted a proton lifetime of about 10^{31} years, immensely greater than the limit set by the existence of life. In fact, it was far longer even than the age of the universe, which was only a paltry 2×10^{10} years old.

One could check this lifetime by taking one proton and watching it for 10^{31} years. Given the short attention span of humans, it was better to assemble 10^{31} protons and watch them for a year, hoping one would fizzle.

Physicists in the United States, Japan, Italy, and India had done that all through the 1980s and 1990s. And no protons had died.

Well, the theorists had said, the mathematics must be more complicated. They discarded certain symmetry groups and thrust others forward. The lifetime might be 10^{32} years, then.

The favored method of gathering protons was to use those in water. Western physicists carved swimming pools six stories deep in salt mines and eagerly watched for the characteristic blue pulse of dying matter. Detecting longer lifetimes meant waiting longer, which nobody liked, or adding more protons. Digging bigger swimming pools was easy, so attention had turned to the United States and Japan . . . but still, no protons died. The lifetime exceeded 10^{32} years.

The austerity of the 1990s had shut down the ambitious experiments in the West. Few remembered this forlorn experiment in Kolar, wedded to watching the cores of iron rods for the quick spurt of decay. When political difficulties cut off contact, the already beleaguered physicists in the West assumed the Kolar effort had ceased.

But Kolar was the deepest experiment, less troubled by the hail of cosmic rays that polluted the Western data. Clay came to appreciate that as he scrolled through the myriad event-plots in the Kolar computer cubes.

There were 9×10^9 recorded decays of all types. The system rejected obvious garbage events, but there were many subtle enigmas. Theory said that protons died because the quarks that composed them could change their identities. A seemingly capricious alteration of quarky states sent the proton asunder, spitting forth a zoo of fragments. Neotrons, the other building blocks of nuclei, were untroubled by this, for in free space they decayed anyway, into a proton and electron. Matter's end hinged, finally, on the stability of the proton alone.

Clay saw immediately that the Kolar group had invested years in their software. They had already filtered out thousands of phantom events that imitated true proton decay. There were eighteen ways a proton could die, each with a different signature of spraying light and particle debris.

The delicate traceries of particle paths were recorded as flashes and sparkles in the house of iron outside. Clay searched through endless graphic printouts, filigrees woven from digital cloth.

"You will find we have pondered each candidate event," Mrs. Buli said mildly on the sixth day of Clay's labors.

"Yeah, the analysis is sharp," he said cautiously. He was surprised at the high level of the work but did not want to concede anything yet.

"If any ambiguity arose, we discarded the case."

"I can see that."

"Some pions were not detected in the right energy range, so of course we omitted those."

"Good."

Mrs. Buli leaned over to show him a detail of the cross-checking program, and he caught a heady trace of wildflowers. Her perfume reminded him abruptly that her sari wrapped over warm, ample swells. She had no sagging softness, no self-indulgent bulgings. The long oval of her face and her ample lips conveyed a fragile sensuality . . .

He wrenched his attention back to physics and stared hard at the screen.

Event vertices were like time-lapse photos of traffic accidents, intersections exploding, screaming into shards. The crystalline mathematical order of physics led to riots of incandescence. And Clay was judge, weighing testimony after the chaos.

7.

He had insisted on analyzing the several thousand preliminary candidates himself, as a double blind against the Kolar group's software. After nine days he had isolated sixty-seven events that looked like the genuine article.

Sixty-five of his agreed with Mrs. Buli's analysis. The two holdouts were close, Clay had to admit.

"Nearly on the money," he said reflectively as he stared at the Kolar software's array.

"You express such values," Mrs. Buli said. "Always a financial analogy."

"Just a way of speaking."

"Still, let us discard the two offending events."

"Well, I'd be willing—"

"No no, we consider only the sixty-five." Her almond eyes gave no hint of slyness.

"They're pretty good bets, I'd say." Her eyebrows arched. "Only a manner of speech."

"Then you feel they fit the needs of theory."

Her carefully balanced way of phrasing made him lean forward, as if to compensate for his judge's role. "I'll have to consider all the other decay modes in detail. Look for really obscure processes that might mimic the real thing."

She nodded. "True, there is need to study such."

Protons could die from outside causes, too. Wraithlike neutrinos spewed forth by the sun penetrated even here, shattering protons. Murderous muons lumbered through as cosmic rays, plowing furrows of exploding nuclei.

Still, things looked good. He was surprised at their success, earned by great labor. "I'll be as quick about it as I can."

"We have prepared a radio link that we can use, should the desire come."

"Huh? What?"

"In case you need to reach your colleagues in America."

"Ah, yes."

To announce the result, he saw. To get the word out. But why the rush?

It occurred to him that they might doubt whether he himself would get out at all.

8.

They slept each night in a clutch of tin lean-tos that cowered down a raw ravine. Laborers from the mine had slept there in better days, and the physicists had gotten the plumbing to work for an hour each night. The men slept in a long shed, but gave Clay a small wooden shack. He ate thin, mealy gruel with them each evening, carefully dropping purification tablets in his water, and was rewarded with untroubled bowels. He sweated away weight in the heat of the mine, but the nights were cool and the breezes that came then were soft with moisture.

The fifth evening, as they sat around a potbellied iron stove in the men's shed, Patil pointed to a distant corrugated metal hut and said, "There we have concealed a satellite dish. We can knock away the roof and transmit, if you like."

Clay brightened. "Can I call home?"

"If need be."

Something in Patil's tone told him a frivolous purpose was not going to receive their cooperation.

"Maybe tomorrow?"

"Perhaps. We must be sure that the devotees do not see us reveal it."

"They think we're laborers?"

"So we have convinced them, I believe."

"And me?"

"You would do well to stay inside."

"Um. Look, got anything to drink?"

Patil frowned. "Has the water pipe stopped giving?"

"No, I mean, you know—a drink. Gin and tonic, wasn't that what the Brits preferred?"

"Alcohol is the devil's urine," Patil said precisely.

"It won't scramble my brains."

"Who can be sure? The mind is a tentative instrument."

"You don't want any suspicion that I'm unreliable, that it?"

"No, of course not," Singh broke in anxiously.

"Needn't worry," Clay muttered. The heat below and the long hours of tedious work were wearing him down. "I'll be gone soon's I can get things wrapped up."

"You agree that we are seeing the decays?"

"Let's say things're looking better."

Clay had been holding back even tentative approval. He had expected some show of jubilation. Patil and Singh simply sat and stared into the flickering coals of the stove's half-open door.

Slowly Patil said, "Word will spread quickly."

"Soon as you transmit it on that dish, sure."

Singh murmured, "Much shall change."

"Look, you might want to get out of here, go present a paper—"

"Oh no, we shall remain," Singh said quickly.

"Those devotees could give you trouble if they find—"

"We expect that this discovery, once understood, shall have great effects," Patil said solemnly. "I much prefer to witness them from my home country."

The cadence and mood of this conversation struck Clay as odd, but he put it down to the working conditions. Certainly they had sacrificed a great deal to build and run this experiment amid crippling desolation.

"This result will begin the final renunciation of the materialistic worldview," Singh said matter-of-factly.

"Huh?"

"In peering at the individual lives of mere particles, we employ the reductionist hammer," Patil explained. "But nature is not like a salamander, cut into fragments."

"Or if it were," Singh added, "once the salamander is so sliced, try to make it do its salamander walk again." A broad white grin split the gloom of nightfall.

"The world is an implicate order, Dr. Clay. All parts are hinged to each other."

Clay frowned. He vaguely remembered a theory of

quantum mechanics which used the term "implicate order," meaning that a deeper realm of physical theory lay beneath the uncertainties of wave mechanics. Waves that took it into their heads to behave like particles, and the reverse—these were supposed to be illusions arising from our ignorance of a more profound theory. But there was no observable consequence of such notions, and to Clay such mumbo jumbo from theorists who never got their hands dirty was empty rhapsodizing. Still, he was supposed to be the diplomat here.

He gave a judicial nod. "Yeah, sure—but when the particles die, it'll all be gone, right?"

"Yes, in about 10^{34} years," Patil said. "But the *knowledge* of matter's mortality will spread as swiftly as light, on the wind of our transmitter."

"So?"

"You are an experimentalist, Dr. Clay, and thus—if you will forgive my putting it so—addicted to cutting the salamander." Patil made a steeple of his fingers, sending spindly shadows rippling across his face. "The world we study is conditioned by our perceptions of it. The implied order if partially from our own design."

"Sure, quantum measurement, uncertainty principle, all that," Clay had sat through all the usual lectures about this stuff and didn't feel like doing so again. Not in a dusty shed with his stomach growling from hunger. He sipped at his cup of weak Darjeeling and yawned.

"Difficulties of measurement reflect underlying problems," Patil said. "Even the Westerner Plato saw that we perceive only imperfect modes of the true, deeper world."

"What deeper world?" Clay sighed despite himself.

"We do not know. We *cannot* know."

"Look, we make our measurements, we report. Period."

Amused, Singh said, "And that is where matters end?"

Patil said, "Consensual reality, that is your 'real' world, Professor Clay. But our news may cause that bland, unthinking consensus to falter."

Clay shrugged. This sounded like late-night college bullshit sessions among boozed-up science nerds. Patty-cake pantheism, quantum razzle-dazzle, garbage philosophy. It was one thing to be open-minded and another to let your brains fall out. Was *everybody* on this wrecked continent a booga-booga type? He had to get out.

"Look, I don't see what difference—"

"Until the curtain of seeming surety is swept away," Singh put in.

"Surety?"

"This world—this universe!—has labored long under the illusion of its own permanence." Singh spread his hands, animated in the flickering yellow glow. "We might die, yes, the sun might even perish—but the universe went on. Now we prove otherwise. There cannot help but be profound reactions."

Clay chuckled. "If we go back to thinking like the early Greeks, there'll sure as hell be reactions."

"Perhaps quantum mechanics is a bit of deception, my friend," Singh said. "A delicate veil dancing before the reality."

Clay was trying to josh them out of this stuff, but they weren't budging. He said sharply, "Look, the world is real, mechanisms work—"

"Do they?" Patil shot back. "Our science assumes all is machinelike. But *we* are not, are we?"

"Uh, well, sure we are."

"Do you feel like a machine?" Patil jabbed a finger at him.

"Well, no, but—"

Patil swept an arm toward the shed doorway.
"Then why should those trees out there be machines?
Just burners of air and makers of wood?"

Singh followed right up. "That word we use—
'thing'—it means something *we* are not, yes?"

Clay kept his glassy smile. "Hey, you got to keep
yourself separate from things, so you can study them."

"Not if the veil is stripped away," Singh said inci-
sively.

"So how does physics get, uh, stripped?"

"We do not know. Perhaps in the end it is a matter of faith," Singh murmured, peering into the dancing, popping flames of the stove. It burned with more
apparent life than the men around it.

"Physics is a matter of *faith*?" Clay was surprised,
disgusted. The sharp savor of ancient soil seemed to
rise up all around him. He reminded himself to be
civil. "Look, let's stick to business."

"Yes yes," Singh said. A certain transfixed quality
left his face and the scientist that Clay knew returned,
his eyes now quick and intelligent. "Our labors must
not cease. The day remains to be won."

He thought he saw what they were driving at. "A
Nobel Prize, even."

To his surprise, both men laughed merrily. "Oh
no," Patil said, arching his eyebrows. "No such trifles
are expected!"

9.

The boxy meeting room beside the data bay was
packed. From it came a subdued mutter, a fretwork of
talk laced with anticipation.

Outside, someone had placed a small chalky
statue of a grinning elephant. Clay hesitated, stroked
it. Despite the heat of the mine, the elephant was cool.

"The workers just brought it down," Mrs. Buli

explained with a smile. "Our Hindu god of auspicious beginnings."

"Or endings," Patil said behind her. "Equally."

Clay nodded and walked into the trapped, moist heat of the room. Everyone was jammed in, graduate students and laborers alike, their dhotis already showing sweaty crescents. Clay saw the three students the devotees had beaten and exchanged respectful bows with them.

Perceiving some need for ceremony, he opened with lengthy praise for the endless hours they had labored, exclaiming over how startled the world would be to learn of such a facility.

Then he plunged into consideration of each candidate event, his checks and counterchecks, vertex corrections, digital array flaws, mean free paths, ionization rates, the artful programming that deflected the myriad possible sources of error. He could feel tension rising in the room as he cast the events on the inch-thick wall screen, calling them forth from the files in his cubes. Some he threw into 3-D, to show the full path through the cage of iron that had captured the death rattle of infinity.

And at the end, all cases reviewed, he said quietly, "You have found it. The proton lifetime is very nearly 10^{34} years."

The room burst into applause, wide grins, and wild shouts as everyone pressed forward to shake his hand.

10.

Singh handled the message to the NSF. Clay also constructed a terse though detailed summary and sent it to the International Astronomical Union for release to the worldwide system of observatories and universities.

Clay knew this would give a vital assist to his career. With the Kolar team staying here, he would be their only spokesman. And this was very big, media-mesmerizing news indeed.

The result was important to physicists and astronomers alike, for the destiny of all their searches ultimately would be sealed by the faint failures of particles no eye would ever see. In 10^{34} years, far in the depths of space, the great celestial cities, the galaxies, would be ebbing. The last red stars would flicker, belch, and gutter out. Perhaps life would have clung to them and found a way to persist against the growing cold. Cluttered with the memorabilia of the ages, the islands of mute matter would turn at last to their final conqueror—not entropy's still hand, but this silent sputter of protons.

Clay thought of the headlines: UNIVERSE TO END! What would *that* do to harried commuters on their way to work?

He watched Singh send the stuttering messages on the big satellite dish, the corrugated tin roof of the shed pulled aside, allowing him to watch burnt-gold twilight seep across the sky. Clay felt no elation, as blank as a drained capacitor. He had gone into physics because of the sense it gave of grasping deep mysteries. He could look at bridges and trace the vectored stability that ruled them. When his daughter asked why the sky was blue, he actually knew, and could sketch out a simple answer. It had never occurred to him to fear flying, because he knew the Bernoulli equation for the pressure that held up the plane.

But this result . . .

Even the celebratory party that evening left him unmoved. Graduate students turned out in their best khaki. Sitar music swarmed through the scented air, ragas thumping and weaving. He found his body swaying to the refractions of tone and scale.

"It is a pity you cannot learn more of our country," Mrs. Buli remarked, watching him closely.

"Right now I'm mostly interested in sleep."

"Sleep is not always kind." She seemed wry and distant in the night's smudged humidity. "One of our ancient gods, Brahma, is said to sleep—and we are what he dreams."

"In that case, for you folks maybe he's been having a nightmare lately."

"Ah yes, our troubles. But do not let them mislead you about India. They pass."

"I'm sure they will," Clay replied, dutifully diplomatic.

"You were surprised, were you not, at the outcome?" she said piercingly.

"Uh, well, I had to be skeptical."

"Yes, for a scientist certainty is built on deep layers of doubt."

"Like my daddy said, in the retail business deal with everybody, but count your change."

She laughed. "We have given you a bargain, perhaps!"

He was acutely aware that his initial doubts must have been obvious. And what unsettled him now was not just the hard-won success here, but their strange attitude toward it.

The graduate students came then and tried to teach him a dance. He did a passable job and a student named Venkatraman slipped him a glass of beer, forbidden vice. It struck Clay as comic that the Indian government spent much energy to suppress alcohol but did little about the population explosion. The students all laughed when he made a complicated joke about booze, but he could not be sure whether they meant it. The music seemed to quicken, his heart thumping to keep up with it. They addressed him as Clay*ji*, a term of respect, and asked his opinion of what they might do next with the experiment. He shrugged, thinking,

'*Nother job, sahib?* and suggested using it as a detector for neutrinos from supernovas. That had paid off when the earlier generation of neutrino detectors picked up the 1987 supernova.

The atom bomb, the 1987 event, now this—particle physics, he realized uncomfortably, was steeped in death. The sitar slid and rang, and Mrs. Buli made arch jokes to go with the spicy salad. Still, he turned in early.

11.

To be awakened by a soft breeze. A brushing presence, sliding cloth . . .

He sensed her sari as a luminous fog. Moonlight streaming through a lopsided window cast shimmering auras through the cloth as she loomed above him. Reached for him. Lightly flung away his sticky bedclothes.

"I—"

A soft hand covered his mouth, bringing a heady savor of ripe earth. His senses ran out of him and into the surrounding dark, coiling in air as he took her weight. She was surprisingly light, though thick-waisted, her breasts like teacups compared with the full curves of her hips. His hands slid and pressed, finding a delightful slithering moisture all over her, a sheen of vibrancy. Her sari evaporated. The high planes of her face caught vagrant blades of moonlight, and he saw a curious tentative, expectant expression there as she wrapped him in soft pressures. Her mouth did not so much kiss his as enclose it, formulating an argument of sweet rivulets that trickled into his porous self. She slipped into place atop him, a slick clasp that melted him up into her, a perfect fit, slick with dark insistence. He closed his eyes, but the glow diffused through his eyelids, and he could see her hair fanning through the air like motion underwater, her luxuriant weight bucking, trembling as her nails scratched his shoulders, musk rising smoky from them both. A silky muscle milked him at each heart thump. Her velvet mass orbited above their fulcrum, bearing down with feathery demands, and he remembered brass icons, gaudy Indian posters, and felt above him Kali strumming in fevered darkness. She locked legs around him, squeezing him up into her surprisingly hard muscles, grinding, drawing forth, pushing back. She cried out with great gulping heaves and lungfuls of the thickening air, mouth going slack beneath hooded eyes, and he shot sharply up into her, a convulsion that poured out all the knotted aches in him, delivering them into the tumbled steamy earth—

12.

—and next, with no memories between, he was stumbling with her . . . down a gully . . . beneath slanting silvery moonlight.

"What—what's—"

"Quiet!" She shushed him like a schoolmarm.

He recognized the rolling countryside near the mine. Vague forms flitted in the distance. Wracked cries cut the night.

"The devotees," Mrs. Buli whispered as they stumbled on. "They have assaulted the mine entrance."

"How'd we—"

"You were difficult to rouse," she said with a side-long glance.

Was she trying to be amusing? The sudden change from mysterious supercharged sensuality back to this clipped, formal professionalism disoriented him.

"Apparently some of our laborers had a grand party. It alerted the devotees to our presence, some say. I spoke to a laborer while you slept, however, who said that the devotees knew of your presence. They asked for you."

"Why me?"

"Something about your luggage and a telephone call home."

Clay gritted his teeth and followed her along a path that led among the slumped hills, away from their lodgings. Soon the mine entrance was visible below. Running figures swarmed about it like black gnats. Ragged chants erupted from them. A *waarrrk waarrrk* sound came from the hangar, and it was some moments until Clay saw long chains of human bodies hanging from the rafters, swinging themselves in unison.

"They're pulling down the hangar," he whispered.

"I despair for what they have done inside."

He instinctively reached for her and felt the supple warmth he had embraced seemingly only moments before. She turned and gave him her mouth again.

"We—back there—why'd you come to me?"

"It was time. Even we feel the joy of release from order, Professor Clay."

"Well, sure . . ." Clay felt illogically embarrassed, embracing a woman who sill had the musk of the bed about her, yet who used his title. "But . . . how'd I get here? Seems like—"

"You were immersed. Taken out of yourself."

"Well, yeah, it was good, fine, but I can't remember anything."

She smiled. "The best moments leave no trace. That is a signature of the implicate order."

Clay breathed in the waxy air to help clear his head. More mumbo jumbo, he thought, delivered by her with an open, expectant expression. In the darkness it took a moment to register that she had fled down another path.

"Where'll we go?" he gasped when he caught up.

"We must get to the vans. They are parked some kilometers away."

"My gear—"

"Leave it."

He hesitated a moment, then followed her. There was nothing irreplaceable. It certainly wasn't worth braving the mob below for the stuff.

They wound down through bare hillsides dominated by boulders. The sky rippled with heat lightning. Puffy clouds scudded quickly in from the west, great ivory flashes working among them. The ground surged slightly.

"Earthquake?" he asked.

"There were some earlier, yes. Perhaps that has excited the devotees further tonight, put their feet to running."

There was no sign of the physics team. Pebbles squirted from beneath his boots—he wondered how he had managed to get them on without remembering it—and recalled again her hypnotic sensuality. Stones rattled away down into narrow dry washes on each side. Clouds blotted out the moonglow, and they had to pick their way along the trail.

Clay's mind spun with plans, speculations, jittery anxiety. Mrs. Buli was now his only link to the Western fragment of India, and he could scarcely see her in the shadows. She moved with liquid grace, her sari trailing, sandals slapping. Suddenly she crouched down. "More."

Along the path came figures bearing lanterns. They moved silently in the fitful silvery moonlight. There was no place to hide and the party had already seen them.

"Stand still," she said. Again the crisp Western diction, yet her ample hips swayed slightly, reminding him of her deeper self.

Clay wished he had a club, a knife, anything. He

made himself stand beside her, hands clenched. For once his blackness might be an advantage.

The devotees passed, eyes rapt. Clay had expected them to be singing or chanting mantras or rubbing beads—but not shambling forward as if to their doom. The column barely glanced at him. In his baggy cotton trousers and formless shirt, he hoped he was unremarkable. A woman passed nearby, apparently carrying something across her back. Clay blinked. Her hands were nailed to the ends of a beam, and she carried it proudly, palms bloody, half crucified. Her face was serene, eyes focused on the roiling sky. Behind her was a man bearing a plate. Clay thought the shambling figure carried marbles on the dish until he peered closer and saw an iris, and realized the entire plate was packed with eyeballs. He gasped and faces turned toward him. Then the man was gone along the path, and Clay waited, holding his breath against a gamy stench he could not name. Some muttered to themselves, some carried religious artifacts, beads and statuettes and drapery, but none had the fervor of the devotees he had seen before. The ground trembled again.

And out of the dark air came a humming. Something struck a man in the line and he clutched at his throat, crying hoarsely. Clay leaped forward without thinking. He pulled the man's hands away. Lodged in the narrow of the throat was something like an enormous cockroach with fluttering wings. It had already embedded its head in the man. Spiky legs furiously scrabbled against the soiled skin to dig deeper. The man coughed and shouted weakly, as though the thing were already blocking his throat.

Clay grabbed its hind legs and pulled. The insect wriggled with surprising strength. He saw the hind stinger too late. The sharp point struck a hot jolt of pain into his thumb. Anger boiled in him. He held on despite the pain and yanked the thing free. It made a sucking sound coming out. He hissed with revulsion and violently threw it down the hillside.

The man stumbled, gasping, and then ran back down the path, never even looking at them. Mrs. Buli grabbed Clay, who was staggering around in a circle, shaking his hand. "I will cut it!" she cried.

He held still while she made a precise cross cut and drained the blood. "What . . . what *was* that?"

"A wasp-thing from the pouches that hang on our trees."

"Oh yeah. One of those bio tricks."

"They are still overhead."

Clay listened to the drone hanging over them. Another devotee shrieked and slapped the back of his neck. Clay numbly watched the man run away. His hand throbbed, but he could feel the effects ebbing. Mrs. Buli tore a strip from her sari and wrapped his thumb to quell the bleeding.

All this time devotees streamed past them in the gloom. None took the slightest notice of Clay. Some spoke to themselves.

"Western science doesn't seem to bother 'em much now," Clay whispered wryly.

Mrs. Buli nodded. The last figure to pass was a woman who limped, sporting an arm that ended not in a hand but in a spoon, nailed to a stub of cork.

He followed Mrs. Buli into enveloping darkness. "Who were they?"

"I don't know. They spoke seldom and repeated the same words. Dharma and samsara, terms of destiny."

"They don't care about us?"

"They appear to sense a turning, a resolution." In the fitful moonglow her eyes were liquid puzzles.

"But they destroyed the experiment."

"I gather that knowledge of your Western presence was like the wasp-things. Irritating, but only a catalyst, not the cause."

"What *did* make them—"

"No time. Come."

They hurriedly entered a thin copse of spindly trees that lined a streambed. Dust stifled his nose and he breathed through his mouth. The clouds raced toward the horizon with unnatural speed, seeming to flee from the west. Trees swayed before an unfelt wind, twisting and reaching for the shifting sky.

"Weather," Mrs. Buli answered his questions. "Bad weather."

They came upon a small crackling fire. Figures crouched around it and Clay made to go around, but Mrs. Buli walked straight toward it. Women squatted, poking sticks into the flames. Clay saw that something moved on the sticks. A momentary shaft of moonlight showed the oily skin of snakes, tiny eyes crisp as crystals, the shafts poking from yawning white mouths that still moved. The women's faces of stretched yellow skin anxiously watched the blackening, sizzling snakes, turning them. Fire hissed as though raindrops fell upon it, but Clay felt nothing wet, just the dry rub of a fresh abrading wind. Smoke wrapped the women in gray wreaths and Mrs. Buli hurried on.

So much, so fast. Clay felt rising in him a leaden conviction born of all he had seen in this land. So many people, so much pain—how could it matter? The West assumed that the individual was important, the bedrock of all. That was why the obliterating events of the West's own history, like the Nazi holocaust, by erasing humans in such numbing numbers, cast grave doubt on the significance of any one. India did something like that for him. Could a universe which produced so many bodies, so many minds in shadowed torment, care a whit for humanity? Endless, meaningless duplication of grinding pain . . .

A low mutter came on the wind, like a bass theme sounding up from the depths of a dusty well.

Mrs. Buli called out something he could not understand. She began running and Clay hastened to follow. If he lost her in these shadows, he could lose all connection.

Quickly they left the trees and crossed a grassy field, rutted by ancient agriculture and prickly with weeds. On this flat plain he could see that the whole sky worked with twisted light, a colossal electrical discharge feathering into more branches than a gnarled tree. The anxious clouds caught blue and burnt-yellow pulses and seemed to relay them, like the countless transformers and capacitors and voltage drops that made a worldwide communications net, carrying staccato messages laced with crackling punctuations.

"The vans," she panted.

Three brown vans crouched beneath a canopy of thin trees, further concealed beneath khaki tents that blended in with the dusty fields. Mrs. Buli yanked open the door of the first one. Her fingers fumbled at the ignition.

"The key must be concealed," she said quickly.

"Why?" he gasped, throat raw.

"They are to be always with the vans."

"Uh huh. Check the others."

She hurried away. Clay got down on his knees, feeling the lip of the van's undercarriage. The ground seemed to heave with inner heat, dry and rasping, the pulse of the planet. He finished one side of the van and crawled under, feeling along the rear axle. He heard a distant plaintive cry, as eerie and forlorn as the call of a bird lost in fog.

"Clayji? None in the others."

His hand touched a small slick box high up on the axle. He plucked it from its magnetic grip and rolled out from under.

"If we drive toward the mine," she said, "we can perhaps find others."

"Others, hell. Most likely we'll run into devotees."

"Well, I—"

Figures in the trees. Flitting, silent, quick.

"Get in."

"But—"

He pushed her in and tried to start the van. Running shapes in the field. He got the engine started on the third try and gunned it. They growled away. Something hard shattered the back window into a spiderweb, but then Clay swerved several times and nothing more hit them.

After a few minutes his heart thumps slowed, and he turned on the headlights to make out the road. The curves were sandy and he did not want to get stuck. He stamped on the gas.

Suddenly great washes of amber light streamed across the sky, pale lances cutting the clouds. "My God, what's happening?"

"It is more than weather."

Her calm, abstract voice made him glance across the seat. "No kidding."

"No earthquake could have collateral effects of this order."

He saw by the dashboard lights that she wore a lapis lazuli necklace. He had felt it when she came to him, and now its deep blues seemed like the only note of color in the deepening folds of night.

"It must be something far more profound."

"What?"

The road now arrowed straight through a tangled terrain of warped trees and oddly shaped boulders. Something rattled against the windshield like hail, but Clay could see nothing.

"We have always argued, some of us, that the central dictate of quantum mechanics is the interconnected nature of the observer and the observed."

The precise, detached lecturer style again drew his eyes to her. Shadowed, her face gave away no secrets.

"We always filter the world," she said with

dreamy momentum, "and yet are linked to it. How much of what we see is in fact taught us, by our bodies, or by the consensus reality that society trains us to see, even before we can speak for ourselves?"

"Look, that sky isn't some problem with my eyes. It's *real*. Hear that?" Something big and soft had struck the door of the van, rocking it.

"And we here have finished the program of materialistic science, have we not? We flattered the West by taking it seriously. As did the devotees."

Clay grinned despite himself. It was hard to feel flattered when you were fleeing for your life.

Mrs. Buli stretched lazily, as though relaxing into the clasp of the moist night. "So we have proven the passing nature of matter. What fresh forces does that bring into play?"

"Huh!" Clay spat back angrily. "Look here, we just sent word out, reported the result. How——"

"So that by now millions, perhaps billions of people know that the very stones that support them must pass."

"So what? Just some theoretical point about subnuclear physics, how's that going to——"

"Who is to say? What avatar? The point is that we were believed. Certain knowledge, universally correlated, surely has some impact——"

The van lurched. Suddenly they jounced and slammed along the smooth roadway. A bright plume of sparks shot up behind them, brimming firefly-yellow in the night.

"Axle's busted!" Clay cried. He got the van stopped. In the sudden silence it registered that the motor had gone dead.

They climbed out. Insects buzzed and hummed in the hazy gloom.

The roadway was still straight and sure, but on all sides great blobs of iridescent water swelled up from the ground, making colossal drops. The trembling half spheres wobbled in the frayed moonlight. Silently, softly, the bulbs began to detach from the foggy ground and gently loft upward. Feathery luminescent clouds above gathered on swift winds that sheared their edges. These billowing, luxuriant banks snagged the huge teardrop shapes as they plunged skyward.

"I . . . I don't . . ."

Mrs. Buli turned and embraced him. Her moist mouth opened a redolent interior continent to him, teeming and blackly bountiful, and he had to resist falling inward, a tumbling silvery bubble in a dark chasm.

"The category of perfect roundness is fading," she said calmly.

Clay looked at the van. The wheels had become ellipses. At each revolution they had slammed the axles into the roadway, leaving behind long scratches of rough tar.

He took a step.

She said, "Since we can walk, the principle of pivot and lever, of muscles pulling bones, survives."

"How . . . this doesn't . . ."

"But do our bodies depend on roundness? I wonder." She carefully lay down on the blacktop.

The road straightened precisely, like joints in an aged spine popping as they realigned.

Angles cut their spaces razor-sharp, like axioms from Euclid.

Clouds merged, forming copious tinkling hexagons.

"It is good to see that some features remain. Perhaps these are indeed the underlying Platonic beauties."

"What?" Clay cried.

"The undying forms," Mrs. Buli said abstractly. "Perhaps that one Western idea was correct after all."

Clay desperately grasped the van. He jerked his

arm back when the metal skin began flexing and re-shaping itself.

Smooth glistening forms began to emerge from the rough, coarse earth. Above the riotous, heaving land the moon was now a brassy cube. Across its face played enormous black cracks like mad lightning.

Somewhere far away his wife and daughter were in this, too. *G'bye. Daddy. It's been real.*

Quietly the land began to rain upward. Globs dripped toward the pewter, filmy continent swarming freshly above. Eons measured out the evaporation of ancient sluggish seas.

His throat struggled against torpid air. "Is . . . Brahma . . . ?"

"Awakening?" came her hollow voice, like an echo from a distant gorge.

"What happens . . . to . . . us?"

His words diffracted away from him. He could now see acoustic waves, wedges of compressed, mute atoms crowding in the exuberant air. Luxuriant, inexhaustible riches burst from beneath the ceramic certainties he had known.

"Come." Her voice seeped through the churning ruby air.

Centuries melted between them as he turned. A being he recognized without conscious thought spun in liquid air.

Femina, she was now, and she drifted on the new wafting currents. He and she were made of shifting geometric elements, molecular units of shape and firm thrust. A wan joy spread through him.

Time that was no time did not pass, and he and she and the impacted forces between them were pinned to the forever moment that cascaded through them, all of them, the billions of atomized elements that made them, all, forever.

Afterword

In science fiction, a good idea is one that conjures up good scenes. Sometimes this means a Big Idea, most times not.

Often all I get is the one scene, an idea that seems worth a slice of another life, a quick, pointed vision—a short story. Other times the idea is really not a concept at all but a person gritty and flawed, somebody from a place and a time which makes him or her interesting, quirky, worth closer study. And still other times, an idea worries my imagination like a dog gnawing at an apparently dried and worthless bone, finally yielding up a sustained plot and interconnected scenes, and then comes the struggle to manhandle the thing into a tale.

I let matters get out of hand now and then, and a story ends up being a novel. Anyone who has been reading my work for a while has noticed that sometimes stories can also turn up in a later novel, when I discover that a piece I had thought stood alone was really part of a larger scheme. I feel a bit odd when that happens. My imagination simply presents me with these conclusions, sometimes reaching back two decades to scoop up an old story and show me that it really was a hint about a lurking novel.

Artistic instincts are seldom orderly, even in a scientist. To readers who find this unsettling, I can only offer some apologies for my rude friend the unconscious, a largely uncontrollable spirit with more animal gusto than manners, who maybe gets out a bit too much. But a writer who is afraid to follow where his craft takes him is as useless as a politician who can't afford to be wrong.

Science fiction has always traded in ideas. In the larger literary world this, and a weakness for exotic setting and event, marks one as a rogue, not to be invited to high culture dinner or even trusted with tea and crumpets. Some critics like ideas and can even recognize a new one, though not many do. They are occasionally surprised when they stumble upon some while staggering down our particular alley. Most keep such discoveries secret, or notice it in public only after a given idea has become respectable.

I like very short stories and you'll find a handful here. Sometimes a notion seems best expressed in one burst. Concepts usually need room, though, and most modern short stories are typically both short and low on intellectual calories. Yet one of the pleasures of fiction is Poe's "ratiocination," and such delights live on in the mystery, detective and other genres, including most definitely science fiction. This collection emphasizes stories with high idea content, for those as likes 'em.

Science fiction is also often about people who are not nice by any stretch of the imagination. It jars, questions, infuriates. Most readers don't like this, so they either stay safely away from it by sticking to fiction about the past—as most "contemporary" fiction really is—or by reading the sort of science fiction which recycles standard props and devices (as do nearly all sf films).

I am afraid that most of what I write lurches through landscapes that please only a few. For one thing, I have never seen any point in keeping a consistent narrative voice, so some of the stories in this book will seem to have been written by different people. "Time Guide" careens even more than most. It's deliberately disorienting.

"Calibrations and Exercises" I wrote to get at a certain antiseptic anomie I sensed. I grew up in rural southern Alabama and for me there is something rather funny about the subject. My apologies to those who will find nothing amusing in this piece. "Nobody Lives on Burton Street" is in here because it is one of my most popular and reprinted stories, though for the life of me I don't know why. Unfortunately its characters seem more plausible now than when I wrote it in the late 1960s.

"Proselytes" is a pointed objection to the common assumption that aliens will have the lofty views of, say, liberal Democrats. "Dark Sanctuary" is a good example of writing a story to display an idea, one that still has some scientific punch, I think. Like other stories in this volume, it is written in clear prose within a genre straightjacket. Its implications for current scientific pursuits such as the radio-listening Search for Extraterrestrial Life, I leave to the reader.

More reflective and general is "Mozart on Morphine," which has big autobiographical chunks in it and reflects one of my likings in fiction—the sense of what a life of work and engagement can be like, framing larger aspects of what it means to be a fairly savvy primate. "Matter's End" is another look at being a physicist, with every scientific detail taken directly from the world. The moist mysteries of its besieged Indian are from life, too, but augmented by some thoughts about how biotech is going to affect the third world. Its philosophical basis is a mixture of the "implicate order" theories of quantum mechanics and Platonist ideas about the nature of knowing. These are not my views, mind, as a working physicist, but they do serve the cause of the story, so I used them.

"Freezeframe" and "Centigrade 233" poke at attitudes I thought deserved fresh inspection. "Touches" and "Sleepstory" reflect my continuing interest in aspects of consensual reality, as does "Matter's End" in a different fashion. Much thinking about how we know the outer world has a claustrophobic feel. Especially so is the latest technological wrinkle, virtual reality. Though it has many practical uses, its fundamental program is to replace our sense of the world, which is analog, with a digital array—which I suspect is doomed to fail, precisely because the world is finer than our ideas about it. As a concept, virtual reality seems to appeal to people who spend a lot of time indoors.

"Sleepstory" arose from a request that I write a war story—indeed, invent the whole war. Since I am fascinated by how much we as a species obviously like to fight each other, I accepted the challenge. It was fun to set on the same Ganymede as two of my novels, *Jupiter Project* and *Against Infinity*, which suggests that maybe this is the first sign of another novel about that wondrous theater, the Jovian moons. The economic speculations in this story may actually make sense; I believe that eventually, running the earth intelligently, with decent standards for all humanity, will demand that we use the resources of the entire solar system. In my opinion the best sf about combat comes from Joe Haldeman and I hesitated to get into the ring with him. Wearing the uniform is not the same as hearing a slug whistle by your ear. I have never seen combat; still, I was surprised that I couldn't write this story in a straightforward way. What this means I don't know, but I am struck by the fact that war is now an entertainment for most of us, as distant as dragons.

I have always liked very short stories, and this explains "Leviathan," "Side Effect," "Time Guide," and others. Several assume a twenty-first century transformed by biological technology, which I use for a bit of fun (yes, I am fond of dogs).

"Knowing Her" was written in the throes of mortality as friends began to slip away; it's one of my major themes: the Great Problem. I wrote "Slices" in an hour, just to see what that was like. Fun, yes, but it resembled driving 130 miles per hour on a freeway, which I've also done, and don't want to have to do again. "The Bigger One" I did as a radio script by editorial direction. It reflects an old, bothersome preoccupation of mine with the oddities of Californian geology. I wrote "We Could Do Worse" after reading the letters of Robert Taft, discovering that he really did consider making Joe McCarthy his vice presidential running mate in 1952 if he got the nomination over Eisenhower. It made political sense; they both held the isolationist views now becoming popular once again.

Sometimes I write a piece simply to mull over a recent scientific finding. "Shakers of the Earth" reflects a discovery made by David Gillette, the state paleontologist of Utah, and others. This marvelous find in the late 1980s was one of those surprises which makes science so delightful. (The story was written before *Jurassic Park* appeared as a novel; the general idea is actually quite old in sf.) It may indeed be possible to get some genetic information out of unfossilized remains found in New Mexico. This is being pursued by physicists and chemists at Los Alamos National Laboratory, which is near the site. In a century or so the notion I present might even happen.

On a less happy note, I also think "Immortal Night" anticipates a very real reaction to come from many people. "Cadenza" comes out of my own experiences with the "health industry" and its curious way of robbing us of our sense of self. We are machines, yes, but that's not all.

Maybe that's what I was trying to say, too, in my first published story from far-off 1965, "Stand-In." Its attempt at light fantasy I include here mostly to encourage those who aim to be writers; see, you can start this awkwardly and still survive. Reading it just now, I was even more thankful that at about this time I decided to keep on with my scientific career and not try writing full-time. That's still the way I work. More advice: do keep that day job.

Short stories have different goals and satisfactions from novels, and I suspect they are not, as some feel, the cutting edge of speculative literature. For that, for depth and sweeping imagination, go to novels.

Short stories are *fun*, and should be enjoyed for what they are. These are gathered from a career now spanning nearly thirty years, which started with a graduate student sitting through a boring lecture, scribbling "Stand-In" in his notebook intended for serious, significant statistical mechanics. I hope they give some sense of my preoccupations, and some pleasure.
January 1994.

ABOUT THE AUTHOR

GREGORY BENFORD has won virtually every major science fiction award, including two Nebulas. He is an internationally renowned physicist and astronomer, a professor at the University of California, Irvine, and has published more than one hundred scientific papers. A Woodrow Wilson Fellow, he served on NASA's Science Advisory Board. He has published thirteen novels, including *Timescape, Artifact, Heart of the Comet* (with David Brin), and *Against Infinity*, as well as a collection of short stories, *In Alien Flesh*.